a
lighthouse
Christmas

BOOKS BY JENNY HALE

Christmas at Fireside Cabins
Christmas at Silver Falls
It Started With Christmas
We'll Always Have Christmas
All I Want for Christmas
Christmas Wishes and Mistletoe Kisses
A Christmas to Remember
Coming Home for Christmas

The Beach House
The House on Firefly Beach
Summer at Firefly Beach
The Summer Hideaway
The Summer House
Summer at Oyster Bay
Summer by the Sea
A Barefoot Summer

a
lighthouse
Christmas

JENNY HALE

bookouture

Published by Bookouture in 2021

An imprint of Storyfire Ltd.
Carmelite House
50 Victoria Embankment
London EC4Y 0DZ

www.bookouture.com

ISBN: 978-1-80019-875-3
eBook ISBN: 978-1-80019-874-6

PROLOGUE

"Mia, dear!" Grandma Ruth's voice called across the wide expanse of marshlands, over the low dunes, and through the sea grass, reaching Mia, despite the crash of the Atlantic behind her and the seagulls squawking overhead.

Seven-year-old Mia Carter set down the bag of seashells she'd been collecting and put her tiny hands, frozen from the winter air, to her forehead to shield her eyes from the light ricocheting off the sea, peering over at the familiar apron-clad figure in the doorway of Winsted Cape lighthouse.

Grandma Ruth beckoned for her to come inside. "I've made lunch!" she called. "And the peach cobbler's ready!"

Mia waved to let her grandmother know she'd gotten the message. She picked up the bag of seashells and sprinted across the sand, her long dark hair ballooning over the back of her thick winter coat as it blew in the coastal wind, like the sails of one of those monohull boats that regularly dotted the horizon. Her heavy boots sinking in the soft sand, she ran the length of the coast that was protected by the lighthouse's beam and then made a sharp right, treading lightly on the old dock that stretched out above the marshes, so as not to trip.

The shells clinking in the bag with every step, she hopped off the dock and slowed to catch her breath in the frigid air, walking through the wide grassy fields of the grounds, past the old oak tree with her favorite swing, along the plank fence separating the yard from the horse field. Delilah, Woody, and Charlotte—Grandma Ruth's horses—were standing together, bundled in their blankets in the barn at the far end of the fencing, their tails swishing.

"Were you plannin' to eat today?" Grandma Ruth asked when Mia had reached her, her affectionate smile as warm as her peach cobbler. The heat from the stone fireplace and the glimmer of the Christmas tree enticed her to leave the cold behind and retreat to the soft heat of inside. "You're gonna waste away to nothin', and you can't do that if you plan to rule the world one day," she said, opening the door wider to let her in. She wrinkled her nose fondly at Mia.

Her fingers and nose numb from the winter cold, Mia came inside and dropped the bag of shells in front of her four-year-old sister Riley, who'd stayed back at the lighthouse to bake with her grandmother. Riley sat on her knees in the chair at Grandma Ruth's kitchen table. "Look what I found," Mia said, opening the bag and pulling out a starfish, lingering grains of sand dropping onto the surface of the table.

Riley gasped at its beauty. "Where did you find it?" she asked in her squeaky, youthful voice, looking up to her sister with awe in her green eyes.

"Stuck in the sand at Lock's Bend," she said, remembering how it had been half buried in the foam of the turbulent waters, at the spot where Grandma Ruth had warned Mia her whole young life not to go past the first break when she was swimming in the summers, as the rip tide was treacherous. "It wasn't in the water," she told her grandmother, to ward off any lectures on the dangers of Lock's Bend.

Grandma Ruth nodded thoughtfully and brought Mia's sandwich over to the table. "Did you know that a starfish symbolizes guidance and intuition," Grandma Ruth said, her gentle command pulling both girls' attention right to her. As she set the plate down and leaned over Mia's shoulder, her familiar scent of lilac and roses was like coming home after a long trip. "Looks like you've been chosen to lead," she said with a knowing smile. "But I knew that before the starfish." Grandma Ruth wrapped her arms around Mia and gave her a soft kiss on her cheek.

"Mia?" Alice Carter's grief-stricken voice broke through the memory like a scratch on an old record. "Are you okay?"

Her vision blurred by tears, Mia focused on her mother's voice at the other end of the phone as she sat in her Manhattan apartment, overlooking the massive skyscrapers that stretched across the city. She tried to answer, but her quivering lips wouldn't allow it. She fiddled with the starfish that she'd had for years and now kept in a dish on the coffee table.

"Honey, it's so hard, I know. But she's in a better place now."

Mia took in a ragged breath, choked by the tightening in her throat, more tears surfacing. Grandma Ruth had been sick for a while. Mia had visited her frail grandmother at her hospital bed a few times, but she'd never been able to come to terms with the fact that life could overtake her grandmother's grit and will. Even in her last days, Grandma Ruth's spirit had always seemed unbeatable.

"How's Riley?" she managed, concern for her sister welling up.

"She's handling it."

Mia nodded even though there was no one there to see.

"I'm going to need your help," her mom said, her tone desperate, overwhelmed by the loss of her mother. "I don't know what to do first." Until then, Mia had never heard the vulnerability in her mother's voice that she was experiencing at that moment.

Even though her heart was breaking, Mia pushed her sadness deep down, a skill she'd mastered over the years, and wiped her tears with the tips of her fingers. Mustering all the strength she had, it was time to lead. "I'll take care of the details, Mom," she said, forcing an evenness into her words.

She'd have to plan the funeral, begin compiling a list of

Grandma Ruth's loved ones. She'd run the will past her lawyer, making sure all the assets were taken care of. She'd put Grandma Ruth's car up for sale. She'd check in with the caretakers and make sure Delilah, their last remaining horse, was cared for until they could figure out what to do with her. She'd get the financial details on the lighthouse and make decisions on how to manage the property... Storing her grief in the dark place at the pit of her soul, she'd focus on what had to be done.

When she'd ended the call, Mia got up and walked over to the picture window in her apartment, peering out at the nighttime city skyline and the massive line of taillights. A constant stream of cars weaved through the vast expanse of skyscrapers to their multitude of destinations, the late summer holiday traffic adding to the usual Manhattan madness. She blinked away more tears, not allowing them to fall. With her husband Milo still at work, the place was silent, but her thoughts were not. Given what she had to deal with in her own life, this might be the worst possible time to be faced with this, and she wasn't sure how to move forward. But she needed to go home to her family.

ONE

"I can't do it," Mia's mother said through her tears.

Alice held her trembling fingers against her lips as if to stifle her grief, while the two of them stood in the inky darkness on the icy cold front porch back home in her small town of Bakers Ridge, Mia's suitcases at their feet. With the threat of a major winter storm on the horizon, the coastal wind cut like razors. The meager strand of Christmas lights that her mother wound around the posts and railings every year blinked off and on under a dusting of snow.

How different this meeting was from their normal life at home. She'd come home for the funeral, but the last time they were *really* together, when they were themselves and not completely grief-stricken, she and her mother had sat around laughing, sharing stories of Grandma Ruth and talking about the possibility of Mia's grandmother coming home from the hospital.

Seeing her mother in this state was unnerving. Unsure of how to console her, Mia wrapped her bundled body around Alice to comfort her, neither of them acknowledging the freezing coastal breeze lashing at them. Growing up, Mia had never noticed how thin her mom was or how her clothes seemed to drape her rather than fit. She'd always seemed larger than life to a young Mia.

"I'll help you. We don't have to think about it until tomorrow,"

Mia said, the role of the strong one—a role she'd become so skilled at, growing up—coming back to her easily.

At the young age of ten, when their father died, Mia had had to push through her pain to take care of her seven-year-old sister Riley while her mother had worked two jobs—one at the local grocery store and the other as a night custodian at the hospital—to make ends meet. Mia had helped Riley with homework, made dinners, and kept her sister entertained whenever the little one got worried about being in the house alone with just the two of them. She'd done what her mother had done, pushing all her fear and pain deep down. The only time it bubbled up was in the dark after she'd gone to bed.

"It's our destiny," her mother had said one night when she'd brushed Mia's hair off her forehead, tucking her into bed after coming home from work too late for any ten-year-old to be awake. "You come from a long line of strong women. Your Grandma Ruth has run the lighthouse at Winsted Cape all by herself nearly her entire adult life."

Mia's grandfather had suffered a heart attack before she was born, as if fate had plucked him out of their lives, ridding them of any male influence whatsoever and priming them for their calling of being independent women. And just like the other women in her family, Mia had never seen Grandma Ruth cry over the loss of her beloved husband.

Just the mention of Grandma Ruth could cause a swell of happiness in Mia's chest. Like an old movie playing in her mind came the memories: running through the green fields that led to the marsh at the edge of the shore; the clothes on the old clothes-line flapping in the breeze like party flags; the way she had to squint to keep the sun from piercing her eyes so she could see the shiny glass at the top of the red-and-white lighthouse, the seagulls circling overhead.

But the grounds outside weren't the only delight about visiting Grandma Ruth when she was a little girl. The lighthouse in

Winstead Cape was only a short drive from her hometown of Bakers Ridge, so she visited her grandmother all the time.

When she'd finished playing out back, flying through the air on the wooden tree swing, her hands raw from holding the rope so long, she'd run through the horse pasture into the lighthouse and throw her arms around her grandmother, the sweet spice of her warm snickerdoodle cookies filling the air. Looking up at the smile on her grandmother's weathered face, Mia hadn't had a clue back then about all the heartache her grandma had gone through in her life.

"We're warriors like her now," her mother had said when she was a young girl.

That protective armor she'd built as a child had slid back up as Mia had gotten off the plane two hours ago and climbed into the rental car, headed for the coastal border between Virginia and North Carolina. With every mile closer to her mother's modest home, nestled in the rural landscape about a block from the Atlantic, far away from Mia's life in New York, she worked to keep her emotions in check. It was time to be resilient for her mother and sister. Packing up the lighthouse, and all their memories, wouldn't be easy for any of them.

"It's freezing out here," she told her mother now as she swam back into the present, swallowing her tears, the winter wind doing a good job of disguising them. "Let's go in and get warm." She opened the old front door of her childhood home and picked up her suitcases, lugging them inside, past the Christmas wreath of faded greenery and red berries.

The glow of lamplight and the crackling fire hid the shabbiness of the living room well. The old sofa where Mia had read stories to Riley before bed looked exactly the same, down to the knitted orange and yellow blanket draped over the arm. A tiny Christmas tree sat in the corner of the room, one of the strands of colored lights not working, the quilted tree skirt underneath empty of presents. It didn't matter how often Mia came; her adult view of the home was surprising every time. It had seemed perfect growing up, but now she could see the years of struggle in the outdated furnishings, the worn carpet, and the faded wallpaper.

"Get settled in your room and I'll make us some Christmas cinnamon tea," her mother said, clearing her throat and sniffling as she tucked a runaway piece of wiry gray hair back into her bun, putting on a brave face. "Riley's in the shower. She'll be out in a minute. She's gonna be so happy to see you."

With a deep breath, Mia nodded and put on her best smile. She and her mother had an unspoken solidarity when it came to protecting Riley, as if they could shield her from everything.

Mia rolled her two Louis Vuitton suitcases across the thin carpet and down the narrow hallway to the back of the house, the faint sound of running water and holiday songs on the radio coming from the bathroom at the end. She pushed open her old door, running her finger along the tape marks that remained from her teenage posters, before clicking on the light. Her twin bed still held a mass of her stuffed animals, the ruffled bedspread had been folded back neatly the way she used to do it, and her gymnastics trophies lined the dresser. She shut the door behind her and dropped down onto the bed. Only then did she let the tears over losing Grandma Ruth come.

But she didn't have long to wallow before her phone went off with a text. She wiped her eyes and fished the device out of her handbag, frowning at the message from her husband, Milo Broadhurst.

> *The venue called. They're already booked. I knew we should've booked it earlier. This trip is terrible timing, you know. Selling the lighthouse at Christmas was a ridiculous idea. I hope you can handle things from there.*

A mixture of guilt and irritation swarmed her like a pack of angry bees. Yes, she knew she should've booked a venue for the corporate party earlier, but it had slipped her mind. This year hadn't been the easiest for her, with Grandma Ruth passing away in August, and Milo's foul moods as well as their impending divorce announcement certainly hadn't helped.

Mia was usually the life of the party. She made a living out of it. She was director of event planning and PR at her husband's marketing and media company Broadhurst Creative, and everyone was looking forward to their yearly Christmas bash on December twentieth—A-list celebs, fashion designers, and all their friends. The Broadhurst Christmas party was *the* place to be in New York, and all their clients and their clients' friends were waiting for the invitations to show up. From early November, it was all anyone in her circle talked about. Last year's had been her best. She'd scored the biggest ballroom in the Arcadia hotel, only available for private parties, and usually with a three-year wait list. It was a large expanse with chandeliers and white-gloved service, dripping in designer tuxedos, furs, and low-cut dresses, the guests putting on their very best.

The pressure to get it right was enormous, and Mia was doing everything she could to keep all the balls in the air. Over the past few months, this had meant trying to keep her emotions in check, managing a funeral for her grandmother and the sale of the lighthouse, as well as being a sounding board for her mother and sister's grief, her mother literally crumbling when they'd come to the conclusion that they had to sell the lighthouse. And then there was the impending divorce that she and Milo were waiting until after the holiday to announce, so as not to put a dampener on the party. For the last six months, they'd been living in the same house while simultaneously trying to avoid one another.

She'd managed to keep everything going without anyone seeing a single crack in her carefully constructed facade. Until she'd forgotten to confirm the venue and officially assign the charity for Broadhurst's annual event, and she'd lost the reservation. How in the *world* could she have forgotten...? To stall and cover up her enormous blunder, she'd announced to the media that the venue and charity were a surprise this year, and everyone was anticipating the big reveal.

Mia texted Milo back: *I'll take care of it.*

A knock on the door pulled her out of her frustration. A smiling, wet-haired Riley poked her head in. The water made her normally blonde hair a soft brown, one of the few differences between the sisters. With their milky skin and green eyes, people mistook them for twins when they were younger, but their hair color set them apart. At twenty-three, Riley's sweet face was so youthful and worry-free. "I missed you," she said, pushing through the door, plopping down in her oversized flannel pajamas and throwing her arms around Mia. Mia closed her eyes and allowed her sister's fresh scent of strawberries and soap to calm her.

"Mama's making us Christmas tea," she said, slipping her phone back into her handbag and grinning for Riley's benefit.

Riley's face contorted into a more serious expression. "Was she okay when you got here?"

Mia shook her head, not wanting to say too much and worry her sister.

"She can't stop crying over losing the lighthouse. I've never seen her like this. She's usually so strong."

Rubbing her forehead, Mia pressed her temples to keep the ache at bay. "I know. I totally understand—I don't want to lose it either." Right before she died, Grandma Ruth had willed the lighthouse to her family, but she'd taken out a couple of sizeable agricultural loans to maintain the grounds because their grandfather's insurance money was dwindling, and it wasn't enough to keep her afloat. "We already have to make those back payments. We can't afford to foot the bill for the loans. We'll all go broke."

"You sure you can't do it?" Riley asked, her words guarded and careful, but hope in her eyes.

"Milo and I make a good living, but not enough to afford that on top of our other mortgages," she said, not wanting to go into everything right at that moment. She needed to catch her breath after Milo's rant.

"You don't want to sell your house in the Cayman Islands to pay off the loans and then keep the lighthouse?" Riley asked with a little laugh, covering up the fact that her question was more pleading than teasing.

The question alone caused shame to wriggle under Mia's skin. Her mother and sister weren't in any position to save the lighthouse. If anyone could afford to fix this, it was Mia. But there was no way, even *before* their plans for divorce, that she'd get Milo to sell their beautiful vacation home to take on a dilapidated, non-working lighthouse in the middle of nowhere, no matter how much she'd loved it as a child. And now... Panic floated through her chest as her gaze landed on those designer bags of hers. Things would certainly be different after the divorce.

"I just can't," Mia said, her head pounding.

Riley nodded, sucking in an anxious breath.

"Tea's ready!" their mother called from the front room.

Her sister stood up. "That's our cue."

As Riley headed to the door, Mia stopped her. "I brought presents," she said, almost as a peace offering, the sentiment withering under the pressure of what they were up against. She pushed her suitcase onto its side and unzipped it.

"You didn't have to do that," Riley said. "We don't have anything for you."

"I don't need anything," Mia replied, pulling four shiny red gifts from her bag. "It might raise Mama's spirits." She reached in again and pulled out a big box of chocolates. "Heads up." She tossed it over to her sister.

Riley caught the box and looked down at it, brightening. "Chocolate ganache truffles!"

"Mama loves them," Mia said with a grin, "so you'd better get a few before they're gone."

Alice poked her head into the room. She'd gotten herself together. The only remnant of their tearful time on the porch was the hint of pink at the rims of her eyes. "Are y'all gonna come get your tea or would you rather me just ice it and serve it in glasses?... Ohhh," she said, her attention turning to the gold chocolate box.

"Sorry, we were a little distracted." Riley waved the package in the air.

"What are those?" Alice pointed to the gifts on the bed.

"They're for you and Riley," Mia replied, grabbing them.

Worry formed in lines along her mother's forehead. "I thought we weren't exchanging presents."

"We aren't," Mia assured her. "I just wanted to do something nice for my family—that's all."

Her mother softened. "You shouldn't have."

"I shouldn't have gotten gifts for my two *favorite* people?" Mia wrinkled her nose playfully at them, the heaviness from earlier lifting for the moment.

As they walked down the hall, Alice put her arms around both her daughters. "Glad you're home," she said to Mia.

"Things always get better when Mia's home, don't they?" Riley said, giving her sister a squeeze.

"Yes," Alice replied said. "They certainly do."

Mia welcomed the happiness that bubbled up in her. She'd lived away from her mother and sister almost ten years now, after going to college and then moving to New York with Milo, only visiting Bakers Ridge to see her family during the holidays. But it had taken something as drastic as losing Grandma Ruth to realize that she should've come home much more than that.

Mia set the gifts under the tree, and the three of them grabbed their mugs and settled on the sofa in a snuggly line, the fire roaring in front of them, overpowering the wintery draft that snaked through the old house.

"I don't want to ever open them," Mia's mother said as she eyed the presents while she was nestled between her daughters, gripping her holiday mug with its printed holly pattern around curly script that said *Merry & Bright*. "They look so pretty under there."

They sparkled beneath the little tree in the corner, the single working strand of lights casting different colors across the shiny paper. Mia had wrapped the gifts herself and tied each one with a silver bow, the tails of the ribbon cascading down the sides of each box.

Alice reached forward and grabbed the chocolates on the coffee table, opening them and pinching one between her two fingers. "You're both such strong, beautiful women. How did I get so lucky to have you two?" she asked, popping the truffle into her mouth.

"We get it from you," Mia said with a loving smile.

"I wish your Grandma Ruth could be here to see you two tonight," Alice replied. "This is our first Christmas without her."

"She's here," Riley assured her mother. "She's right here."

"It always felt so festive with Grandma Ruth around," Mia said, recalling the nights they'd spent at the lighthouse over the holidays. "She always had snickerdoodle cookies in the oven when we got there."

"Oh, it's been so long since she made those," Alice said wistfully. "I'll bet the recipe is in her recipe box at the lighthouse."

Riley bit her lip, her eyes sparkling. "They're so delicious... We should make them this year."

"I'll go make us a note right now to look for the recipe when we're there," Alice said, pushing against Mia's knee as she got up off the sofa and went into the kitchen.

"Have you been to the lighthouse at all since..." Mia asked, unable to finish the sentence, the memory of the drive into the small town of Winsted Cape coming to mind. Passing the historic Winsted Hotel with its lanterns and stone archways, going down Main Street, past all the little shops that looked like something out of a storybook with their striped awnings and individual typography etched on their glass windows...

Riley shook her head, worry pulling at the corners of her mouth. "I meant to stop by to make sure the cleaning crew you hired is doing an okay job for any showings, but I've been so busy at the hospital... And I didn't want to go there alone. I need you with me."

The idea of it sent another wave of anxiety through Mia, although she worked to hide it. Would Grandma Ruth approve of them selling the lighthouse that had been in their family for generations?

Mia's mother came back in, the low light almost hiding her bloodshot eyes. She sniffled and gave Mia a squeeze with her free arm, sitting down and balancing her tea on her knee with the other. "You know, I go through ups and downs about what's supposed to happen at this point. I know selling the lighthouse is the right thing to do. It's just that it's the last piece of her, you know?"

Mia nodded, taking a warm sip of the rich cinnamon and cream tea, the flavors as delicious as Christmas morning. She totally understood how her mother felt. The lighthouse, which had been in their family since 1870, passed down from generation to generation of Carters, had always been a glittering existence in their mundane, blue-collar lives, a towering representation of Grandma Ruth's love for people and the world. Growing up, it had been the view of the wide blue horizon from the top that had made Mia wonder what else was out there, and eventually apply to Columbia University in New York, only one of the many high standards she'd set—and met—for herself.

Despite her bouts of sadness, their mother seemed more at ease now that they were all together. She was much better than Mia had imagined she'd be only four months after Grandma Ruth had passed.

"How's the real estate agent? Have you spoken to him yet?" her mother asked Mia before sipping her tea.

"Yes, quite a few times. Will Thacker's his name. He was a lucky find. Mr. Thacker came highly recommended from one of my colleagues at Broadhurst. It was a complete fluke. I happened to mention selling the lighthouse over general conversation and she said she knew someone who might be able to help me. He's well-versed in selling sizeable properties, and he's got family in this area, so even if he wasn't able to sell the lighthouse, he could probably put me in touch with someone who could. I was floored when he said he'd take it on himself."

As she spoke, she could see the conflict of relief and guilt on her mother's face.

"The right buyer will come along," Riley said. "Will you get it all done by Christmas?"

"It's a pretty tight timeline, but the agent and I have had a ton of phone discussions over the last few weeks and it might just pay off. We want to make it a showstopper right at the holiday, hoping to capitalize on Christmas magic." She dared not say out loud that they'd probably need nothing short of magic to sell it. The rural area was hardly full of potential lighthouse owners.

"What does he want to do?" Riley asked, grabbing a chocolate.

"We're going to repaint the exterior and renovate the inside just slightly—fresh paint and new kitchen and bathroom fixtures, cabinets, and counters to update it. I've also got a designer who's a great friend of mine coming in to stage furniture and decorate it for Christmas. Then we put the photos online, price it competitively, and pray we get an offer."

"Do we have money for all that?" her mother asked, the lines between her eyes creasing.

"I've taken care of it," Mia assured her, although she no longer shared a bank account with Milo, and she could actually see the dent it had made in her savings. But it was the least she could do, since her mother and Riley had taken on the brunt of Grandma Ruth's care for most of her time in the hospital while Mia was in New York.

She could still remember the day that she'd gotten into Columbia. She'd applied mostly to see if she had what it took to get in; a test of her warrior status, so to speak. When she'd actually received the acceptance letter, she'd run over to Grandma Ruth's to show her.

"I can't really live in New York, can I?" she'd asked her grandmother breathlessly.

Grandma Ruth sat down in the chair on the lighthouse porch. "Why not? You can do anything you set your mind to."

"But I have responsibilities here," she said. "Riley still has a few years of high school left. Who'll help her with her homework?"

Grandma Ruth smiled at her. "Who helped you with yours?"

she asked.

Mia considered this.

"Maybe it's time to let Riley learn her own power." She leaned forward, putting her hand on Mia's knee. "Go. Spread your wings and fly. It's what this life has been preparing you to do. You were born to lead, remember? Maybe it's time to lead outside of your family."

"There are a lot of Grandma Ruth's belongings to go through," Riley said now, pulling Mia out of her memory. "We'll want to divvy up the mementos and really take our time with it."

"I know," Mia agreed. "I'm driving into Winsted Cape in the morning to start packing things in the lighthouse." Just saying it out loud gave her a pang of unease.

"We'll meet you there after your meeting," her mother said, that wall of strength that Mia had seen throughout her childhood sliding back up.

"All right." Feeling the heaviness returning, Mia took in a deep breath and then grabbed a chocolate herself. "So, Riley. Tell me about this guy you're dating—Russell? How's it going?" she asked, attempting to lighten the mood.

Riley made a face, locking eyes with their mother for a second. "It isn't. We broke up."

"Oh no. I didn't even get to meet him."

"Yeah. He wasn't the one." She looked completely deflated, blinking away tears. "I just can't seem to find my person, you know?" Riley said, both hands wrapped around her mug as it sat in her lap, nestled in the pile of orange and yellow blanket that she'd pulled off the arm of the sofa.

Growing up, Riley had big dreams, just like her sister. She'd talked about living in faraway places, being a princess, and she'd even spent a summer wanting to go to Space Camp to learn how to be an astronaut. Mia wished Riley could've gotten out like she had, but after high school she'd stayed, worked to get a nursing degree at the college a town over at night while she ran the desk at the local hotel, and then after graduating she went to work at the hospital in town. Her shifts were long, and Mia struggled to watch the years slip away as her dreamer of a sister worked crazy hours and treaded water in her life.

"It's the women-warrior gene," Mia replied. "We're destined to be solitary creatures. It's why we're so strong." She popped a truffle into her mouth, the milky creaminess of chocolate and caramel mixing with the sprinkling of salt on top.

Her mother grinned and set her tea onto the table. "That's not entirely true," she countered. "You found Milo."

Maybe it was the pressed, fabricated smile or the lie in Mia's eyes, but Alice immediately noticed.

"Everything okay with Milo?"

She felt like she should be sad about a future without her other half, but life with Milo had become so unpleasant that she was numb to the idea of living without him. She'd often recall the blissful early days of their relationship and wonder what went wrong, rehashing everything and coming up empty. Her tenacity and determination couldn't save them. The fact that there was something this huge that she couldn't muscle through ate at her every single day, until she'd shut off completely from it in some sort of feeble attempt at self-preservation. She took in a deep breath and let it out. "We weren't going to say anything until after the holiday, but we're getting a divorce."

Alice's eyes were the size of saucers and Riley gasped. "Oh Mia, are you okay?"

"Surprisingly, yes. We can't even communicate properly anymore. We grew apart, and no matter how hard I try—and believe me, I *did* try—I can't fix it."

"Maybe the space will give you both perspective," her mother offered hopefully. "You know, with you here and him in New York... Absence makes the heart grow fonder and all that."

Mia smiled for her mother's benefit. "Maybe. I do have to go back for the holiday party on the twentieth, but I'll return right after and stay until the lighthouse is sold."

"No matter what happens, let's make this Christmas one of our best," Riley said. "We're all three together and I'd like to believe that Grandma Ruth is here too. There's nothing better than that."

"Definitely," Mia said, the warmth of her family breathing life back into her.

With the heat from the fire, the Christmas lights twinkling, and the people she loved next to her, Mia couldn't help but hope that, despite everything, Christmas might just have a little magic after all.

TWO

"Milo, I haven't even had breakfast yet," Mia said quietly into her phone the next morning, squeezing her stinging eyes shut as she lay under her thin childhood bedspread, the draft from the old window giving her a chill. Between the cold temperature and the firm mattress, she hadn't slept well.

"We'll have the same issue after you eat," he said, in a tone that she knew meant he was shaking his head and had a disappointed look in his eyes—the same eyes that used to swallow her with interest when they'd first met.

"That's not the point." She rubbed her thumping temple, her gaze falling on a picture of her as a child—her proud youthful smile as she rode Delilah, her grandmother's chocolate-brown horse, a blue ribbon hanging from the bridle. Mia's muscles relaxed in surrender as a wave of sadness flooded her. "How did we get here?"

"We got here by you missing the deadline to book Arcadia for the party," he spat. His voice was miles away from the soft whispers he'd once uttered at her neck just before she'd fallen asleep at night in the early years of their relationship. She twisted her head toward her pillow, trying to recall how his chest had smelled against her face, but she couldn't conjure it up. It had been forever since he'd held her like that.

"You're not angry about the party," she told him, emotionless despite his jab.

"The hell I'm not!"

"No," she disagreed calmly, despite his aggressive response. "You're angry about how *we* turned out. We put five long years into this and it didn't work." She bit back tears, the numbness burning off at the thought of the hope she'd had when she'd met him.

The first time she'd laid eyes on Milo Broadhurst, in the heat of the summer, he was outside her favorite coffee shop in the city. She'd walked out with her iced latte—the drink she got every day—and noticed him. He had his phone to his ear, pacing around his Range Rover, when he'd noticed her. It was an instant curiosity. He ended whatever call he was on and smiled apologetically, as if he'd offended her by not immediately noticing her.

"I think my car battery's dead," he said—for lack of something better to say, he'd told her later. When they'd reminisced about that day, he'd said that he spit out whatever words he could conjure up to keep her from walking away.

"I see," she said. "My car's just down the road. Do you need a ride somewhere?"

"You let just any old random guy in your car?"

She'd laughed. "How do you know *you're* safe with me?"

The curiosity intensified, turning into full-blown interest. "How about I buy you lunch first and we can make sure we won't kill each other? There's a great place called Marco's we could go to."

Mia came to from her memory and realized that, uncharacteristically, Milo had gone silent. She knew he remembered the good times too.

"I haven't been the greatest either," she admitted. "I said things I shouldn't have. I'm so sorry we let it get this bad." She rolled over, cradling her phone against her ear. "Remember when we used to meet each other after work for drinks at Marco's?" She honed in on a memory of him two years after they'd met, sitting at their table at

Marco's Italian restaurant in the red sweater she'd bought him for Christmas. The thought of the way the corners of his mouth had turned upward and the late-day shadow on his face caused her chest to tighten. "You always had a martini waiting for me when I got there."

A twinge of nostalgia fluttered around in her stomach when she recalled how he used to look at her when she walked through that door. Then, without warning, their last night out a few weeks ago flooded her mind. She squeezed her eyes shut to get the image out of her head. She didn't want to remember the softness in his face when he'd looked at his coworker, Elaine, his lingering smile. The woman had made him laugh—something Mia hadn't been able to do in a long time.

Milo cleared his throat and let out a heavy breath through the phone.

"Can we talk when I get home?" she asked. "Just strip away all the baggage and talk? You and me."

"What will it change, Mia?"

"Nothing if you won't let it." A fighter by nature, she couldn't allow this to end without one last battle. "We used to be great together."

The line buzzed between them before he finally asked, "What are we going to do about the party?" His voice was more controlled now.

"I'll figure it out," she said, the tiny bit of confidence she'd had that they could save their relationship withering away. "I promise."

Milo was the first to hang up. Mia flipped onto her back, dropped her phone on her chest, and stared at the ceiling. If they could just have some time together with no other demands, could they make things work between them? Was there anything left of what they'd had? Or were they completely different people now?

The bedroom door squeaked as it opened. "Hey," Riley said from the doorway. She was dressed in her scrubs already. "I thought I heard you talking. Everything okay?"

Mia sat up and rubbed her face, trying to wipe away the entire call, if that was possible. "It was Milo," she croaked.

Riley sat down on the bed, pulling the bedspread taut against Mia's legs. "Not good, huh?"

"Definitely not."

"Sorry." Riley rubbed the blanket covering Mia's shin sympathetically.

"Don't be." She forced her eyes open wider and pushed a smile across her face to bury her issues with Milo. "It's Christmas—the best holiday of the year. Maybe getting out of bed and on with the day will help pep me up."

Her sister brightened. "Well, if you've got time before you meet the real estate agent, breakfast could take your mind off it. Mama's made her famous French toast with honey and bananas, and there's a hot pot of coffee waiting."

"That sounds amazing." Mia rolled out of bed and slid on her fuzzy slippers. She twisted her hair into a clip and dug out her oversized cardigan from her suitcase, slipping it over her pajamas. "Do you have time to eat before your shift?" she asked Riley.

"Barely," her sister replied. "But I can't *not* eat Mama's French toast."

"True. How about Mom? Does she have time before work?"

"They've been real flexible with her hours at the bank lately. She seems fine with it, but they might have cut them back. I never see her rushing off anymore," Riley said, a hint of worry in her voice.

"As long as she's okay with it," Mia said.

"I've never heard her complain. What about you? What time are you meeting the agent?"

Mia looked over at the clock. "Nine. So I've got about an hour."

"In an odd way, I'm looking forward to being back in the lighthouse. I miss it. And I've only been as far as the barn when I had to sell Delilah."

Mia stared at her wide-eyed. "You sold Delilah? Why didn't you ask for my help?"

"You had enough going on," her sister said.

"Did she go to a good family?" Mia asked, apprehensive about the horse's old age, remembering the long summer days she'd spent brushing her mane, her tail swishing gently in the salty air as she led her back to the stalls.

"Yes, Farmer Owens in town bought her. Remember him from the funeral? Big guy..."

"Oh, yes," Mia replied, recalling Mr. Owens and his wife. "They brought us all the bouquets of wildflowers."

"I know, that was so sweet. And they're just as kind to Delilah. She has a pasture full of buttercups in the summer and a warm barn at the back of the farm."

Mia smiled with relief, remembering how the horse waited with her head over the whitewashed fence for Grandma Ruth's afternoon visits with her handful of garden-grown carrots. The memory caught her off guard, the absence of Grandma Ruth so palpable that it stabbed her right in the heart. She still couldn't believe that her grandmother was gone.

"Sit down, you two," Mama said, fluttering around when they entered the kitchen. She always got buzzy when she was trying to keep her emotions at bay.

The gas burner on the stove had warmed the small room considerably, and a platter with a stack of French toast sat in the center of the wooden table. Mia took a seat, breathing in the sweet, buttery smells and letting the moment relax her.

Mama pulled a chair out for Riley like she used to do when the girls were young. "I hope you're hungry. I made enough for an army." She grabbed the pot of coffee and filled their mugs, the nutty aroma filling the air. "Cream and sugar are beside the syrup."

"You've outdone yourself," Mia said, eyeing her mother protectively, as if she could keep her from falling apart with her stare while they slid into their seats.

"Only the best for my girls." She blew her daughters a kiss and then scooted her chair up to the table, taking the platter and serving herself two slices before passing it to Riley. "So, what exactly is on the agenda today?" her mother asked with a cautious edge to her question.

"I'm meeting with the agent to talk about the timeline for the sale of the lighthouse and take a look at remodeling plans at nine," Mia said. "And then I'm going to start packing it up. Riley's coming by after work." She tried to gage the uneasiness on her mother's face, but she was covering it well. "You don't have to—there's no pressure—but if you want to, you're more than welcome to pack up Grandma Ruth's things with me."

"I think it would be good to be there," their mother said. "It's hard, but it might give me some closure."

"We can do this, Mama," Riley said, reaching across the table for her hand. "We've always done everything we could for Grandma Ruth—together. We took care of her when she started to get sick and the chemo wasn't working; we helped her through her long hospital stay when all she wanted was to jump out of that bed and head home... We need to do this one last thing for her. *Together*. Strength in numbers, right?"

Alice nodded, resolution in her eyes.

Strength in numbers.

Mia shrugged her heavy coat off and set it, along with the roll of paper towels and a bar of hand soap she'd brought for the day, on the old Formica kitchen counter of the main house. It was attached to the lighthouse on Winsted Cape, half an hour's drive from her mother's. She rubbed her cold hands together, the snow coming down outside turning the grounds into a winter wonderland.

She fiddled with the thermostat, upping the temperature, and then looked around for the first time in a year. The cleaning crew had done a good job. Grandma Ruth's teacup collection still lined the far wall; her rolling pins remained in the giant ceramic bowl she'd kept them in on the counter; the hummingbird sun-catcher glittered in the window above the sink. It was as if she would putter around the corner any minute to make Christmas cookies.

Mia closed her eyes for a second, trying to summon the smell of her cherry pie, but nothing came, a fresh wave of grief hitting her.

From the kitchen, Mia walked into the living room, a wide expanse with vaulted ceilings and exposed beams. A stone fireplace stretched upward along the far wall, where they used to roast marshmallows. Everything was in order, down to the tapestry throw pillows on the sofa. She headed down the short hallway to the bedrooms. There were three: Grandma Ruth's and one for each of her grandkids, she'd said.

Mia went into hers first, dragging her fingers along the thin yellow bedspread that had been on that bed since she was a little girl. A wooden vanity sat in the corner next to a window with a view of the horse pasture. Under the window, the modest dresser still held photos of when Mia and Riley were young. Mia picked up a silver frame with a picture of her and her sister sitting in front of the Christmas tree in their candy-cane pajamas.

Riley's room was also just the way Mia remembered it to be, with a navy-blue comforter and extra pillows because Riley always liked to sleep surrounded by them. The bathroom had a lacy hand towel draped over the edge of the sink and a vase of silk flowers on the back of the toilet—all the way Grandma Ruth had left it.

Finally, she peeked into Grandma Ruth's room, the lilac and roses scent of her grandmother stronger in there. That, coupled with the pair of slippers still next to her bed, made the hair on Mia's arms stand up. She stepped inside and took in a steadying breath, the whisper of the little tune that Grandma Ruth used to hum coming to mind. Mia walked over to the oak dresser with ornate brass pulls, and fiddled with a pair of pearl earrings that were still sitting in a porcelain dish as if they were waiting to be worn again. Slid under the dish was a folded piece of paper. Mia opened it, finding a phone number and the name Mildred. The area code wasn't familiar. Was this person still waiting for a call from Grandma Ruth? Mia refolded it and placed it back where it had been.

She paced back into the kitchen and peered outside at the wild waves of the Atlantic on the edge of the property. Dull sunlight filtered in through the window, muted by the snowfall. Glancing at her watch, she looked out the beveled panes in the door at the blanket of snow, the real estate agent's sign jutting out of it. The bright red "FOR SALE" letters screamed at her, and the tracks from her rental car were already buried by new snow. She turned away. It was after nine; the agent should be here any minute.

Between the eerie quiet of the house and the immense expanse of snow as far as she could see outside, there was a stillness to it all that put an exclamation point at the end of the fact that this was it. These would be their last few moments in the house that had been Grandma Ruth's whole life, the place that had carried their family through its ups and downs over generations. The beacon light on the lighthouse tower would remain dark until another owner decided to turn it on.

Ruth had insisted from her hospital bed that the lighthouse stay in the family, no matter what. They didn't know how they would manage it, but they'd promised her they'd do everything they could. In the end though, it just wasn't possible. Surely Grandma Ruth would understand that? It didn't stop Mia's lurking fear that, once the lighthouse was sold, it would cease to be their family refuge—just disappear like Grandma Ruth, time moving on around it.

The kitchen door flew open, startling Mia. Snow blew onto the mat that lay under two large boots. She followed them up to a pair of jeans and then a coat, an arm holding a laptop and a small cardboard container with striped red lettering, finally resting on the face of a guy that looked to be about her age. Snowflakes dotted his light brown hair, and his electric-blue, sultry eyes seemed frazzled —which didn't match his commanding presence—as he shut the door behind him.

"Sorry I'm late," he said in a low but gentle tone, slightly breathless. He took her in with interest for a brief moment as if he were processing the visual of the voice he'd heard over the phone during their calls. Almost as though looking at her had helped him to gather himself, he smiled warmly, shifted his items to one arm and stretched his hand out. "Will Thacker."

There was a sincerity in his gaze that made her indifferent to his lateness.

"Mia Carter." She shook his hand. "This snow slows everything down, doesn't it?" she said, trying to lessen any unease he had.

He smiled again, his eyebrows rising in agreement, but there was something heavy behind his gesture that made her wonder if the snow had had anything to do with his arrival time at all.

For an instant, they stood together, their separate worlds needing a moment to melt away and leave just the two of them.

"Great to finally meet you. I come with a peace offering. I thought it might help our creativity." He held out the box, which she realized was from The Corner Bakery.

Mia laughed at the sight. She knew The Corner Bakery well. Originally owned by two brothers named Thomas and Edwin Platt, it had been around since the 1900s; it was the town jewel and somewhere she hadn't been since she was a girl. She'd gotten cupcakes with chocolate bars baked into them every summer that she visited Grandma Ruth in Winsted Cape.

Mia had fond memories of rows of candy containers forming an enormous rainbow on the bright white walls, and the red-and-white striped lettering painted in curly script that spelled out the shop's name. Her mother always let them get one treat, and she could still feel her indecision as she leaned on the large glass display window at the register, ogling over the vast array of confections.

"I can't decide between the double chocolate cookie with white chocolate chunks and mint sprinkles or the orange cream truffles," she'd said once to Grandma Ruth.

"Well, you know how to handle that situation, don't you?" Grandma Ruth had said.

A ten-year-old Mia shook her head. "No, how?"

"You buy both!"

Mia and Riley had doubled over laughing, while Grandma Ruth asked the baker to fill an entire box of treats for them that day.

Curious about what was inside, nostalgia bubbling up, Mia took the box from Will and opened it. Nestled in white parchment were an array of sweets: little bell-shaped donuts dusted with powdered sugar, Santa hat cookies with red-and-white trimming, buttery biscuits and croissants—all of it pulling her into a more festive mood.

"These look fantastic," she said, inhaling the sugary sweet smells. "They'd be really great during showings, laid out on a platter here on the island. We could light some vanilla and clove candles, maybe add a holiday runner to the farm table…"

"Ah, they worked," he said, chewing on a grin as he opened his laptop on the table, the screen coming to life. "You're full of ideas already."

Mia brought the box over next to him and dipped in for a donut. "And I haven't even eaten one yet," she teased, their light and easy banter a breath of fresh air, given her circumstances.

Her comment amused him, and the playfulness that surfaced in his eyes somehow made her feel like she'd known him forever.

"They're very helpful," she said, holding the bite-sized powdered dough between her two fingers. "My morning started off a little crazy, so thank you for bringing me back into the Christmas spirit."

"I totally understand." He shot her a look of solidarity, and only then did she notice the slight fatigue lingering behind his stare.

Clearing whatever it was before she could ponder it too much, he pulled a chair out for her, and the two of them sat down.

"I'll definitely get some more pastries come showing time. We can tick that one off the list. Were you able to book a designer?" he asked.

"Yes," Mia replied, trying not to think about how nice it was to have a normal conversation with someone. "I've got one flying in from New York. Her name is Leah Gatwick. She's worked with me on quite a few occasions, and she's a good friend."

"That sounds great. May I?" He gestured toward the paper towels.

"Of course."

Will ripped one off and took a croissant from the box. "Thanks. I didn't get a chance to have breakfast this morning, but then again I never do." He smiled at her again, lifting her mood even more.

"I'm staying at my mother's, and before I'd even gotten out of bed, she'd made enough French toast to feed a small country."

Will grabbed a pen and a pad of paper from his laptop bag. "What's the address? I'll be sure to stop by tomorrow morning then," he teased.

She laughed at his joke but before she knew it, her smile fell. The memory of her and Milo on their first date, walking down a cobbled alleyway behind her apartment in the city, snow falling around them, floated into her consciousness—he'd made her laugh with something silly just the same way Will had now... And look how that had turned out.

After a calming breath, Mia said, "My plan is to pack up everything that we don't need and let Leah, the designer, create a really inviting, beautiful atmosphere." There was a natural softness to his expression that surprised her, as if he legitimately wanted to know about her plans. She broke eye contact and turned her attention down the hallway toward the living room. "My grandmother has some great furniture in the house. We just need to get rid of the clutter. Then we're coming in and decorating for Christmas."

"Sounds perfect," he said, typing on his computer. "As I mentioned on the phone earlier, I have three options for the kitchen remodel."

He turned his screen toward her and shuffled closer. His scent, a delicious mixture of sage, pine, and spice, caused her breathing to become shallow and she wouldn't allow herself to inhale it. She kept her eyes on the screen, focusing on the estimates while nearly holding her breath.

"This company here wants to do a slate tile backsplash with quartz countertops and light gray cabinets." He tapped the screen to pinpoint the estimate, forcing her to stop thinking about his blue eyes. What was wrong with her? She squinted at the screen. "In my opinion, it's the strongest design, but I'll let you decide." He zoomed in on the other two and Mia leaned forward to take a closer look.

"I think you're right," she said. "The first one's a great look for in here. Can they carry it through the bathrooms?" She took a bite of the soft donut, the vanilla dough melting in her mouth.

"Of course."

"What's our timeframe?" she asked.

"All three companies would love the recognition for a job like this. Because of that, the kitchen cabinet installation can be done in a day, counters would come in the next day, and then spot painting. It would be done by next week. All three companies are willing to put a rush on it, and they'll begin the minute we give them the word. Demo can start as soon as you're packed. Will that give your designer enough time?"

"It should work out perfectly as long as the snowstorm holds off."

"I know someone with a snowplow. We'll plow the drive if we have to."

"Awesome. Leah can come right in after them. She only needs a few days. That will allow us to have a finished product before Christmas."

"Excellent. I'll have a photographer do a video shoot and stills when the designer's done so we can get the listing up."

"Perfect. Thank you."

"No problem. I'll do everything I can to help you get this property off your plate."

She pushed down the panic that came over her at the finality of the situation.

As Will opened another screen, she tore herself from the

thought. "I also found you some spots that take donations. I know you wanted to do some research."

"Oh, wow. Thanks for doing that."

"No problem at all. I can help you deliver the donations as well." His eyes met hers and it was as if he were trying to subtly figure her out right then and there. By the look he was giving her, she was worried he could read her entire life story without her having to say a word.

She nodded uneasily, and he finally let her off the hook, turning his attention back to the laptop. Their easy chemistry wasn't something she'd expected, and she needed to keep it from becoming a distraction. She was there to sell the lighthouse, that was all.

"This charity takes books." He redirected her to the screen. "And this one allows furniture donations as well as clothing."

He offered her an inquisitive half-smile, and all of a sudden, she wanted to get on with packing things up. She needed to be alone with Grandma Ruth for a while to calm her chaotic mind. Her entire life, she'd been in complete control, but right now, it was as if everything were spinning around her in a frenzy, and she was unable to grab hold of it all.

"Great." Mia rummaged around in her handbag, retrieving the extra key to the lighthouse. "On the phone, I promised you a universal key. Here's the key that opens the kitchen door, which—as you know—is the main door we use, since it's by the drive, the front door, and the door to the lighthouse, although that one isn't usually locked. I guess we should lock it."

"Perfect," he said, digging out the spare key he'd gotten from under the mat outside, which only worked the kitchen door.

He set it on the table and took the new key from her. When he did, she pulled her hand away quickly to avoid contact, sending his thoughtful gaze her way once more and causing her heart to beat like a snare drum.

"I'll let the contractors in once you give me the go-ahead, and I'll get the lockbox with the key installed for other agents," he said.

"I can give you a code to get into the box if you need the key for any reason."

"Awesome. Thank you." She stood up and pushed in her chair in an attempt to signal for him to go. "I'll actually be here," she announced. "I have a second key so I can come and go. And if, by some miracle, we get a showing before the listing, I'll be happy to clear out for you." She reached out her hand. "It was nice to finally meet you, Mr. Thacker."

With a searching frown, he stood up and slipped his laptop into its bag. "I'd better get going. The snow's really coming down. It was very nice to meet you... Ms. Carter." He tried to hide it, but she caught a flicker of a look down to her bare ring finger and then away before he ran his thumb under his own.

"Goodbye, Mr. Thacker," she said, not offering for him to call her by her first name. She had enough to deal with right now without getting caught up in some sort of flirtation.

THREE

By lunchtime, Mia had eaten half the box of bakery items and, while she'd sorted a ton of her grandmother's belongings, she'd barely scratched the surface of packing Grandma Ruth's things. She had two large piles in the middle of the living room in front of the sofa: one full of old clothing from the bedroom closets, and one with housewares that she'd collected throughout the various rooms.

Setting a vase on the pile, she maneuvered around it all and peered outside at the snow that was coming down with a vengeance. The back side of the house that held a sitting room and a small office jutted out toward the sea, connecting the lighthouse to the main home. Against the pristine white snow, the towering red-and-white lighthouse looked dingy, and she couldn't wait for the painters to come freshen it up. The heavy clouds moving across the gray sky made the lighthouse look like it was swaying, rocking back and forth, as if consoling itself without Grandma Ruth.

Feeling dusty from moving her grandmother's belongings around, she sat cross-legged on the worn braided blue-and-tan rug in the living area, with sheets of paper spread out around her. All of them held lists of New York venues, charities, and their phone numbers that she'd scratched down. She'd yet to find a venue for the party, and it was supposed to happen in just over a week. She closed her eyes and rolled her head on her shoulders, trying not to imagine the conversation when she told Milo she had nowhere to host the party.

She leaned on her elbow, at a loss, when something across the room on the credenza caught her eye. She walked over to a framed photo and picked it up. It was a black-and-white picture of a little girl with curly hair and a gauzy sundress, holding an ice cream cone. "Wonder who this is?" she said out loud, hoping to hear Grandma Ruth answer her.

"He-ey!" Riley's voice meandered in from the kitchen. "Mia?"

"In the living room," she called back, returning the frame to its spot.

Riley came in with a pile of folded cardboard, stacking it against the wall, and put her hands on her hips, surveying the piles. "The stores are crazy right now because of the snowstorm coming." She huffed out an exhausted breath and pushed a lock of hair away from her face. "Glad I bought more boxes. You've been busy," she said.

"Yeah. There's still so much to go through, though." Mia grabbed the lists off the floor and shoved them into her pocket as she greeted her sister. "You're off early."

Riley sat down on the old tweed sofa, running her hands over her scrubs, along her calves. "I took a half-day. My legs are killing me."

"That bad a day already?"

"Yes, but that's not why I took off.'

"Getting a head start on the impending snow?"

"Not that either."

Mia kept her attention on her sister.

"I wanted to give you some support. I know you're trying to be resilient, but I could see it on your face this morning at breakfast— this is tougher for you than you're letting on."

"I'm fine," Mia countered. She wasn't used to having her little sister doing the supporting, and the fact that Riley could see the cracks in her strength made her feel like she'd crumble at any minute. She couldn't crumble.

"I'm sure you are. You make a point of being fine. But you aren't *good*."

"I'll be good when I can get all this stuff out of the lighthouse," she said, attempting to shift the focus.

To Mia's relief, Riley slipped off her winter coat and lumped it on the sofa before walking over to the large built-in bookcase that stretched along the wall, leaving the discussion right there. She tipped her head up to see the books that Grandma Ruth had collected over the years. "Some of these travel memoirs look good," she said, her back to Mia. "This one is set in Italy. I've always wanted to go there."

"Mm-hm," Mia said, her mind clouded by everything. She pulled a book off the shelf and flipped through it. "There's a message in this," she said, running her finger over the page. "It's in Italian. '*Il tuo preferito*. All my love.'" She closed the book.

"I only took two years of Italian in school, but I think that means 'Your favorite,'" Riley said. "Wonder who it's from?" She grinned. "I used to adore Grandma Ruth's stories about traveling the world when she was a girl. Remember when she said she rode around the vineyards in the south of France on the back of a moped?"

"Oh yeah," Mia replied. "She told me once that she'd fallen madly in love with a man named Philippe. He was two years older than she was, and he taught her how to read in French. They spent that whole summer together."

"Ooh la la, what happened after that?" Riley asked, tucking the book under her arm.

"Her father had finished his tour and she had to go back to school here in Winsted Cape... She had so many great memories," Mia said, eyeing the book in Riley's hands and suddenly not wanting to part with it. If she closed her eyes, she could still see Grandma Ruth in an elegant summer dress in the rocker on the front porch, her legs crossed at the ankle, a book on her lap, with that smile as Mia came bounding up the front steps.

Grandma Ruth's life had always seemed so glamorous. She

told the girls stories about how she traveled while her father was in the military, how she'd encountered so many vibrant cultures, and all the things she'd learned along the way. Every now and again, when Mia was a kid, Grandma Ruth would rattle off phrases in Italian or French, filling Mia with excitement.

Riley walked the book over and slipped it into her purse. "I'll keep that one," she said. It was clear that neither of them wanted to dwell too long on Grandma Ruth or they'd break down into tears.

"So, where should we start?" Riley asked.

"There are a bunch of unmarked boxes in the hall closet. We could begin with those and then pile the items we're giving away in the empty boxes."

"Sounds good."

Mia unlatched the hall closet door, swinging it wide open, the space full of boxes, and the two sisters dragged them into the living room. Riley opened one of them, digging down inside it.

"This one's full of photo albums," she said with excitement, pulling one out and opening it up. "Oh, is this Grandma Ruth?" She squinted down at a picture of their grandmother making a silly face for the camera, but even her pursed lips and goofy eyes couldn't hide her beauty.

Mia laughed. "This will take us years if we go through everything like that. Let's make a new pile of personal items. We'll have a look at them later."

"You're right," Riley said, shutting the book and setting it back in the box. "I just miss her."

Mia bit her lip. "Me too."

"We could try to sort the personal items now before Mom gets here," Riley suggested. "It might be easier on her that way."

"That's a good idea," Mia agreed. "Did she say when she was coming?"

"I thought she'd be here already."

"Well, let's go through these boxes as quickly as we can and get Grandma Ruth's personal things tucked away." The emotion of the situation settled around her like broken glass—if she dared to touch it, it would hurt her.

"I'm starving," Riley announced, as they stacked the last box of Grandma Ruth's personal things in the bedroom.

They'd been going strong for the last two hours, and they'd found all kinds of interesting items in those boxes. They'd discovered a journal full of recipes that she'd kept while living in Germany when she was sixteen. She'd hated having to eat Schweinshaxe, some sort of pork dish, but she said she'd loved the Apfelkuchen, a kind of apple cake that sounded delicious. They'd also found a collection of envelopes with stamps from different countries and photos of various members of the family. Mia was dying to take a closer look at it all, but they'd been trying so hard to shield things from their mother that they'd rushed through it.

She went over to the window and peeked out. The snow was still steadily falling down, and the grounds were completely blanketed. "It's weird that we haven't heard from Mom yet." She grabbed her phone and put it to her ear. "We can invite her to go to lunch," she suggested as the phone rang. "We could go to the little café in town."

"Murphy's? I love that place," Riley said, grabbing her coat and slipping it on. "Let's head that way and we can call her en route."

Mia held up her finger when the line stopped ringing.

"Oh, Mia," her mother answered without a hello. "Are you all right? Is Riley with you?"

"Yes, we're fine," she replied. "Why wouldn't we be?" She put the phone on speaker so that Riley could hear the conversation.

"Are you still in Winsted Cape?" her mother asked urgently.

"Yes, we're at Grandma Ruth's, why?"

"I'm sitting in a tow truck right now. I slipped into a ditch in the snow, heading your way. It's treacherous out there. It's really coming down."

"Are *you* okay?" Riley asked.

"I'm fine, but I worry about the roads. The main ones are bad enough, but leaving the lighthouse... Can you and Riley get your cars through the snow to reach the main road?"

Mia's gaze met Riley's. "I have no idea... Mom, we'll call you back once we figure it out. Are you safe at the moment?"

"Yes. The driver's taking me and my car home."

"Okay. Sit tight. I'll keep you posted."

Mia ended the call as they both made their way into the kitchen to view their cars through the glass door.

"Oh, great," Mia said, as she stared at the mounds of snow that had accumulated throughout the morning, completely covering the winding drive leading from the road, through the fields, and to the house. The evergreen trees on the property drooped with the weight of the snow, the bare branches lined in white. The only visible color was the meandering plank fence that outlined the horse pasture and the deep blue waves at the edge of her view. While they'd been packing, the storm had dumped a ton of snow on them, only half the tires of Mia's rental showing above it.

"The storm came faster than the forecasts said it would," said Riley. "How are we supposed to get out of this? At the very least, I'd like to eat. I was hoping for an early dinner."

"I've got half a box of bakery items," Mia replied weakly, looking around the dated kitchen. She opened the old maple cabinets but came up empty so she went over to the pantry door, grabbing the glass knob and checking for anything edible. The cleaners had gotten rid of everything, as she'd instructed them to do. All that was left was a canister of sugar. "Grandma Ruth has rice. That keeps forever. It might still be okay..."

"Great. Old rice and Christmas cookies." Riley made a face. "Wait! I have a power bar in my purse!" She ran into the living room and returned with the bar. Flipping it over and folding back the flap on the package, she read, "Thirty grams of protein. That's fifteen each if we split it. With the rice and cookies, we've almost got ourselves a meal."

Mia laughed. "This is a disaster."

But then Riley's laughter died, and she went quiet. She looked up at the ceiling as if she were trying to find something.

"What are you doing?" Mia asked.

"What if it's not a disaster? What if Grandma Ruth wants us here by ourselves?" She set the bar on the table and looked seriously at her sister.

"What?"

"We're stuck here without Mom—just the two of us. What if there's something Grandma Ruth wants us to know? What if she planned this? It would be just like her."

"So, she sent a snowstorm that propelled Mom into a ditch? Poor Mom—what did she ever do to Grandma Ruth?" Mia asked with another laugh.

"I'm serious!" Riley playfully smacked her sister on the arm.

"Well, if Grandma Ruth wanted to trap us here, I'd have thought she'd leave us more than old rice to eat."

"You have a point there..." Riley put her hands on her hips and gazed out the window again at the winter storm that surrounded them, shaking her head. Then she turned back to Mia. "I haven't told you yet, but that last week in the hospital, when Grandma Ruth was in and out of consciousness, she said something that I was supposed to tell you."

Mia's heart raced at the thought of a message from her grandmother. "What was it?"

"As I was collecting all her paperwork and trying to get the last bit of information from her before we took over the lighthouse, she reached out for me and grabbed my hands urgently. I could barely hear her whispers between long breaths, but she said, 'Tell your sister, hope is where you find it. If you'll look.'"

"*Hope is where you find it?* That doesn't make any sense."

"Maybe she wanted us to stay hopeful in all this."

Mia chewed on the inside of her lip, biting back the sadness that seemed to surface without warning. "I should've been there. I could've asked her myself."

"You had that big PR thing," Riley said.

A wave of guilt overtook Mia. "Big PR thing," she said through clenched lips. "I put a work event over coming to see my grandmother."

"You didn't know those were her last days," said Riley softly.

Mia blinked back tears. "It doesn't matter. I should've been here for her." She leaned against the window, the snow falling at her back. "And now I'll never know what she wanted to tell me... *Hope is where you find it?*"

"But you know how she was at the end," Riley said. "They had her on so much medicine to keep her comfortable while she battled the cancer. Who knows if she even had a clue what she was saying?"

"Yeah..." Mia said for Riley's benefit. It didn't matter what her sister said, Mia still felt awful.

"It's not Christmas without her."

Mia walked over, put her arm around Riley's shoulder, and gave her a squeeze, the weight of returning to New York for the party next week settling heavily on her shoulders. She didn't want to make the same mistake again. She needed to be here for her family. "Let's do something special this Christmas," she offered. "Let's really make it feel like the holidays used to feel—do it for Grandma Ruth."

"How? What do you want to do?"

"I don't know yet," Mia answered honestly. She walked over to Grandma Ruth's old radio and flipped the switch, sending fuzzy static into the room. Turning the dial, she found "Frosty the Snowman."

"I'm not making a snowman," Riley said with warning.

"No," Mia giggled. "But we can eat the Christmas cookies and listen to the music. It's a start, right?"

"Definitely," Riley said as they both smiled at each other.

FOUR

Mia offered Riley the last donut just as a knock at the door sent them both jumping. Who could have gotten across the vast snow-filled acreage to reach them?

"Hello?" Will Thacker's muffled voice called from the other side as he peered into the kitchen, meeting Mia's gaze.

"It's the agent."

Mia opened the door and let him in, along with a gust of frigid air. He was dressed more casually this time, in a rugged flannel peeking out from under his coat and a battered baseball cap. "I worried you'd gotten stuck out here," he said with a shake of his boot, depositing snow onto the small mat. "I came out to put the lockbox back on the door, figuring I could check to see if you were all right."

"That was nice of you to check on my sister," Riley said, with a loaded look to Mia. "We haven't met. I'm Riley Carter."

Will shook her hand. "Nice to meet you."

Mia peeked out the window to find a big sapphire-blue truck in the driveway, its tires resting easily on the snow.

"Do you all need a ride into town?"

"We'd love one," Riley replied before Mia could say anything. She grabbed her sister by the arm. "We'll just gather our things. Be right back."

They hurried into the living room, where Riley pulled Mia close and whispered, "You didn't mention that he's totally gorgeous."

"What did you want me to say, 'Glad you made it to Grandma Ruth's. Oh, and by the way, the real estate agent is hot?'" She picked up her handbag. "And it doesn't matter what he looks like anyway."

"Why not?"

"His job is to sell the lighthouse."

Riley gave her sister a playful grin. "And get us to town. Should we ask him to have a drink?"

"That wouldn't be very professional."

"No, but it would be a great way to say thank you for rescuing us from the snow."

"We don't need rescuing," Mia said with a frown.

Riley rolled her eyes. "Yeah, warriors and all that—I know. But there's a bowl of Murphy's house broccoli cheddar soup that makes me feel otherwise. I *need* rescuing."

Mia considered spending a meal with Will, thoughts of their easy chemistry returning. "It's probably not a good idea..."

"Let's let *him* decide." Riley strode off in the direction of the kitchen. "You're so thoughtful coming back out here to make sure my sister was okay..." Mia heard Riley telling him.

With a deep breath, Mia fixed her eyes on a photo of her grandmother standing on the shore behind the lighthouse, the dune grass swaying in front of the ocean, Grandma Ruth in a sundress, holding a sun hat in front of her with both hands. "You're gonna let her get away with this?" Mia asked the woman in the picture, relenting and allowing a grin.

Grandma Ruth's bright eyes stared back at her.

"Oh, fine. So, you're on *her* side," she teased. "Traitor. I suppose in order to find hope, you have to look, right? But I'm just *looking* tonight. I'm not ready to find it yet." Mia adjusted her handbag on her shoulder and met Will and Riley in the kitchen, always following Grandma Ruth's wishes.

. . .

Mia scooted into the booth at Murphy's. She'd already had to sit in the middle of the bench seat of Will's truck, between Will and her sister, pressed against the side of him on the way there, taking in his spicy aftershave. Now, he was sliding in beside Mia as Riley lowered herself down across from them.

Odd circumstances aside, it was warm and cozy in Murphy's, making her feel festive. White string lights hung from the dark ceiling above them, and twinkles from the Christmas trees flanking the large bay window, with letters that spelled out Murphy's in curling gold script, were reflected in the glass. A large brick fireplace sat at the back, warming them with roaring flames while festive music played over the speakers. With the snow coming down like feathers outside, it was as quaint as a holiday card.

Mia's phone buzzed in her bag. "That could be Mom," she said, pulling it out and peering down at it only to find another barking text from Milo: *No word from you means you've gotten nothing accomplished?*

"What's wrong?" Riley asked, clearly noticing the knit of her eyebrows.

"Nothing." Mia twisted her expression into a pleasant look, despite the fact that Milo was texting to scold her. "Just work." She dropped her phone back into her bag.

The waitress arrived with their menus, handing them out. "Welcome to Murphy's. Glad y'all are here," she said with a friendly nod of her head, pulling a pencil from the pocket of her white apron, which was tied around the signature pinstriped dress uniform. "Just to let you know, we have our hot cocoa with bergamot drizzle and spiced chocolate sticks on special. Chocolate orange tastes so good it'll make your head spin."

"Definite yes from me," Riley said.

Mia nodded in agreement. "I'll have one too."

"How about you, Will?" Riley asked.

He looked over at Mia with interest. "Sure," he said. When Riley caught his eye, he quickly glanced down at his menu.

Mia shook her head subtly at her sister to ward off any thoughts of playing matchmaker. She wriggled her ring finger, only to remember that it was bare. It had been a few months since she'd taken her ring off for good, only wearing it at work, but she kept forgetting that it wasn't there. It wasn't like she'd had a husband over the last year anyway. She and Milo had barely crossed paths outside of the office. The ring she'd worn had been more of a place-holder to tell people that she was off the market rather than a symbol of their love. She'd actually stopped wearing it around the house before she'd seen a lawyer to end the marriage, after Milo had had one outburst too many over trivial things. Milo hadn't even noticed she'd taken it off.

"What's going on with work?" Riley asked, pulling Mia out of her thoughts.

"Oh, just this Christmas party I'm planning." She addressed Will to explain. "I work for a media company."

"What's going on with the event?" Riley asked.

"I have to find a location for it, and after Thanksgiving, it's tough—everything's booked. I should've found one earlier..."

Riley had turned to Will. "Their Christmas parties are full of famous people." Riley had always been enamored with Mia's celebrity friends. "Both Justin Timberlake and Jay-Z have been there."

Will offered another quick glance over to Mia, curiosity on his face.

"Our usual spot in the city is already booked. *Every* venue in New York is booked." She shook her head, disappointed in herself.

Riley leaned on her hand. "Does it have to be in New York? What about that time you all had it in Vail?"

"I've been checking everywhere, even outside of the state, but we're two weeks away from Christmas. I have a feeling that this close to the holiday, we're going to need a miracle to find something big enough to hold everyone."

"How big does the place have to be?" Will asked.

"It has to accommodate at least two hundred people. And if it's outside New York, we also need a hotel that can hold that many reservations. Know any empty buildings? I'd take literally anything at this point," she teased.

Riley chewed on her lip as she considered the question.

Mia twisted toward Will, hoping he had an idea or two, his brows pulling together in thought. Then, an idea hit her. It was definitely a crazy thought, but could it work? "Do you happen to know if the Winsted Hotel has anything going on next week?" Surely in that small town, and off season, they wouldn't be full...

"I can check for you, if you'd like," Will replied. "But I know for a fact that they don't have a gathering space that size."

"I just need the rooms so people would have somewhere to stay," she replied.

"I know that face," Riley said. "You used to get it before you asked me to sneak out of the house when we were in middle school. What are you thinking?"

"What if we had the party at the lighthouse and on the grounds? The barn's empty already. Maybe we could heat it in some way and have a band out there?"

Riley shrugged optimistically.

"I once did a party for Chris Stapleton in Tennessee—he's one of our clients. We completely transformed his barn, and he had twenty-five cows."

"How do you keep everyone from dying of allergies?" Will asked.

"We'd need to clear out the whole barn, paint, and pressure wash it. That could be tricky with the plunging temperatures, but all we need is a day above freezing and it could work."

"If it doesn't, we could do ice skating out there," Riley suggested playfully.

"Broadhurst Creative does have liability insurance," Mia said with a laugh before continuing. "We could provide outdoor heaters lining the paths, and decorate the inside of the barn. It's definitely big enough..." She paused, her mind whirring, "Will, you said we could get the renovations done in the lighthouse in a week, right?

Leah can be here to decorate and stage the space as soon as I give her the word, and we could get someone to clean the barn. If we rush, we could get the place ready."

"Could we get the barn ready *and* get all Grandma Ruth's things packed in time?" Riley asked enthusiastically.

"I'll give it everything I've got," Mia replied.

"And thinking as your agent," Will added, "if this party is promoted, it could give the lighthouse a lot more visibility."

"We may even find a buyer in the crowd," Mia said, hope lifting a bit of the weight off her shoulders. Maybe this was the Christmas miracle they'd been searching for.

The waitress came back with their hot cocoas, setting an enormous mug full of whipped cream and sprinkles with sticks of chocolate and a red-and-white striped straw protruding from it in front of Mia.

"I think we should celebrate," Riley said. "Let's get a bottle of champagne." She consulted the waitress. "What do you have by the bottle?"

"What are we celebrating?" Mia asked.

"Finding a venue for the party! And being together at Christmas. If you have the party here, you don't have to leave us. That's exactly what Grandma Ruth would've wanted."

"That's definitely worth celebrating," Mia said.

"We have a house champagne on the menu," the waitress suggested.

Riley clapped her hands. "Excellent. We'll have a bottle of that."

"All right." The waitress flipped to a clean page on her hand-held pad of paper, her pen poised to jot down their choices. "Are you all ready to order?"

"Could we have a few more minutes?" Mia asked, still holding the menu that she hadn't had a chance to look at.

"Of course. Back in a second with your champagne," the waitress said, leaving them to their conversation.

"We'll really need to sell this idea to get people here. They're all waiting to find out where it'll be," Mia said, a mix of relief and excitement bubbling up. "What could be our angle?"

Riley made a face and then sipped her hot cocoa. "An old lighthouse and an old horse barn? I have no idea."

"A country Christmas by the sea?" Will offered.

"Yes!" Mia agreed. "But do you think people will be able to get here in the snow?"

"Flights haven't been grounded yet. Everything seems to still be moving," Will replied.

"But what about accessing the lighthouse?" she countered.

"We can plow the drive, remember?"

"That's right!" she said, getting butterflies. "Could we get some white paint for the walls inside? Maybe the painters could leave some for us? I can do it myself."

"Of course," he said, firing off a text to them right then and there. "I'm sure they'd deliver it for the cost of the paint since they're already contracted."

"A coastal getaway from the hustle and bustle of the city. You're a genius!" she said, twisting toward him, unable to hide her happiness.

Their eyes met like they had earlier at the lighthouse and a thrill quivered through her chest. She broke eye contact and focused on her mug of cocoa, drinking the rich, sugary drink down too fast and clearing her throat to keep from coughing against the fiery liquid.

"I just thought of something," Riley said. "Do you think Milo will go for it?" She leaned across the table and addressed Will. "Milo is Mia's husband."

Will sat up a little straighter.

"He's my *ex*-husband, and he's going to have to be okay with it because he has no other options."

The waitress returned with the champagne, popping the cork and filling glasses, the fizz bubbling up to the rims before sliding back down into the gold liquid beneath. "Y'all want a minute with your bubbles or are you ready to order?"

Mia still hadn't looked at her menu. "Do you two know what you want yet?" she asked Will and Riley.

"Is anyone up for sharing a pizza?" Will asked, pointing to a woodfired option with feta cheese and spinach.

"That sounds amazing," Riley said.

"Works for me," Mia agreed.

The waitress scribbled it down and left them alone once more.

"Hang on," Mia said, positioning the bottle and her popping and fizzing glass of bubbly. She snapped a photo. "Let me text this to Milo." She sent the picture along with a message that said, *I've found a venue, and digital invites will go out tonight.*

Then, she raised her glass. "To great ideas," she said, allowing herself a glance at Will out of the corner of her eye. She could've sworn he was looking right at her.

"To great ideas," Riley repeated, and the three of them clinked their glasses.

"Here's your leftover pizza," Will said, as he stood at the door to Mia and Riley's childhood home, his truck running behind them in the snow-filled driveway.

"Thank you for coming to check on us today," Mia said. He looked so handsome standing opposite her, that small smile playing at his lips. She'd definitely had too much champagne.

"You're welcome."

The three of them stood in the icy coastal wind under the frosty porch, unsaid words resting on Will's lips. With a fluttering glance to Riley, he handed Mia the triangular to-go box as Riley opened the door, all three of them distracted by their mother.

"Hey there!" Alice said, with a warm sparkle in her eye at the sight of her daughters.

"This is Will Thacker, the real estate agent," Mia explained, introducing him to her mother. "He brought us home since our cars are buried in snow back at Grandma Ruth's."

"My goodness," she said, beckoning them in. "Thank you for

getting my girls home safely. What have y'all been doing?" She took Mia's pizza and put her arm around Riley, heading inside. "Y'all come in," she called through the glass front door from the entryway.

"Want to come inside a minute?" Mia asked, the champagne buzz helping her to forget about everything she was dealing with for the moment. "We can talk about renovating the barn."

He stared at her, clearly deliberating. "I can't stay," he finally said. "I have somewhere to be in about forty minutes, and the snow will already slow me down."

The breeze picked up, swirling the falling snow like a powdery funnel cloud. "How will I get back to the lighthouse tomorrow?" she worried aloud.

"I can take you back to Winsted Cape tomorrow if you need me to."

"Oh, no," she blurted, realizing her blunder. "I didn't mean to imply you'd take me. That's not in your job description."

"Which one isn't—driving you around or renovating barns?"

"Both." She allowed a little laugh before scolding herself for letting him have that effect on her. He could have her smiling in a snap. Dangerous...

"I don't mind," he said, that interest that she'd seen in his eyes returning. "How about if I pick you up at eight?"

"Okay," she replied, the icy air giving her a shiver.

"You'd better get inside before you become a block of ice."

He reached around her and twisted the knob, his woodsy spiced scent wafting toward her like it had when she'd first met him. She held her breath to keep herself from committing it to memory. "Thank you."

As the glass door closed behind her, he walked back to his truck. With a quick wave, he got in and pulled out of the drive, the engine rumbling as he went.

As she went inside, her phone pinged with a text from Milo that simply said, *Thank God.* It occurred to her that through all the personal things she had going on, Milo hadn't once acknowledged that this might be hard for her. Who had he become? And what kind of person was she to have allowed it? She pushed the question away and focused on her family.

"The real estate agent sure is easy on the eye," her mother said, as Mia came into the living room and dropped down onto the sofa beside Riley. "Definitely beats my tow truck driver," she continued. "I'd be liable to get stuck in the snow quite a bit if Will Thacker's the one coming to the rescue."

"Don't say rescue," Riley whispered teasingly. "Mia doesn't get rescued. She finds a ride."

Alice laughed and then wrapped her arm around Mia. "That's my girl." Then, she twisted toward her. "You look like you've got something on your mind."

"Hm?" Mia realized then that she was staring at the small Christmas tree, zoning out as she thought about Milo against her will.

"What's up? You worried about the lighthouse?"

"No, it's not that."

"Tell us," Riley urged her.

"I sort of feel stuck at the moment," she said, "but I'll be fine."

"Fine isn't always best," her mother said. "Sometimes it's okay to get things off your chest and out into the open."

"I don't want to worry you with it. It's really okay."

"Who are you to worry if not your family?" Riley asked, leaning toward her and blowing her little kisses.

Mia took in a breath, debating how to verbalize what she was feeling. It wasn't like her to show her soft underbelly, even if it was to her sister and mother, but for some reason it felt right to talk about it. Maybe it was the champagne, or maybe it was because she didn't have the answers and she was hoping for some guidance. *Hope is where you find it...* Was that what Grandma Ruth had meant?

"For the last five years, I've helped to build Broadhurst Creative with Milo, and I've kept my calendar so busy that I haven't stopped to get a hold of who I am once it's all gone."

"That's a normal thing," her mother said. "Divorce is a big change. It takes time to figure out all the answers."

"But there's one thing that terrifies me."

"What's that?" Alice asked, sliding the blanket off the arm of the sofa and draping it across her legs.

"When I married Milo, I signed a prenup," she told her mother. "When the divorce is final, I walk away with nothing. Before I came home, I'd put in for some jobs in the city... I really want to stay in New York. It's where my life is. But I don't know who I am anymore," she admitted. "I feel lost."

"Mmm," her mother said with a smile. "You know what Grandma Ruth always used to say, right?"

"What's that?"

"The boats coming in would lose their way in the darkness, so they plodded along until they could see the light of Winsted Cape lighthouse to get their bearings. Just keep swimming in the darkness until you see the light, and you will. There is no darkness without light."

"But I can't swim. I'm stuck," Mia said, fighting back tears. "I'm stuck between the good memories of what I had and the here and now."

Riley leaned in and patted her arm lovingly. "You're the strongest person I know. You're a fighter and you want to fix this, to make it right. But sometimes, the best way to fix it is to leave it and move on. Maybe you don't have a plan—that's okay. But one thing I know for sure is that you *will* figure it out."

"I hope so," she said as her mother clicked on the Christmas lights outside, filling the room with a soft glow that filtered through. "Maybe Christmas will bring me what I need this year." Mia grabbed the box of truffles that was still on the coffee table and offered them to her mother and Riley. "If not, these might be just as good."

"Oh, she made a joke," her mother said with a loving grin. "It's a start."

FIVE

"Will Thacker isn't one for being on time," Mia said to her mother the next morning, after Riley had caught a ride to work. Mia and Alice stood at the front door with their bags packed to stay at Grandma Ruth's, waiting for Will to pick them up. "He was late yesterday, too."

She didn't want to make her mother any more anxious than she already was. Mia could tell that she was fretting over having to go into the lighthouse for the first time; she was doing a great job trying to hide it, but Mia knew by the slight crease in her forehead and the way she buzzed around as she packed that this wasn't as easy as she was letting on.

Alice fiddled with the handle of her suitcase. They'd decided to stay over at the lighthouse so Will wouldn't have to keep driving them back and forth and they could work longer hours. "Maybe he's a busy man," she offered.

"At 8 a.m.?"

"You never know," Alice said with an uneasy smile. "He could have a house showing. Or it could be the snow."

"Yeah..." Mia squinted to try to see to the end of the street across the small patch of grass they had for a front yard, past the little black mailbox with its red Christmas bow, and through the falling snow. "He's been so kind that I'm willing to overlook his lateness. It's just weird. He's always so attentive to details in everything else."

"I could make us a cup of coffee while we wait."

"Sure. I think we can have Grandma Ruth's things packed up in the next few days if we really work, so we can take our time."

"I agree. If he comes before we've finished our coffee, I'll offer him one. It's been a long time since I've had a new face around the table."

In all her own grief and stress, Mia hadn't stopped to think about how her mother had spent countless years by herself in that little house. What had it been like in the days after Grandma Ruth's death? Without Grandma Ruth's endless chatter about how she was convinced the tides were changing, or her rundown of the last article she'd read about the increase in travel abroad, the silence was probably deafening. Did she sit around their empty kitchen table with the three plastic placemats, having dinner all by herself? Had she walked the short hallway to her bedroom, passing Mia's and Riley's empty rooms, the silence loud in her ears? Thank goodness Riley lived nearby at least, Mia thought with a tug of guilt.

Like clockwork, the minute they'd filled their mugs, the doorbell rang.

"I'll go ahead and pour a third mug," Alice offered. "You get the door."

When Mia answered, Will had that same slightly ruffled look that he'd had when she'd first met him, but he was clean-shaven, his hair was combed, and he was otherwise completely put together.

"Sorry I'm late. Again."

He didn't offer any more than that, and she didn't want to pry.

"My mom's making you coffee," she said, opening the door wider to let him in, a few snowflakes drifting down around him. "Maybe I can pick your brain on a few things for the party."

"All right," he said, coming inside, that curious gaze staying on her a little longer than she wanted it to.

"Morning," her mother sang from the kitchen, as she clinked a mug down onto the table for him. "Cream and sugar are on the plate right there." She pointed to the small serving tray in the center of the table, her entertaining skills on full display. "How are the roads?"

"Not good," he said, taking a seat. "I'm hoping the salt trucks will come through soon. But it looks like most people are staying home, so getting around isn't too difficult. We should be able to drive into Winsted Cape just fine."

Mia sat down next to him, making sure she didn't sit too close.

"Well, let's take our time then. Maybe we'll get lucky and the trucks will come down our road. I'll put some cinnamon rolls in the oven," Alice said, clearly procrastinating. "I've got a roll of premade ones in the fridge. It's absolutely freezing. Let me grab a sweater from my room and then I'll make us some yummies."

"Sounds delicious," Mia said as her mother hurried back to her bedroom.

"I'm not sure the salt trucks will arrive so soon," Will said quietly.

"It isn't that. She's struggling going back to the lighthouse."

"Ah," he said, nodding.

Still worried about her mother, Mia reached for the cream, the sleeve of her oversized sweater dipping into her coffee. Realizing it right away, she yanked her arm back but proceeded to tip her coffee mug over, the brown liquid eating up the table toward her. She shuffled her chair to the side quickly to avoid it, sliding into Will and nearly knocking him over too. He caught her with his steady hands, his face right at the side of hers, their cheeks touching, and it took her a minute to collect herself enough to assess the situation. Coffee cascaded off the table, dripping on the floor at her feet while Will's hands were on her arms. She peered down at the gentle way his fingers wrapped around her bicep. Softly, he let go.

"Oh," she said with a sigh, wriggling away from him in an attempt to regain her composure. "I'm so sorry. Did you get any on you?"

"No," he said, his brows pulling together as he seemed to be reading some sort of invisible message on the surface of the table.

Mia went over to the sink and grabbed a roll of paper towels, sopping up the coffee and dumping the towels into the trash. She couldn't remember the last time she was this clumsy. She was definitely losing it.

"Goodness," Alice said, returning with her blue-and-white snowflake cardigan. "I step away for a second and you're dumping coffee on everyone," she teased.

"I know. I'm such a goof." Mia finished cleaning up, blotted the arm of her sweater, and poured herself a new mug of coffee. "You sure you didn't get any on you?"

"I'm sure," Will replied, looking as though his mind were elsewhere for a second.

Mia scooted back up to the table, feeling jittery all of a sudden. "Last night I went ahead and sent out the invites for the party," she told him, sticking to business as she added sugar to her coffee and stirred.

Alice pulled a sheet pan from the oven and ripped a piece of aluminum foil off the roll, smoothing it out.

"But we still need catering for two hundred. Any ideas this late in the game?"

Will pouted while he held his mug in both hands. "Not sure. I could ask at the bakery, but it would be light confections. What kind of food are you thinking?"

"The party starts at seven, so that might work. We usually have light hors d'oeuvres. Maybe Murphy's could do it?"

"It's worth checking," Will said. "I'd be happy to ask around at other places, too, while you all are working on the lighthouse."

"Would you? That would be fantastic."

"No problem." He set down his mug. "I did find someone for you who could clean out the barn and get it into shape."

"You did?" Mia asked, surprised. "Thank you so much."

He smiled.

"What company is it?"

"It isn't a company. It's a single contractor."

"Who?" she asked.

"Me."

Mia stared at him, her eyes rounding. "What?"

"I called around and couldn't find anyone on such short notice, and I know you need the space to have your party, so I'm willing to roll up my sleeves. I know a guy who has a pressure washer. I've used it before."

"You don't need to do that. We can find someone, surely."

"I really don't think you'll be able to find anyone; the three contractors we found for the kitchen all penciled you in weeks ago. And it's no problem. I've rescheduled two of my other showings already to free up my schedule. This is a big sale for me, and I'll do what I can to make it happen."

Even though the renovations to the kitchen and bathrooms were minimal, and she felt pretty good about having enough time to finish working through Grandma Ruth's things, Mia knew that *everything* had to go right for her to be able to pull this off. And then there was the lingering fear that this whole thing might actually work, and she'd have to give up the special place that held so many memories.

Pushing away the unsettling thought, Mia turned to her mother. "Let's see if we can get Grandma Ruth's things completely packed by tomorrow. It'll mean a long night tonight, but we need the contractors to be in as soon as possible so Leah can start designing. Will, could you help us deliver some things to charities?"

"Of course," he answered.

The scent of brown sugar and spicy cinnamon filled the air, taking Mia back to her Christmases as a child. It hadn't escaped her attention that her mother still had cinnamon rolls on hand. Even in her grief, she was ready for the holiday, her excitement over having both her girls back home clear.

When they were done, Alice served them on the holiday plates she'd used for Santa's cookies over the years—delicate white saucers with little painted holly leaves around the edges. Mia inhaled the sweet icing that her mother had drizzled over the top, the scent like Christmas morning.

"These look delicious," Will said, cutting a piece of his with the side of his fork.

"It's one of her specialties," Mia said, giving her mother a wink.

Alice seemed calmer now; an adoring look in her eyes had replaced the anxious one from earlier. Mia was glad that they'd taken the time to slow down. This was a big day for her mother—it was best to ease into it. Together, maybe they'd find the hope that Grandma Ruth had been talking about.

Things seemed to be going along fine until Alice had to go inside the lighthouse. When she got to the door, Mia's mother finally broke down. She started to shake, her eyes filling with tears as the angry winter sea lashed the shore behind the house.

"This morning, I got up and thought I could do it, but I'm not sure now," she said, her lip wobbling as her hair blew around her forehead.

Will looked on, concerned, the three of them standing at the stoop to the kitchen door in the falling snow.

Mia let her gaze roam upward to the lighthouse, the glass dome at the top of the striped brick dark, as if mirroring the fact that Grandma Ruth had vanished from their lives. "I'll help you," Mia offered, taking her hand.

Her mother hung her head, sucking in jagged breaths, the air puffing out around them in the icy wind that hurled itself at the lighthouse from the far reaches of the Atlantic. The weathervane in the field squealed out its warning as it moved in rapid circles. "Give me a minute."

After a long pause, Will caught Mia's eye, and with a cautious stare asked if he should let them in. Mia nodded and slipped her arm around her mother. "It'll be okay. I'm here," she soothed.

Will punched the code on the lockbox and took out the key, slipping it into the lock quietly behind them, and opening the door.

Gently, Mia walked her mother inside, shutting out the frosty temperatures. Without even having to ask her mom, she knew immediately how it must feel. She was certain her mother could smell the unique fragrance of mild cedar mixed with the lavender and rose perfume that Grandma Ruth used to wear still saturating the house; she could hear the buzzing kitchen light and the tick-tock of the Italian-made cuckoo clock on the wall like an old tune from her childhood.

"She was my strength," her mother whispered, still not looking around, her eyes squeezed shut, her lashes wet with tears.

Will nodded at Mia to let her know he was heading into the living room, to give them a minute.

"I have to face the fact that she's gone," Alice said, "but it's so much easier to forget when I'm at my own house." She finally opened her eyes, the tears now spilling down her cheeks as she took in her surroundings—Grandma Ruth's checkered towel still hung from the stove, her reading glasses case sitting next to the fridge. "I miss her so much," she croaked.

Mia offered a soft, sympathetic smile. "Like Riley told us, she's still here. We just can't see her."

Alice nodded with a sniffle.

"Remember the last day we all went to visit her together and she admitted that she hadn't cleaned before going into the hospital? She said, 'If you all don't make sure my house gets cleaned, I'll come back to haunt you.'"

Alice tipped her head back and chuckled despite herself. "Maybe we should've left it dirty then."

Mia laughed. "Maybe."

Alice rolled her head on her shoulders and then squared them with renewed focus. "I can do this."

"*We* can do this." Mia took her mother's hand, and the two of them walked into the living room where Will, who had been waiting on the sofa, stood to greet them.

She surveyed the boxes she and Riley had packed yesterday—

the most personal things from the hall closet and her living areas out of sight.

"Okay," Mia said, clapping her hands together. "We've got boxes of old clothes there." She pointed to the cartons in the corner by the window. "Boxes of books in the one by the door, and knick-knacks in those."

"It looks like the snow is finally tapering off," Will said. "I could start filling the back of my truck and taking loads into town."

"Perfect," Mia said. "You can start with those there." She pointed to the books. "Mom, why don't you work on packing up the dishes in the kitchen that we won't be using, and I'll go through the bedroom."

"Yes, that's a good plan," her mother said, her gaze roaming the hallway toward Grandma Ruth's room.

"There are more boxes by the table. Just yell if you need me."

Once her mother was working and Will had started loading his truck, Mia grabbed a cardboard box and walked into Grandma Ruth's bedroom, shutting the door behind her. Her grandmother's frilly yellow bedspread was folded along the bottom of the bed rather than pulled up under the pillows, which made it clear someone else had done it. Her slippers were set neatly under the chair in the corner with a view of her favorite painting of an Italian villa, and a book sat unopened on the table beside it. She'd had a tough enough time getting rid of Grandma Ruth's old clothes and items in the trunk in the living room, but hanging in the closet were all the things she'd worn over the years leading up to her final days. She and Riley hadn't had a chance to get to them yet.

Mia walked over to the closet door and opened it, Grandma Ruth's scent overwhelming her. She ran her fingers down her grandmother's yellow sweater with the pearl buttons that she always wore when she got dressed up, then pressed the chiffon sleeve of one of her blouses to her nose and took in a deep breath, closing her eyes. She could almost feel her grandma's arms around her.

With resolve, Mia dragged an empty box over and started

pulling out the clothes, setting them delicately into the container, working quickly to get it done before her mother finished in the kitchen. Grandma Ruth's short pumps were lined up at the bottom of the closet. Mia set them in the box, along with a pile of belts and scarves that were also hanging.

When she got to the very back of the closet, she found a flower-patterned box. She pulled it out, set it in the middle of the floor, and opened the lid. It was full of the photos and letters they'd found yesterday. Riley must have stashed them back there so her mother didn't see them. Looking over at the door, Mia sharpened her hearing. When she was sure Alice wouldn't open the door, she pulled out the stack of letters tied with a red ribbon and smiled, realizing now that they looked like old Christmas cards from around 1950.

Under them was a pile of black-and-white photos. She held one of them up. It was a very young Grandma Ruth in a pencil skirt, standing in a park with another woman in a lace dress who was holding a swaddled baby. Mia flipped the picture over, looking for a label, but there was nothing written. Grandma Ruth only looked about eighteen at the most. Was this an old friend?

"What is that?" Alice's tentative voice came from the doorway, making Mia squeal, shoving everything back into the box. But her mother didn't seem to have registered it yet. Her gaze searched the room before landing back on Mia and the box on the floor beside her.

"It's a box of Grandma Ruth's," Mia said, coming clean. Tentatively, she picked up the photo of Grandma Ruth leaning against a building with the sea at her back, and brought it over to Alice. "This was in there," she said, holding out the picture. "Wasn't Grandma Ruth gorgeous?"

Her mother ran her finger around Grandma Ruth's pin curls in the black-and-white photo before flipping it over, both of them leaning in to read the description: *Praiano, Italy; Summer 1958*. "She certainly was... I remember her telling me about this picture. She'd just come to Italy from Germany and she didn't know a bit of

Italian. A young tutor named Antonio spent every afternoon with her at a café by the water, teaching her. In turn, she taught him English."

"I think she told me this story," Mia said. "She was shy because she didn't know the language and when he spoke, she shook her head. The first word he taught her was *impavida*. The two of them went down to the water, and he stripped off his shirt and yelled it out as he dove off the cliff into the sea."

"Yes," Alice said, nodding as she wiped a tear. "*Impavida*. Fearless." She smiled through her tears. "It's hard to believe she was ever that young." Tears welled up in her mom's eyes again.

"I know. She was always so full of wisdom."

"I wonder what she was like as a girl," Alice said.

"I'll bet she was fearless—even if she didn't think she was back then."

Her mother offered a sad smile. "What else is in the box?"

"I was just sifting through it when you came to the door. Do you feel like you want to take a look?"

With slow steps, her mother went over to the flowered box and peered inside. She grabbed the faded stack of Christmas cards on the floor and flipped through them. "These are all from the same person," she said. "Mildred Beaumont, Cedar Lane... South Carolina."

That name ran like a familiar tune in Mia's mind. "Do you know her?"

Her mother shook her head as she opened the Christmas card. "Merry Christmas—love, Mildred and family." She set it aside. "Must be old friends or something."

"Hang on." Mia went over to Grandma Ruth's dresser and retrieved the phone number she'd seen. "Yes. This says Mildred." She held it out to her mother.

Her mother pouted with interest. "Could be the same person."

"Unless she had lots of friends named Mildred."

Alice leaned over the box and dipped into it again, but they were interrupted when Will came into the room, his cheeks rosy from the cold.

"I've got everything loaded up for the first run, and I'm heading into town. Need anything?"

"We might want to get a few groceries to have here while we're working," her mother suggested.

"You're probably right," Mia agreed.

"Why don't you go with Will and pick some things up for us?" her mother suggested. "I'd like to spend a little time in the lighthouse by myself, if that's okay."

Mia didn't really want to leave her mother, but she knew that they should have some food ready—especially with another storm coming in. It would probably be good to give her mom some time.

"Okay," Mia said, standing up and grabbing her coat and scarf. "Want anything in particular?"

"Just a few nibbles to get us through. You choose. We could have coffee." She eyed the photo of Grandma Ruth in Italy. Her grandmother had told her that she'd brought back a few life-changing things from Italy, one of them being her love of coffee.

"I wonder if Grandma Ruth's coffee maker still works. Have you packed it up yet?"

Her mother offered a knowing smile. "I left it out just in case. Grandma Ruth wouldn't have us in her house without offering us a cup of coffee."

Mia beamed at her mother, delighted to hear her making a little joke. She put on her coat and wound the scarf around her neck. "We'll be back soon. Sure you're going to be okay?"

Her mom nodded. "I'm sure."

"Text me if you need anything."

"All right."

As Mia left the room, her mother was digging around in the box again. She followed Will to his truck which was already running, the engine purring, and climbed into the warmth inside, Will's spicy scent lingering. As the ocean raged under a darkening sky, the radio announcer warned of the upcoming storm. "*Get your groceries, folks. You won't want to go out in this. We've already had to close several bridges. The I-76 bridge is closed in Knightsbridge and we have reports of closures happening in Rocking Creek and Belview."* She peered up at the lighthouse, the old red-and-white paint peeling. The whole thing seemed to be swaying in the clouds tumbling above it.

"The exterior painters are supposed to be here Monday," she told Will. "I scheduled them from New York before I left. But now I'm worried that the storm will delay it."

"Fingers crossed it blows over us like some of the models are predicting," he said, fastening his seatbelt. "We'll have to just wait and see."

As they bumped down the winding, snowy drive through the grounds, Will's cell phone went off in the center console. Clearly trying to keep his focus on the road, he slowed down as he attempted to view the phone.

"Want me to get that for you?" Mia asked, reaching for it.

"It's fine," he said, pulling over and stopping the vehicle, grabbing his phone and peering down at the text before clicking it off quickly. He took in a deep breath, thoughts behind his eyes, setting the phone in his lap.

"Did you need to get that?" she asked.

"No," was all he said. But the tension in his shoulders told her that there was more to the story.

As they took off again, Will turned up the radio, "We Wish You A Merry Christmas" filling the air. In silence, they stared ahead at the white expanse of road, both of them lost in their own thoughts.

SIX

"Oh, I'd forgotten about this place," Mia said, her eyes on the shop next door to the market after they'd come out with their bags of groceries.

The display windows were draped with greenery and white starfish, and Christmas music played from the outdoor speakers. But behind the festive flair were clocks of all kinds: grandfather clocks, brass clocks that showed the time all over the world, clocks with toy trains running around them, and others in the shapes of animals.

"My grandmother was beside herself when her prized Italian cuckoo clock stopped working. She had to get it fixed once when I was probably five or six," she said, peering inside. "She took me in here to drop it off for repair and could hardly get me out."

"What did you find so interesting about it?" Will asked as he stood beside her, holding the grocery bags, the whole street glistening with the Christmas lights in all the storefronts.

"I remember the lulling sound of all the clocks as they ticked. It calmed me." She put her hands on the glass to see inside better, shielding her eyes from the glare of the holiday lights. "Oh my goodness, Mr. Morris is still there. He was friends with Grandma Ruth."

"Shall we go in and say hello?" Will asked.

"Would you mind?"

"Not at all." Will allowed her to go first, opening the door for her.

Inside, the walls ticked and clicked in a rhythmic way beneath the light holiday music that played over the speakers. Mia took in all the various clocks—a round one, one with roman numerals, another that only had the hands, all the numbers in a pile at the bottom of the clock. She smiled at that one.

The old man behind the counter straightened as they came in. When the rush of winter air chased Mia and Will inside the shop, he pulled his open cardigan around his thin body, crossed his arms to keep the sweater in place and glanced over his readers at them. He looked exactly the same as she remembered except his bald spot had now expanded, and there was a ring of white wispy strands around the back of his head and over his ears.

"Happy holidays," he said in a cheery tone, setting the book he was reading onto the counter and removing his glasses.

"Same to you," Mia said.

Will's phone went off again, and worry slid down his face. "I'm so sorry. Mind if I take this?" he asked.

"Go ahead."

He headed back to the door, stepping outside.

Mia tried to keep her mind off Will and turned to Mr. Morris. "You probably don't remember me, but I came in some years ago with my grandmother, Ruth Carter."

The corners of his eyes crinkled with fondness. "Ah, Ruth. That must make you Mia or Riley."

"Mia," she said. "You fixed my grandma's cuckoo clock once."

"I remember. It only cooed from behind its doors." He smiled at his own joke but then sobered. "She was a wonderful woman, your grandmother. I'm so sorry you lost her."

Mia nodded, afraid to speak for fear her voice may crack with emotion, thinking about Grandma Ruth.

"I knew Ruth her entire life," he said. "She was a great woman."

"Wait," she said, refocusing on Mr. Morris. "Her whole life?"

"Mm-hm. We were great friends. Your grandfather and I used to play chess every Tuesday at the lighthouse before he passed away."

"Did you?"

"We sure did."

Hope swelled up from the pit of her stomach. "Did my grandmother or grandfather ever mention anyone named Mildred Beaumont?"

The skin between his round eyes wrinkled and he shook his head. "Doesn't ring a bell."

"You've never heard of that name at all?"

"No, why?"

"Uh, no reason," she said, forcing a smile. "I just found the woman's name in my grandmother's things. It's probably no one."

Disappointed, she looked down at the counter, Grandma Ruth's words like a puzzling echo: *Hope is where you find it.* Every time she hoped for answers, they escaped her. As the message rolled around in her mind, frustration welled up again, and she was angry at herself once more for not being there to talk to Grandma Ruth those last days. She deserved to be confused.

"I wish I could go back and talk to my grandma one more time," she admitted.

"Time is a funny thing, isn't it?" he asked, his head still but his eyes darting around to all the clocks on the walls. "Just as we're standing here now, unaware of the time, yet it's slowly slipping away from us second by second, minute by minute."

"That's a bit terrifying," she said with a fearful chuckle.

"For us, *maybe*," he said, clearly unconvinced, "but time continues. It ticks on forever. I like to think that we do too somewhere. If you want to talk to her, *talk* to her. She might be listening."

"Do you think she's still here?" Mia asked, feeling a flare of hope again.

Mr. Morris got up from his stool and held out a weathered

finger toward one of the clocks. Its enormous brass hands were set at 3:00. "See this one here? It's stayed at three o'clock. Whatever was happening that day at three, this clock still marks it." He walked over to another one that was an hour ahead. "And this one wants us to move faster than we are. It's already in the future, but we haven't gotten there yet. However, the clock has gotten there. It's sitting in the future right now."

Mia took in the hands of the clocks in question.

He gave her a knowing smile. "The past, the present, and the future are all here." He walked back over behind the counter and took a seat, picking up his book. "I've blabbered on quite enough," he said jovially. "Feel free to look around, Mia. Let me know if you need anything."

"Thank you," she said, walking through the shop. She pretended to be looking at the clocks, but she was trying to make sense of what Mr. Morris had said. Were the past, the present, and the future right here all along? She eyed Mr. Morris, taking in this present moment and admitting that she wouldn't have come in were it not for the past. But what about the future? Could we really find our future in our present moments? Her mind was whirring as the bells on the door rang, pulling away her attention.

"Sorry," Will said, returning.

"It's no problem," she replied, ignoring the timing of his entry in answer to her question. "Everything okay?"

"Yeah, it's just family stuff—you know..."

Obviously he had something going on, yet he was there with her, shopping and walking around town. She should probably get back to the lighthouse. "Thanks for letting me look around, Mr. Morris," she said, waving over to him.

"I'm glad you came in," he said.

"Me too." Then she turned to Will. "Ready to go?"

Will opened the door and the two of them stepped out into the glacial air. "Would you be okay if I made a quick pit stop at the bakery on our way back to the lighthouse?" he asked.

"Of course. I wouldn't mind getting a few more of those donuts. Riley and Mom would love them, I'm sure."

He smiled.

"Why don't you stay this evening and have some with us? It'll be my treat." Had she really just said that? Mr. Morris's words were getting the better of her.

"I wouldn't want to impose," he replied.

"You wouldn't be interrupting anything. We're just packing up my grandma's things. You could help us sort."

"I'd love to stay and help, as long as I wouldn't get in the way."

"Definitely not," she said, as they made their way to the truck. "It would be good to get your opinion on things as we move forward, since you're experienced in staging to sell."

Will set the groceries in the back of the truck and opened Mia's door for her. She climbed inside and he started the engine, pulling away from the glittering stores, headed for The Corner Bakery.

"I haven't been to the bakery since I was a kid," she said, as they drove through the snow that had started falling again, covering everything in its wake. All the quaint little restaurants and cafés around town were abuzz with people rushing into the warmth from outside. "We used to go every time I visited my Grandma Ruth," she continued.

He looked over at her briefly and then back to the road, listening.

"My favorite treat as a kid was their double chocolate cupcake."

He nodded, his mind clearly elsewhere, so she looked out the window, watching the flakes fall delicately onto the Christmas banners that had been put up on the streetlights through town.

"I'll leave the truck running for you," he said, as they pulled up at the bakery. "Be right back."

"Okay," she said, slightly deflated that he hadn't asked her in.

He jumped out and jogged up to the door, disappearing inside.

As the truck hummed quietly, the heat filling the space since Will had shut the door behind him, she pulled out her phone and texted Milo.

Did you need me?

Her phone rang immediately, and she answered it.

"I saw the invite—we've hit rock bottom with this year's party," he said without a hello. "Do you really expect our guests to fly out to no-man's land to stay at your grandmother's house? My God, Mia."

"Did you have any better ideas?" she asked defensively.

"I think no ideas are better than this one."

"We're renovating it, and I have Leah coming in to design it. It'll be amazing," she told him. She went on to explain the plans for the barn and the DJ that she didn't mention she still needed to find. "It'll be the perfect Christmas escape from the city."

"We'll see when the RSVPs start coming in," he snapped.

She shook her head, the space between them toxic. "Milo, I don't know what I've done to make you so angry; I've forgotten at this point what we're even fighting about... If we didn't work out, that's okay, but can we at least be civil? It's Christmas."

"I'm seeing Elaine," he blurted.

"From work?" she asked, clenching her fist, unsure of what else to say. She knew it was Elaine from the office. It didn't take a genius to figure it out.

"Yes, from work," he said, his tone finally softer. "We're being discreet about it. She won't be coming to the party. She didn't want to overstep our plan to let everyone know after the holiday."

Mia shouldn't have been surprised, and Milo had every right to move on, but it still floored her how he could throw away five years together in an instant. Their relationship had been the first thing in her life that she'd fought for but hadn't gotten.

"If that's what you want," she said, turning her gaze out the window, so lost in thought that she barely noticed how hard the snow was coming down.

"I think I'm in love with her."

Mia squeezed her eyes shut to keep the sting from swarming her body. Even though she knew she was better off without him, it still hurt to hear him choose someone else over her. It made her feel lesser in some way. Like she wasn't enough.

"Mia?" Milo's voice came through the phone, pulling her from her thoughts. "I'm sorry..."

"You don't need to be," she said.

"I was frustrated, not knowing how to tell you. It's recent—we only just started to make things official. Nothing happened while you and I—"

"Milo, it's fine," she said, blinking back tears. "I need to go. We can talk more later."

"All right," he replied.

She got off the phone and quickly wiped her eyes, taking in steadying breaths. Only then did she realize now how long she'd been in the truck. Even with the heat running, a chill had wound its way inside.

Wasn't Will going to just run in and run out? After dragging her fingers under her eyes and peering into the mirror on the visor, she fluffed her hair and turned off the truck, jumping out into the snow, her boots sinking down into it. It would be nice to go inside and see the place from her childhood again, and she should probably offer to pay one more time...

Pulling open the large glass door, she went inside.

To her surprise, there were no customers in the shop; the old display case was nearly empty and the rainbow of candy jars barely full. Her gaze roamed the wall of old photos of happier times, when the place was full of kids holding ice cream cones and buying penny candy over the counter. Will was in deep discussion with a woman in the corner, neither of them noticing that she'd come in. The vibrance of The Corner Bakery that she remembered was gone, the letters on the wall faded, and the floor tiles were cracked and in need of repair. But it still looked clean and, with the sparkling Christmas tree in the corner, it managed to feel cheerful.

"Hello," she said aloud, announcing her presence.

Will turned around. "Oh, Mia. I'm so sorry to have left you in the truck." He beckoned her over. "This is my sister Kate."

"Hi," Kate said, with a smile that looked just like Will's. "It's nice to meet you."

"Kate runs the bakery," he explained.

"I didn't realize that," Mia said. "Have you owned it for long?"

"It's been in our family for five generations," Kate said, but Mia noticed sadness in her eyes when she said it.

"I'm splitting my time between selling the lighthouse and getting this property ready for the market. Know anyone who wants an old bakery?" Will's words were light, but she could sense that he was covering up his real feelings.

"Will tells me you like my donuts," Kate said, producing a big smile and heading behind the counter, where she washed her hands at a small sink. "I'll fill a box for you. On the house."

"Oh, you don't have to do that. I'd be happy to pay for them," Mia offered.

"No, no. It's fine." Kate waved her hand in the air. "You're keeping my brother in town longer than I would have, so it's on me."

"That's not true," replied Will. "I'll stay as long as you need me."

"Right," Kate said, while piling donuts into the box in her hand. "But you can't stay forever."

"Mommy!" said a little boy of about five from the door, with sandy blond hair peeking out from under his winter cap and adorable freckles as he ran behind the counter and wrapped his arms around Kate. A young woman joined them, shaking the snow off her coat.

"Hi, Jackie," Kate said, setting the box on top of the counter and walking around to the other side with her son in tow.

He gave Will a giant hug, grabbing around his legs. Will scooped him up and spun him around before setting him down at the candy counter, where the little boy slipped off his hat and mittens and set them in front of him.

"Thanks for grabbing Felix off the bus. I'm sure the walk here was freezing." Kate grabbed her son's hands. "Are you cold? I can make you some hot cocoa."

"Yes, Mommy, can I have one, please?" Felix climbed up on one of the red stools that sat along the back bar area, his little feet dangling above the floor as he shrugged off his coat.

"It's fine," the young woman named Jackie said.

Kate turned to her brother. "Will, do you mind taking Jackie home so she doesn't have to walk in this snow? It'll only take a minute."

"It's no problem," he said. "Mia, do you mind staying here a sec and I'll be right back—I know it's taking longer than expected..."

"It's fine. I'll just message my mom and my sister and let them know."

Will and Jackie headed out while Kate moved back around the counter and started making the hot cocoa.

"Mia, would you like some?" she asked, as Mia fired off a quick group text.

"I'd love one, thank you." Walking to the back, Mia pulled out a stool next to Felix. "Mind if I sit down?"

"No," he said, his face brightening. "I'm in Kindergarten."

"Big boy school," Kate said, as she grated chocolate into a bowl and folded it into the whipped cream.

"How do you like Kindergarten?" Mia asked him.

"It's fun, I guess." Then he lit up. "We get to paint pictures in art. I painted a Christmas tree today."

"Oh, that sounds festive," Mia said.

"Beside the tree, I painted my family: Mommy and Uncle Will."

Kate set two large mugs of hot cocoa topped with whipped cream and dusted chocolate in front of them, sinking a peppermint stick and a paper straw into each one. Mia wrapped her hands around her beverage to keep warm. "How wonderful," she replied, pondering why he hadn't mentioned his father.

Kate seemed to see the question on Mia's face. "Jackie is Felix's sitter—she helps me out while I'm working," she explained, holding her own mug of cocoa. "Will pitches in when he can... But most of the time it's just me and Felix, right, buddy?"

"Yep," the little boy said before licking whipped cream off his finger.

Mia nodded, getting the picture, and then stirred the hot liquid with her peppermint stick.

"With the winter storm, business is slow," Kate said, clearly trying to change the subject. She set down her mug and began wiping the counters. "I was hoping for a busier holiday season. But it's still early, I suppose."

Was just before Christmas early? Mia took a sip of her hot chocolate. The rich, creamy thickness of it mixed with the peppermint was divine.

"I've been forced into selling this to unload the burden of it." Kate cleared her throat and turned away to fiddle with something behind the counter. Mia could've sworn her lip wobbled as she did, but she'd put on a brave face when she faced Mia again. "I just can't keep it going at the rate it is."

Mia frowned. "I hate to hear that. I remember this place from my childhood. It was so full of life."

"It was. My grandmother, like her father and her uncle, was a natural. And so was my mother. When my mother passed away, I took over. It took a turn, and I just can't get it back." Her voice cracked and a line formed between her eyes. She took in a deep breath and seemed to be steadying herself. "I don't know what I'm doing wrong. We aren't turning a profit and, because of that, I don't have inventory to bring in customers. I have a limited menu right now, but I need customers to afford the inventory." She shook her head. "I told Felix that we'll do something wonderful if we sell it. Maybe go on vacation, right, Felix?"

"Yes, but I want to stay here," Felix said, his little lips turned down in sadness. "I don't want to sell the bakery. Where will I get Gran's chocolate?"

"I can still make all the recipes for us at home," Kate said. "I know them all by heart."

"But it'll taste different at home," Felix worried. "I miss Gran and when I come here, I don't miss her so much."

Mia finished her hot chocolate and set it down on the counter. She understood that too well, and her heart ached for Kate and Felix. She wished there was some way she could help, but just like what she faced with the lighthouse, there wasn't anything to do but move on. "You know, I'm dealing with the same thing," she told Kate. "We're selling my grandmother's home—the lighthouse that has been in our family for generations. I know what it's like to part with something so valuable."

Kate sighed and nodded, an unspoken bond now between them.

The door opened and a gust of icy wind blew in. "Hey," Will said. "Whatcha got there, buddy?" he asked, pacing over to Felix and peering down into the boy's drink.

"Hot chocolate," Felix said as he wobbled the heavy mug, trying to hold it up to show him, his face brightening at the sight of his uncle. "Want some?"

"No thanks, big man. That's all yours." He ruffled Felix's hair. "I'll catch up with you and your mom tomorrow, okay? I'm gonna take Miss Mia home."

"Okay," Felix said, giving Mia a little wave. "Bye."

"Bye," Mia returned. "Nice to meet you, Felix."

"You too," he said, his lips already around the paper straw in his drink.

"I'll swing by in the morning," Will told his sister.

Kate walked around to where they were standing with the box of donuts. Through the clear top, Mia could see the array of sweet treats. Some were covered in chocolate chips, others drizzled with caramel. "Here you go," she said, handing them to Mia. "Come in any time."

"Thank you." Mia took the box and zipped up her coat.

With a wave over his shoulder, Will opened the door for Mia and they headed out into the falling snow, leaving footprints behind. Mia climbed up into the truck and set the donuts in her lap. As they made their way down the icy roads, she thought about her own family and how similar the circumstances were. She was about to give up the lighthouse, and while she was doing a great job of making everyone think she had it all under control, she was silently battling the sadness of it.

SEVEN

"Oooh, what did you get?" Riley said, digging into the grocery bags that Will and Mia brought inside the lighthouse as they took off their snow-covered boots and set them by the door. The snowflakes in Mia's hair began to melt in the heat of the kitchen so she tucked it behind her ears.

"Chardonnay for you." Mia pulled the bottle out of one of the bags. "And cheese and crackers—which I know you love to nibble with your wine."

"Thank you!" Then, under her breath, Riley added, "Having a nice snack might take Mom's mind off the fact that she's parting with Grandma Ruth's things. She's being a trooper, but I know it's harder for her than she's letting on. She's made a to-keep pile..."

"I'll open the wine," Will offered. His phone went off again but he silenced it, his shoulders rising the way she'd seen them do before.

"The corkscrew is in the drawer to the left of the sink," Mia told him, Will's presence already feeling very natural—more natural than it should; he was a stranger, rooting around in Grandma Ruth's kitchen drawer. But it was as if there were empty spaces in Mia's day that she hadn't known needed filling until he was there to fill them.

"Hello." Alice padded into the kitchen, holding a small collection of photographs. The rims of her eyes were red, but she smiled as if nothing were wrong.

"Hi, Mom." Mia opened the box from the bakery. "We brought you donuts."

"Oh, that sounds delicious," Alice said, coming over to the counter and setting down the pictures to pluck a donut out of the box. "I finished working through the bedroom. Look what I found while you all were gone." She gestured toward the pictures with her fingers around a ball of powder-sugared dough.

Mia flipped through them. "They're all of the same woman that was in the other photo with Grandma Ruth and the woman's baby."

Her mother took a bite of the donut and nodded. She swallowed and nudged the third picture with her knuckle so as not to get sugar on it. "Turn that one over."

Mia did so, reading the penciled inscription scratched on the back: "Two years." She looked up at her mother, wondering why the number was significant.

"There are seven Christmas cards and seven photos. They go together."

"So, Grandma Ruth must have been relatively close to Mildred Beaumont if they were sending Christmas cards with pictures of the family over the years," Mia said, connecting the dots.

Will found Grandma Ruth's stemware and handed Mia a glass of wine.

"Thank you," she said, taking it from him. "I hope you got yourself a glass."

"Not yet," he said, "but I will, if you don't mind. Just one." He took in a deep breath and let it out, setting glasses in front of Riley and Alice.

"Of course."

Not noticing the subtle exchange, Alice continued, turning the photos toward her. "I wonder why I've never heard of these people, yet my mother kept these seven cards specifically? She had tons of acquaintances. What's so special about them?"

Riley picked at the cheese wrapper, opening it. "Maybe she liked the front of the card—I sometimes keep pretty ones. Or maybe it was an old school friend or something."

"She told all kinds of stories about her growing up and never once mentioned Mildred," her mother countered. "And the cards don't look like anything special."

"If the woman *was* someone who was close to Grandma Ruth, she may want to know of her passing," Riley said. "We didn't invite anyone named Mildred to the funeral." She took a plate from the cabinet and rinsed it off. Drying it with a towel, she added, "Maybe we should try to tell her."

"I'll call her," Mia said. "We have her number."

"That's a good idea," her mother replied. "I have to admit that I like the idea of chatting with someone who knew my mother. It would make me feel even more connected to her."

Riley dumped a pile of crackers onto the plate and set the cheese beside it, along with a knife she'd rinsed from the silverware drawer. "I've told you before: she's here, Mom. I know it." She picked up a cracker and sliced a piece of cheese. "If she were here to help us pack, what would she do?"

Alice laughed. "She'd packed up so many times in her young life that she'd probably turn on Christmas music, drink way more wine that we would, and stay up all night until it was done without a worry in the world."

"She could make anything fun," Mia said, the idea warming her. "Why don't we do this *her* way then?" She walked over to the radio and flipped the switch, turning up the Christmas music, "Silver Bells" playing loudly. She grabbed her sister's hands and twirled her around. "I say we see how long we can stay up tonight and make a party out of packing. Just like Grandma Ruth would want us to do."

"Let's do it," Riley said, holding up her wine glass.

Their mother's laughter as she raised her wine was the best sight Mia had seen in a long time. They clinked glasses, dancing to the music. Will took Mia's hands and gave her a spin, surprising her. The alcohol warmed her cheeks, and she felt a buzz seeing everyone so happy.

"Will, you should stay too," Alice said.

"I could probably stay a little while," he replied, looking over at the three of them with a warm smile playing at his lips. "My next house showing isn't until noon tomorrow."

"Stay as long as you like!" Alice told him.

Delighted to see her mom smiling, Mia grabbed the bottle of wine and began topping up everyone's glasses.

When she got to Will's, he stopped her kindly. "I'd love to, but I'm driving at some point."

"What do you have to do tonight?" she asked, feeling suddenly festive, her worries melting away for the moment under the spell of Christmas music and a family reunion.

"Not much. I'm staying on my sister's couch."

"We have a couch and blankets," she heard her mother offer. "Stay and help us pack things up—it'll be fun! And if you get too tired, crash here."

Mia considered the fact that any professionalism that they'd built would certainly be strained if she had to see Will with disheveled hair and sleepy eyes in the morning.

"I wouldn't want to intrude," he said, his eyes cautious but that flicker of interest surfacing.

"It's fine with us," Riley said, tossing a suggestive smirk over to her sister.

Mia wanted to protest, but the truth was that she was having such a nice time that she remained silent.

"All right," he relented, smiling over at Mia.

With a thrill zinging through her, Mia reached over and filled his glass.

Mia and Will sat among the boxes, an empty bottle of wine between them after Alice and Riley had gone to bed. They'd been sorting out more things to put in his truck for the charities, but most of the time, they'd been making small talk. She'd found out that his favorite food was shrimp and grits, he'd rather hold a spider than a snake, and he'd collected baseball cards as a kid.

"I'm so sorry to hear about the bakery," she said. "Kate told me that she might sell it."

"Yeah." He tipped up his glass and drained what was left in it. "It used to be the place where the whole family would congregate, but over time, our family has gotten so small that it's just the three of us now. And the customers aren't the same either. We used to have so many people from town stopping in, but now it's just the random tourist here and there. The locals don't stop by anymore because the menu has gotten so limited. We only stocked a bunch for the holiday, hoping to capitalize on the season, but it hasn't worked."

"Different generation," she noted, her eyes feeling heavy from the alcohol. "You know, I work in PR—if Kate needs anyone to try to drum up business..."

"It might be too far gone," Will said. "But thank you for the offer."

"So, when will you list it?"

"Felix is really upset about us getting rid of the bakery, and he's had a tough time adjusting to school, so we're waiting until after Christmas to officially put it on the market. He needs a good holiday with no uncertainties."

"He's having a hard time at school?" she asked, sipping the last bit of her wine slowly to prolong the evening. She was enjoying talking to Will. It took her mind off everything.

"He's really bright, and he gets bored. They're struggling to keep him focused so he gets into trouble for getting the other children off task. A few of the kids' parents have complained."

She nodded, thinking. She barely knew Felix, but she didn't like the idea of that sweet little boy getting into trouble at school. "I hope he can get into the groove of it," she said.

"Me too..."

They sat in silence for a moment, as Mia drank the last of her wine, setting the glass on the table. She smiled at him, the wine doing its job of deleting all the issues weighing on her. She hadn't had a real conversation with someone other than her family in months. The way Will paid attention to her was nice. He wasn't rushing around, half listening like Milo always had been.

"The wine went down a little too easily tonight," Will said, getting up and gathering the bottle and their glasses. "It was nice. Although, I'm not sure I should be drinking on the job."

She smiled through the buzz of alcohol, feeling the same way, but nothing about this Christmas was normal. Her shoulders were slack, her racing mind calmed, and she couldn't shake the thought that she'd needed this. "I'm opening another bottle," she decided.

"With just the two of us to drink it?"

She brightened. "You're having some, then?"

"Well, I can't let you drink it alone, can I?" he asked, following her into the kitchen. "Although there's no way I can drive home tonight."

"Grandma Ruth's sofa is as good as any," she said, letting her guard down.

Before he could reply, his phone went off in the other room. "Hang on a sec. That could be Kate."

While Will answered the call, Mia paced through to her bedroom, passing him on the way. His head was down as he listened intently to the caller. She went into the room where she'd be sleeping and grabbed a pillow off the bed. Then she gathered up a few folded blankets that Grandma Ruth always kept in the closet and brought them into the living room, stacking them on the sofa. Excusing herself so as not to disturb Will's conversation, she went back into the kitchen and filled their wine glasses.

When she turned around, Will was leaning against the doorframe.

She didn't want to end their time together; it had been one of the best nights she'd had in a while. And as soon as she tucked down under her covers, all the things weighing on her would swim through her mind, keeping her aching eyes from closing—she just knew it.

"Everything okay?" she asked.

His slight pause didn't go unnoticed. "Yep," he said, walking into the room and taking one of the glasses. "I'll help."

After they made their way to the living room, he sat down on the sofa, moving the blankets she'd left for him so she could join him.

To avoid those piercing blue eyes, she looked out the window at the black of night and sipped her wine. It was as if she were being sealed in the lighthouse, a silent force giving her reason to stay there. "When do you think this snow will finally go away so we can get our cars out of the drive?" she asked, although she really didn't mind. There were worse places to be stuck. She forced her gaze back over to him.

"Not sure." Those eyes landed on her again, and she had to work to keep the butterflies from flapping in her stomach. She wondered if the emotions were surfacing because it had been a while since anyone had treated her like a human being. For so long, she'd been on autopilot, trying to avoid Milo's jabs, taking each day as it came and not focusing at all on the future.

"For the first snow of the season, this is a pretty big storm."

He twisted toward her, his glass of wine dangling from his fingers. "We used to have a family tradition on the first snowfall of every year."

"What was it?"

"When Kate and I were little, every time it snowed, we ran outside and made snow angels. We were convinced it brought us good luck. Know why?"

"Why?" She beamed from behind her wine glass.

"Because right after we ran out the first time and made the snow angels, Kate found a ten-dollar bill in her pocket. She swore she didn't know it was there. The next year, we did it again and—I'm not lying—a puppy showed up at our house that afternoon. He ended up living with us for the next fifteen years. His name was Bucky."

"That's amazing," she said.

"Yes, it is, but that's not all that happened."

She scooted closer, taking a drink of her wine.

"Every year we made snow angels, something good would happen. It wasn't always material. Our mom was sick one year with the flu and the day that we made snow angels, she felt better. Another time, we lost Kate's parakeet and we thought it had gotten out. She was devastated. But then we found her in the basement." He pursed his lips. "I can't remember when we stopped doing that."

"What about Felix? Have you continued the tradition with him?"

"You know, I don't know if Kate has or not. We should definitely show him how."

"Absolutely." She set her glass down on the floor by the sofa. Under the spell of the wine, she felt freer than she had in what felt like forever. "We should go out and make snow angels right now. Maybe we'll sell the lighthouse!" She reached for his hand and pulled to get him up.

With a laugh, Will stood and looked down at her. "It's awfully cold out there. And dark."

"Who cares?" She took the wine out of his hand and set it down on the floor next to hers. "We need all the luck we can get."

He took her coat from the chair and handed it to her. "You'll definitely need this." Then he picked up his own, sliding it on. "I've done a lot of things for my clients to help them sell a house, but this is a first."

"And staying over isn't? Plus, I need your magic," she said, taking his arm again and leading him to the door. She opened it, the air hitting her like icy spikes to the skin and making her wince. "It's freezing," she said, dancing up and down on the spot, making him chuckle.

"It was your idea."

She ran out into the darkness and fell back into the snow with a thud, the cold shocking her and taking her breath away. Clumps of snow slid into her boots and down the neck of her coat as she swished her arms and legs back and forth. "Do it with me!" she urged him. "It's *your* magic."

He crunched his way over to Mia, falling down beside her with a laugh and sliding his arms and legs in the snow.

"How long do we have to do this?" she asked, the wine making her dizzy now that she was lying down.

"I think we've done the job." He hopped to a standing position and pulled her up beside him, sobering. "It's been a long time since I've felt..."

She waited for him to finish, but he never did. "Felt what?" she dared.

"Happiness," he replied, meeting her eyes.

That look terrified her because she knew that she wasn't ready for it, but at the same time, she couldn't get enough of it. She opened her mouth to say something but she couldn't make any words come out. The two of them stood there, the snow drifting down around them, the only sound the angry waves crashing relentlessly onto the beach behind them.

"Time to get inside and warm ourselves up by a fire. I saw some wood on the porch," he said, pulling them both out of the moment. Think it's dry?"

"It usually is," Mia replied, relieved, brushing the snow off her backside. "That's where Grandma Ruth has always kept it."

"I'll grab a few logs on the way in. Do we have any way to light it?"

"I think there are some matches in one of the kitchen drawers."

The two of them went back in, the warmth hitting her and making her shiver.

Will lumped two logs into the fireplace while Mia got the matches. She pulled some old newspaper from one of the boxes they were still filling and balled it up, stuffing it around the logs before lighting a match and throwing it in. Flames crawled across the paper, spreading to the wood. When they finally caught fire, she held her hands out to warm them, lowering herself down on the large stone hearth. Will sat down beside her and the two of them slid their coats off.

"Think the snow angels worked?" he asked.

"You tell *me*," she teased.

There was a depth in his look that she hadn't seen before, as if he'd finally let his guard down.

"This was fun tonight," she said, her tone soft, giving away her growing fondness for him.

He swallowed, drinking her in with his gaze, that curiosity of his consuming her. His lips parted just slightly, and she was suddenly painfully aware of their proximity. He seemed to want to tell her everything and nothing at the same time, his silent breaths like an unspoken language between them. It had been a long time since she'd found herself in a situation like this. Promising herself she'd be thankful for it in the morning, she shuffled away from him and walked over to get the wine that was left in her glass. She sat down on the sofa and when she looked back at him, he seemed to be processing something of his own, his smile absent, his eyes searching.

Their night aside, maybe it was the kind gestures he'd offered since she'd gotten there, or the way he'd made this whole thing easier on her with their effortless chemistry, but she felt like she should repay him in some way.

"I was thinking, you should come to the company Christmas party," she suggested as he came out of whatever it was he was thinking about, and got up and joined her, grabbing his wine glass. After all, they were working on selling the lighthouse, and there may be potential buyers in the crowd.

"Oh, thank you," he said, looking surprised by the invite. "But... um. I'll be back home in Seattle for the holiday."

Seattle? That was completely across the country. "You're not staying in Winsted Cape for Christmas?" she asked. "I'd just assumed..."

"No, I've been working and living here for the last six months, helping out with Felix and the bakery and getting the building ready to be sold, but I live in Washington."

"Oh," she said, trailing off into thought. It was probably just as well. She'd need to be on her game with Milo on the premises. "When are you going back?"

"As soon as I can."

She tried to fight the feeling that she didn't want that day to come, though it was clear by his answer that he didn't want to stay.

"What are you thinking?" he asked.

She could feel the fire in her cheeks, and she didn't dare admit to him what had just gone through her mind. "I'm just tired," she said, tipping her head back and closing her eyes. She *was* tired. Tired of fighting with Milo. Tired of the stress from the party. Tired of holding herself up over the grief of missing her grandmother when she wanted to crumble.

"Me too," she heard him say in a whisper. "Me too..."

EIGHT

A tiny gasp from across the room pricked Mia's consciousness, but her eyes felt as though they were cemented shut so she couldn't view the source. She took in a long, steady breath, the faint spice of it calming, the sounds around her becoming clear. The coastal wind howled outside, rattling the latch on the screen door of the lighthouse the way it always had, and her mother's faint whisper floated over her, too quiet to decipher. She wriggled comfortably, only then feeling a foreign hand under her own. Trying to swallow, she was aware of her dry mouth.

The end of the evening came back to her in snippets—talking with Will on the sofa, him making her giggle with a little joke about the snow angels despite the fact that she could hardly keep her eyes open, and then laying her head back on the sofa just to rest for a second... *Oh no.* She'd asked Will to the Christmas party. Thank goodness he'd declined. What had she been thinking? All she needed was to have to try to balance entertaining Will while being a fake wife to Milo for everyone's benefit. And right now, she was—

Her eyes flew open and she froze, Will's relaxed lips breathing quietly against her, as he slept. She was suddenly aware of the gentle rise and fall of his breathing, his hand on his chest, her fingers over his. It was intoxicating while simultaneously mortifying.

Carefully, she engaged her core muscles and kept them tight to lift herself up and away from his body without having to push off of him. Their legs were intertwined, so she put a hand on the back of the sofa to steady the first leg as she hoisted it off him, planting one foot on the floor. With one leg to go, she hovered over him and his eyes flicked opened, meeting hers. The lips that had been slack with sleep turned upward just slightly as he took her in.

"Morning," he said.

Riley coughed conspicuously from the kitchen, and Mia knew they were probably being watched. Will heard it too and his smile spread wider.

But while Mia grinned back, internally she was scolding herself for letting this happen. She'd just spent the night draped across the real estate agent. *Have mercy.*

She pushed herself to a standing position and straightened her crumpled clothes.

Will sat up and stretched his arms before running his fingers through his hair. "What time did we fall asleep?" he asked, as the two of them maneuvered around the half-filled boxes to get to the kitchen.

"I don't remember," she said, cringing when she saw the line of empty wine bottles on the counter.

"I know why you don't remember," Riley said with a loaded look.

Their mother nudged Riley's arm. "Good morning," she said pleasantly. "I found the toaster oven and popped in some cinnamon bread. I figured I could scramble up some of the eggs you bought yesterday."

"That sounds perfect," Mia said, her tummy rumbling after falling asleep on nothing but crackers and cheese. And wine. Lots of it.

Will's phone went off and he pulled it from his pocket. "Oh," he said with a frown. "Jackie had an issue and had to cancel on Kate, so I'm late to watch Felix."

"Oh no. I'm so sorry," Mia said, worried about the little guy.

"I need to run. Will you all be okay here until I get back? Shouldn't be more than a few hours."

"Of course," Alice said.

Will rushed out the door in a flash, leaving the three of them in the kitchen.

"Well, this has been an interesting start to the day," Riley said, pulling the small carton of eggs from the refrigerator and handing it to their mother. "Want to tell us how you ended up spooning with our agent?"

"It was completely innocent," Mia explained, but it was clear by Riley's sideways look that she wasn't buying it. After the way she'd acted under the influence of the wine, her answer felt flimsy even to her.

"There's a lot of wine gone." Riley eyed the empty bottles.

"You all drank some of those," Mia retorted.

Alice put the bread in the toaster and pushed down the lever. "You don't usually drink that much. Everything okay?"

"I hadn't meant to. I just got to talking to Will... and it was so nice to spend a night not thinking about Milo." She rolled her head on her shoulders, just the mention of him causing a pinched nerve. "He's seeing someone already," she said, that wave of self-doubt that there must be something wrong with her washing over her again. "He told me yesterday while I was out getting groceries with Will."

"And being with Will helped?" Alice asked carefully.

Mia shrugged.

"It's okay to take an interest in someone, you know," her mother said. "It isn't a crime."

"It's a complication I don't need right now. I have a property to sell and a Christmas party to plan." Mia pulled a glass from the cupboard and filled it with orange juice, taking it over to the table and sitting down. "And anyway, he lives in Seattle. Did you know that?"

"Oh, wow," her mother said. "I didn't."

"There's nothing stopping you from visiting Seattle if things were to progress," Riley said.

"They're not going to progress! And I don't want to go to Seattle. If I leave New York, it'll be to go somewhere warm, where it's sunny ninety percent of the year." She took a drink of her orange juice, the sweet tangy nectar biting at the sides of her dry mouth. "And it's just bad timing," she said. "The universe has *terrible* timing."

"I don't know," Alice said, bringing her a piece of buttered cinnamon bread, the warm spice wafting toward her. "I think the universe has perfect timing. We just don't always understand it." She went back over to the stove and cracked the eggs into a bowl. "I was so upset about coming to Winsted Cape, but now that I'm here, I'm glad I did. I feel close to Mom here, and while we're packing up some of her things, we get to walk in her world as if she's right here with us. It feels so good to be near her again."

"It *is* nice to be together at the lighthouse again, isn't it?" Riley said, putting her arm around Alice.

Their mother pulled her into a hug. "It's unbelievably great." She clapped her hands together. "Who wants coffee with our eggs?"

Mia sat on her grandmother's bed and dialed the number on the little paper from Grandma Ruth's dresser while her mother and sister watched. After several rings, she got an automated message, telling her the caller wasn't available and to leave a message after the beep.

"Hello, my name is Mia Broadhurst and I'm looking for Mildred Beaumont. I have some news about Ruth Carter. If this is the right number, please give me a call back," Mia said, before leaving her number and hanging up.

"No one there?" her mother asked.

"Nope. And it doesn't sound like her voicemail is set up, so I'm not even sure it's Mildred." She folded the paper and slipped it back under the dish where Grandma Ruth had left it.

Riley scooted a pile of clothes out of the way. "Well, we'll wait to see if she calls back, right?"

Mia flipped through the Christmas cards again and put them back into the box. "Yep. All we can do is wait."

"Grandma Ruth definitely wasn't a pack rat," Riley said. "Her things are so organized." She folded one of Grandma Ruth's sweaters and set it on the pile of clothes in the charity box.

"Packing's been pretty easy, hasn't it?" Mia agreed.

They'd been sorting Grandma Ruth's clothes all morning, and were now making their way through her jewelry. They were dividing up the most valuable pieces between them so they'd each have something of hers to remember her by.

"Look at this," their mother said, holding a delicate gold chain with half a heart dangling from it. She caught the pendant in her fingers and squinted down at it. "It says, A. H. C. Those aren't your grandmother's initials. Wonder whose they are..."

Mia came over to view it. "No idea."

"Put it with the Christmas cards we found. We'll call that box the mystery box," her mother said with a lighthearted grin. "I'm not sure what we'll do with it, but it seems strange to part with the items. Let's just hold on to them."

"Yes." Riley gently took the necklace from her mother and wrapped it in tissue, securing it with a piece of tape. Then she carried it over to the floral box, setting it inside.

"The snow looks like it's finally slowing down," Mia said, walking over to the window and peering out of it at the expanse of white that led to the gray Atlantic Ocean. The waves lashed against the shore as if they were taking out their aggression on the unseasonably snowy weather. "I wonder if I should start looking for someone to shovel the paths and maybe dig our cars out."

"I agree," Riley said matter-of-factly. "I'm dying for some lunch, and Will isn't back yet."

"We still have grapes... and crackers and cheese," Alice offered. "Mia, did you all finish the donuts?"

Mia shook her head. "No. We still have those too."

"And more cinnamon bread and eggs," Alice added. "Shall we stop and make ourselves a snack?"

"Definitely," Mia replied. "And I'll text Will to see if we can run out for more groceries once he gets back. He's taking longer than he said..."

She gazed out the window again, her eyes falling on the angels they'd made, the imprints barely visible in the newly fallen snow. She laughed, recalling the two of them lying there in the snow. "Will and I made those snow angels," she said, pointing out the window and telling them the story. "I wonder if it'll bring the lighthouse any luck in selling it?"

"I hope so," Alice said.

"You do?" Mia's question went unanswered, however, when Alice began to falter, tears in her eyes.

Both Mia and Riley rushed to their mother's side. "What's wrong?" Mia asked.

Shaking her head and biting back tears, Alice walked over to the kitchen table and took a seat. "I haven't been completely honest." She put her head in her hands. "I didn't want to burden you two with this, but Grandma Ruth took out a home equity line that is more than my savings. I'm out of money."

"Okay," Mia said, kicking into overdrive, racking her brain for how to fix this.

"The next payment on the lighthouse is due and..." Alice began to sob. "We have to keep making payments so we don't incur fees. I can't afford it. I'm at the end of my savings already."

Riley looked up at Mia helplessly. "We could let the bank take the lighthouse and settle the loan."

Alice hung her head. "I was hoping to sell it so we could get some of my savings back." She misted over again. Mia grabbed a napkin from the counter and handed it to her.

"How much is it over and above your usual paycheck, once you've paid everything for your house and this one?" Mia asked.

Alice's lip wobbled and then she crumbled into tears.

"Is it that much?" Riley asked, putting an arm around her mother.

"I..." Alice sucked in a long, jagged breath. "I lost my job."

The blood drained from under Mia's skin. There was no way she could afford two mortgages and living expenses for her and her mother. Even if they let the bank take the lighthouse, it wouldn't change the fact that she had no savings and another mortgage to pay.

"I thought they just cut back your hours?" Riley asked.

"I didn't want to tell you. It's *Christmas*. And you two have enough to worry about."

"I can cover next month," Mia said, not really sure how she was going to pay for all of this. "Hopefully, we'll sell the lighthouse by Christmas and we won't have to worry after that."

"If anyone can fix this, you can," Alice said to her daughter, putting a hand on Mia's cheek. "I love you."

"I love you, Mom." Mia wrapped her arms around her mother and Riley did the same. "No matter what, we'll figure it out together. We're warriors, remember?"

Alice hugged her daughters tighter. "Yes. Warriors, we are."

It was nearing dinnertime when Will had finally arrived, so he and Mia rushed right out to get more food. With Mia's mother feeling better about packing Grandma Ruth's things, it looked as though all three of them would be staying until the task was complete, which was a blessing, since they needed to get the lighthouse on the market as soon as possible.

"As you know, Kate's a single mom. Felix was a surprise and Felix's dad was only dating Kate before Felix was born. He was long gone by the time Felix arrived. So she's been handling things on her own," Will explained quietly, as he and Mia pushed the cart down the frozen aisle at the town grocery store.

Mia blew out a breath of empathy. "I totally understand that. My mom raised me by herself, and it was really hard on her."

"Yes," he said, nodding. He opened one of the refrigerator doors and pulled out a six-pack of bottled water. Mia checked it off on her list. "She's struggling. She decided to get a college degree in business, hoping to get some insight into how to save the bakery, but that means she's juggling running it, being a mom to Felix, and finishing her classes. Her final exams for the semester are coming up."

"Oh my goodness," she said.

"I've been watching Felix when his sitter Jackie isn't available to take care of him, and I've been helping Kate study for her finals."

Now his perpetual lateness made sense... "I feel awful that I pulled you away. We can figure out how to get our cars unstuck. I really shouldn't be asking you to cart us around. You've got enough going on."

His blue eyes darted over to her, a kind smile playing at his lips. "It's good to feel needed."

"I know what you mean," she said. "I was raised to be completely self-sufficient." She perused the cheese selection, looking for the cheddar. "At an early age, with my mother always at work, I learned how to cook food for my sister and me, iron our dresses, and braid our hair. I could get completely ready for school, pack our lunches, and make it to the school bus with Riley in tow. Not a single person questioned it because I'd become so skilled at it all, I could manage better than most parents." She plucked out a pack of cheese and tossed it into the cart. "I grew up thinking I didn't need anybody. But one day, I realized I did. When I moved to New York, without Riley, I didn't have anyone to take care of anymore. I needed someone to care for."

"You mentioned your husband. Did you feel better once you were married?"

She shook her head. "Milo had his own brand of self-sufficiency. He was strong-willed and direct; he took care of everything he needed. After years of it, I found it isolating."

"Mm," Will said.

"It feels good to be home with my sister and my mother because I'm needed again."

"Have you ever thought about staying in Winsted Cape for good then?"

"I hadn't planned on it. My whole life is in New York..."

They stopped at the yogurt aisle, and as she sifted through various flavors, she considered her response. She had her weekly meetup with the ladies at her club back in New York—Mia would self-destruct without their coffee dates. Mia's fitness trainer was the best around, and she still had at least six more months of paid sessions. Where would she ever get sushi like Wild Umi's? She might not survive without their maguro nigiri... While her family was here, there wasn't much else in the way of work or her lifestyle to keep her afloat. Her life was definitely in New York.

"How about you?" she asked.

Will moved over for a woman reaching around them for the swiss cheese.

"You've come here to help your family too. What's keeping you in Seattle?"

He gritted his teeth in thought, his face becoming serious. "I've had good luck with the real estate market, so it's lucrative from a work perspective."

"What originally took you there?" she asked, as they started walking toward the paper products aisle.

"A girl," he said with a poignant smile. "About ten years ago."

"Is she still there?"

He shook his head and then turned toward the paper towels. "You needed a roll of these, right?" he asked, handing her the package.

Even though she knew he had better things to do, she was glad he enjoyed helping her. "So, you two aren't together anymore?"

"No." He rolled the cart over to the next aisle. "I live alone."

"Sounds like there are lots of reasons keeping you there then..." she said teasingly.

But Will didn't answer. He just pushed the cart along, picking up the next few things on their list. She wanted to press him more, but something told her to let it go. Better not to get to know him any more than she already had. That was far too dangerous.

NINE

By evening, Mia was sweaty and dirty after helping to load the rest of the boxes into Will's truck. Before he left for the final trip to the charity shop, Mia turned to Will, her mother, and her sister.

"I'm exhausted. Why don't we skip cooking tonight?"

"But you just brought home all those groceries," her mother said.

"I did," Mia agreed. "And I got all the ingredients for Grandma Ruth's snickerdoodle cookies, so we can bake later. But tonight, I want to go out. Will, if you would drive us, why don't we get ready and go somewhere wonderful for a nice holiday dinner? On me," she offered. "We can all squeeze into Will's truck, can't we?"

"We can totally fit," Riley said. "Although I can't promise anything *after* I eat... I'm going to buy one of everything on the menu."

"You're always hungry," Mia said with a laugh while Will looked on, amused as he worked a little on his laptop at the table, answering a quick email about a new property for sale.

"It was the same way when she was young," Alice said. "But it never left her as she aged."

"Where does it all go? She's thin as a rail." Mia pinched her sister's side, making Riley laugh.

Will peered at the calendar on his laptop with a look of contemplation. "I have to watch Felix tonight while Kate studies."

"Could you bring him?" Mia asked. "We could come back here and he could help us bake cookies."

"You wouldn't mind?" he asked.

"Of course not," she replied.

"Kate has an SUV with four-wheel drive. Let me see if I can borrow it." He typed a text to his sister and waited for an answer.

This was just what Mia needed. All she wanted was to be dressed in a comfortable pair of jeans and an oversized sweater, enjoy the people around her, and forget about everything she'd been through over the last month.

"Kate said it'll be no problem to use her car," Will said. "She'll be studying all night anyway." He slipped his phone in his back pocket. "Why don't I go home and get cleaned up, switch vehicles, get Felix ready, and then come back in about an hour and a half?"

"That works," Mia said, delighted that it wouldn't be just her and Will at dinner. That would be way too much like a date, given the flutter he gave her that she was trying her best to ignore.

"You're supposed to be getting ready," Riley said, coming into Mia's bedroom. Her hair was curled and she was wearing makeup. She never wore makeup and when she did, it made her instantly look about ten years younger. She plopped down on the yellow bedspread beside Mia and the open floral box, and looked at the delicate gold necklace with the pendant A. H. C. that Mia was currently holding.

"I know. I'm nearly ready, but I just keep thinking about this." She held up the pendant and let it dangle in front of her. "What if these initials have something to do with the pictures we found?"

"It's a real possibility."

"Our best way to find out would be to talk to Mildred," Mia said. "But what if that number over there is no longer Mildred's? I haven't gotten a call yet."

"Maybe that's why Grandma Ruth had the number tucked away under that plate. She tried to call it but it didn't work."

Mia squinted in thought. "That's not like her. If that wasn't Mildred's number, Grandma Ruth would've thrown it away right then. But she didn't."

Mia pulled out her cell phone, located the number, and dialed it again.

"You're calling her right now?" Riley asked, fiddling with one of her dangly earrings.

The line rang and then suddenly, someone answered. It sounded like an old woman. Mia sat up straight and set the necklace on the bedside table. "Hello, is this Mildred Beaumont?" she asked.

"Yes, it is," the woman replied.

"Hi... You don't know me, but my name is Mia Broadhurst. I'm Ruth Carter's granddaughter." Mia widened her eyes excitedly at her sister. Riley clapped a hand over her mouth.

The old woman sucked in a breath and then stayed silent, the buzz of the line causing Mia to tense up.

Alice came to the door, wearing her best red sweater and matching lipstick. Riley shushed her and waved her into the room, pointing to Mia's phone at her ear. "It's Mildred," she mouthed. Alice gasped quietly before coming into the room and sitting down on the other side of Mia.

"I found some photos in my grandmother's things and I'm wondering if they are of you and your daughter. Did you send any in your Christmas cards?" She held the phone away from her ear so her mother and sister could hear, the two women leaning in.

"Uh, yes. I always sent a photo of myself and my daughter."

"How did you know my grandmother?"

Another breath. Another bout of silence. "She hasn't told you?"

"No. And... She passed away this past summer before she could."

"Oh..." Mildred said, that one word heavy with thought.

"We were hoping you could shed some light on it for us."

Mildred cleared her throat. "I'd rather tell you in person. Is there a time when my daughter could bring me to the lighthouse? I think being there would give us closure."

Mia eyed her mother and sister, the two of them shrugging. "Of course. When would you like to come?"

"Give me a week," Mildred said. "I'm ninety-two and I no longer drive, so I'll have to give my daughter enough notice to be able to drive us there."

"All right," Mia said. "That sounds good."

"Thank you for calling me," Mildred said. "This is an answer to our prayers."

"Of course," Mia answered, with no idea what Mildred meant.

"I'll be in touch."

Mia ended the call. "Well, that was interesting," she said.

"It sounds like they might have something to tell us. I'm glad we can help them," Alice said.

Mia couldn't wait to find out how.

Why the Sea Shack Inn had the word "shack" in its title, Mia would never know. It was a sprawling building sitting in the sand. Normally, Mia could see the deep blue Atlantic behind it showing off the whitewashed clapboard like a rare pearl, but the snow was falling all around it, blanketing everything in white, the snowstorm unrelenting.

"Oh, that looks so beautiful," Alice said, getting out of the car and pointing to the wide porches that stretched along the front of the structure.

Typically lined with rows of rocking chairs, this time of year the space was dotted with brightly lit Christmas trees, their glittery ornaments shimmering against the golden light coming through the windows. The two stone chimneys flanking either side of the building were working overtime, their fires clearly roaring inside.

Candles flickered on tables, sparkling against the glass of the windows.

Felix hopped out of the car and trudged through the snow to meet Will. The little boy had talked nonstop the whole ride there, so thrilled to be with them. "Do you think they have chocolate milk?" he asked excitedly, looking up at his uncle, wearing a pressed Oxford shirt and slacks.

"We can definitely ask," Will assured him, taking his nephew's hand as they all crossed the icy parking lot. Felix tugged on the tails of his button-up under his coat as his little docksiders kept pace with Will.

"Yay!" the boy cheered.

Will opened the door for them. The old fireplaces blazed under oversized mantles dripping with fresh greenery and red ribbon, with starfish suspended from the ends of the swooping bows. An enormous Christmas tree, adorned with blue and silver, reached for the driftwood-lined vaulted ceiling.

After Will gave the hostess his name, she showed them to a table for five. Mia sat down next to Will, with her mother and Riley taking seats across from her.

Felix climbed into one of the chairs and the hostess set a child's menu in front of him with some crayons. "Do you have chocolate milk?" he asked her.

"I believe we do," she replied.

"Oh, I'm so happy about that. May I order one, please?" he asked, his feet swinging above the floor.

"I'll tell you what," the hostess said with a wink toward Will, "I'll send my friend over to take your order and you can tell her."

"Okay," he said, picking up the blue crayon and working on the maze on the paper menu in front of him.

Mia peered down at her own menu. "The soups look so good," she said, her stomach growling. "And they have warm Christmas cider."

"Oh, that sounds fantastic," Alice said excitedly. It was nice to see her mother dressed up and happy. "I'm definitely getting the Christmas cider."

The waitress came and took their drink orders, and then Mia settled into her space, draping her cloth napkin across her designer jeans, the fire warming her back. A vanilla candle flickered in the center of the table. As she allowed her body to relax, she couldn't remember the last time she'd felt this comfortable.

Will grabbed the dish of sugar packets and set them in front of Felix. "When I was your age, I used to try to build a house of sugar. I could never get it very high but it was fun to see if I could make the walls and a roof." He set up four sugar packets to make the tiny walls, balancing them carefully on their sides. "Think we can put one on top to give us a flat surface for the roof?"

"It's gonna fall!" Felix said with a giggle as Will carefully placed a packet on top. It stayed put.

"Now, we need to set two of them up as the roof." Will handed two packets to his nephew. "Think you can build it?"

"I don't know," Felix said, unsure as he held the two packs of sugar between his fingers. "It might fall."

"It might," Will told him. "But you'll never build anything if you're afraid of it falling. You have to build it afraid. You might surprise yourself."

Felix stared at the little box of sugar packets, a pout of consideration on his lips. "If we put support in the middle, we could make it two stories," he said. "But it needs a packet in the middle." He took a few from the dish and carefully removed the top one, inserting one of the sugars diagonally from corner to corner. Then he replaced the lid, added another pack the same way, and built four more walls on the top. Finally, he added an A-line roof with two more.

"Wow," Will said. "I've never made a two-story house before."

Alice leaned forward to see what the boy had built. "He's so smart. That's impressive, Felix."

Beaming, Felix took the house apart and placed the sugars back into the dish, his chest puffed out in pride.

"What are you going to order?" Riley asked him, clearly enchanted by the little boy. None of them had been around kids, and having him there was like a breath of fresh air. So much so that it made Mia consider how much life she'd actually missed out on with Milo.

"I'm gonna get the macaroni," he announced, pointing to the photo of the pasta on Will's menu.

"That sounds yummy," Will said with a chuckle, as he picked up a crayon and marked an X on the Tic-Tac-Toe board. "Do you want some chicken to go with it, or maybe a burger?"

"What are *you* going to have?" Felix asked him, lighting up as he took the yellow crayon and drew an O. Then he looked at his uncle with adoring eyes.

"I thought I might have scallops."

Felix made a face. "Yuck. I'm not gonna have the same thing then."

Will laughed, marking another X. "That's okay. What sounds good to you?"

"Just the mac and cheese," he answered. "And then we can go to the bakery for dessert." Felix drew an O in the center of the board.

"Oh, sorry, buddy. The bakery's closed. Remember, your mom's at home studying?"

"The bakery's always closed," Felix said, his lips downturned. "Grandma never closed it this much."

"Maybe we can talk about it later," Will suggested gently. "You blocked me." He tapped the center O before writing an X in the bottom corner.

"That's what Mom always says, but we never do talk about it later." He drew an O. "I got you two ways."

Just in time, the waitress brought Felix's chocolate milk and their cinnamon ciders. The woman squatted down by the boy's chair. "We've got a special visitor tonight," she said. "Did you see the sign?" She pointed to an A-frame chalkboard that had the word

"Santa" in curly script. "He's going to sit right over there in that fancy red chair."

Mia followed Felix's gaze over to a red velvet wingback chair, trimmed in gold.

Felix's eyes grew round, his mood dramatically changing. "Santa?"

"Yep." The waitress stood back up and ruffled his hair. "He'll be here any minute."

"Can I sit on his lap?" Felix asked her.

"If you want to."

"How about that?" Alice said, clapping her hands as she smiled over at Felix. "It's been a long time since I've seen Santa." She turned her attention lovingly to her daughters. "It'll be nice to feel the magic again."

Just then, the sound of jingling footsteps clomped toward them, followed by a bellowing, "Ho Ho Ho..."

Felix turned around with a gasp and threw his hands over his mouth.

Santa took a seat on the large throne, straightened the fur lining on his red-and-white suit, and pushed his booted feet into position to hoist himself up, getting comfortable in the chair. He stroked his long white beard.

"May I go see him?" Felix asked, already wriggling down out of his chair.

"Of course," Will told him.

Santa opened his arms as Felix climbed up onto the man's lap. "Well, look at you," he said. "How have you been this year?"

"Okay," Felix said with a sweet smile.

"Just okay?" Santa asked, bouncing him on his knee.

Felix nodded.

"Well, hopefully Christmas will help to make it more than *just okay*," Santa said. "I think you've been a good boy."

Felix burst into a grin.

"What would you like Santa to bring you this year?"

"I want everybody to be happy."

Santa tilted his head to the side and peered down at the child. "That's a tall order," he said. "Could we maybe narrow it down to a few people at least?"

"Okay." Felix's little brows pulled together. "I want the kids in my class to be nice. I want them to be happy to see me."

"Mm," Santa told him, pensive. "You could definitely remind them that I'm watching. And maybe ask them to tell you their favorite thing to do after school. You might find things you have in common."

"That's a good idea." Felix leaned in. "And I want to keep my gran's bakery," he said quietly. "My mom and my uncle want to sell it, but I want to keep it. My gran's cookies make people happy."

"What bakery is it?" Santa asked.

"The Corner Bakery."

Santa's eyes rounded. "I used to get my cookies from there when your grandmother worked the counter." He looked over at the table, meeting Will's eyes with a question, probably wondering how to handle this one. Will broke eye contact, the topic clearly sitting heavily upon his shoulders.

"Sometimes our lives have a big shake-up," Santa told him. "Do you know what that is?"

Felix shook his head.

"A shake-up is when things seem to go wrong, but really, they're just moving out of the way for something even better. Like with your gran's bakery. What if something even bigger, even better takes the place of it?"

Felix's eyes rolled around as he tried to understand this. "So, like, instead of a bakery, it would be a candy shop?"

Santa shrugged, producing a grin under his white curls. "Maybe!"

Skepticism lingered on Felix's little face before he continued. "I have one more person to make happy: my mom. She works really hard on her studies and she stays up past my bedtime. I want her to get her favorite job so she'll be happy that she did all that learning."

Santa pursed his lips. "I'll definitely be on the lookout for jobs your mom might want." He bounced Felix again. "How about *you*?

You've asked for a lot of great things for everyone else. Is there anything I can get *you*?"

"Puppy Barks-A-Lot," he replied. "My mom says we can't get a dog because she doesn't have time to care for one, so this is a stuffed animal that moves and barks like a real dog."

"All right. One Puppy Barks-A-Lot is now on my list of possibilities."

"Thank you, Santa!" Felix hopped down and ran back to their table. He climbed up onto his chair and twisted around to give Santa a wave before happily wrapping his hands around his chocolate milk and taking a drink. After swallowing a gulp of it, he whispered, "I can't believe Santa is here." His gaze darted back to ol' Saint Nicholas, who was busy meeting another child.

"Those were really nice things you asked for," Will told him.

Felix gave him a big smile.

"I really hope you get them," Will said, but his eyes were troubled under his pleasant demeanor.

Riley wrapped her hands around the cinnamon cider. "Your family owns The Corner Bakery?" she asked. "We used to love going there as kids."

"Are you sure I can't help Kate with some PR for the bakery?" Mia offered again quietly, while Alice worked on the maze with Felix, diverting his attention. Although, with everything she had going on with the lighthouse and the party, as well as Mildred's visit, she had no idea how she'd fit in a project of that size.

"I just don't think she can keep it going with all the classes she's taking," Will replied.

Mia nodded, contemplative. She knew that Grandma Ruth would've managed to save the lighthouse and the bakery, and somehow make it all look easy. She could really do with some of that hope right about now...

After dinner, Felix was tired so they dropped him back home before Will drove Mia, Riley, and their mother back to the lighthouse through the snow that had begun to fall heavily, covering the roads. It seemed like the storm would never end.

"It's late," Alice said, as they all entered through the kitchen door. She stifled a yawn and dropped her handbag on the counter, the calm of the night out still evident in her tired features. "I'm going to head to bed."

"Me too," Riley agreed.

"Will, the pillows and blankets are still on the sofa," Alice told him in her motherly tone. "Don't drive home in this mess. It's too late."

Will huffed out a little smile. "I'll be fine," he assured her.

"I insist," Alice said. "Don't you dare try to drive in the dark. There's a layer of ice under that snow and you're alone. I felt the few slips we made trying to get back. I'd be beside myself if anything happened."

"I should leave a toothbrush and a bar of soap over here," he teased.

"Not a one of us would care if you did," Alice added with a playful wrinkle of her nose. "You two kids keep it down out here, okay?"

"All right," Mia told her mother, kissing her on the cheek. "Night, Riley."

Riley put her hands on her mother's shoulders to lead her out of the room. "Goodnight." Then she flashed a grin to Mia before nodding in Will's direction.

Mia shook her head.

"I have an idea," she told Will after Riley and her mother had left the room, as she settled at the kitchen table under the yellow light of the old fixture above them. "I've been pondering Kate's predicament all night, and I thought of something to help her. Why don't we have a nice cup of warm apple cider and I'll tell you?"

Mia took two mugs from the cupboard and grabbed the jug of cider from the fridge, pouring it into a pan and heating it on the stove. When it was warm enough to send a cinnamon-scented steam into the air, she made them each a cup.

Will sat down opposite Mia and scooted one of the glasses her way. "What's your idea?"

"We have to have a charity for our Christmas party…"

He eyed her curiously, his blue eyes dark like sapphires in the low light.

"What if our Christmas charity this year was the preservation of the historic Corner Bakery?" She stood up, waving her arms out wide, pretending to make a speech. "Our goal tonight is to safeguard a slice of Americana, to maintain the ideals that built this country: family, friendship, and community. Tonight, we celebrate a small-town legacy, generations of hard-working people who built the foundations of our childhood." She sat back down. "They'll all be pulling out their checkbooks, and if this charity is anything like all the others, they'll donate way more money than we even need."

Will leaned on his elbow, his fingers hiding the smile that had spread across his lips, his gaze swallowing her. "Thank you," he said. "But I'm not sure I feel great about taking the place of an actual charity."

"But it *is* an actual need in the community," Mia argued. "And it fits perfectly with our small-town Christmas theme… I could even have Kate do the baking for the party so the guests could see what they're saving, if she's up for it. And anything that we make over and above what you all need can go to a charity of Kate's choice."

Mildred's words came back without warning: *This is an answer to our prayers.* Mia wondered if Grandma Ruth was behind all of this, guiding her, showing her how best to help people just like she would. Maybe, just maybe, there would be happy endings all round this season.

TEN

"Mia." Her mother's voice swam through her consciousness. "The contractors are here."

"Already?" she croaked, forcing her eyelids open.

"It's nine o'clock. The rest of us have all had breakfast, and we've cleared off the countertops. They said we can leave everything in the cabinets because they're able to cover it all with plastic before they paint."

Mia raked her hands through her tangled hair, piling it on top of her head in a messy bun and securing it with the clip on her nightstand. "It's nine o'clock?" She hadn't slept that long in her entire adult life. She wondered if it was because she'd stayed up so late getting the party and the charity organized. After everyone had gone to bed, she'd checked the digital invite list, sent out emails to three different DJs, inquired with a company about wait staff for the event, worked on menu options and contacted local restaurants for catering, set up a car service to partner with the hotel to shuttle people over, asked for quotes from a florist for table arrangements in the barn—and that was just the list of things she could remember off the top of her head.

"Why didn't you wake me up?"

"You needed the sleep." Alice went over to the windows and raised the blinds, the bright blue sky a stark difference from the storm that had followed Mia into town. "You've been running yourself absolutely ragged since you got here."

Mia climbed out of bed, pulled the covers up, smoothing them, and straightened the pillows. "Will's up already?"

"Yep. He's chatting with the contractors. The rest of the team is outside, preparing to paint the exterior. Did you want to show them what you'd like them to do with the lighthouse? They were asking whether you want horizontal stripes or diagonal when they repaint it."

"What do you think?" she asked, still trying to wake up.

"You've got the design talent in the family—you choose."

Mia nodded. "Would you tell them I'll be right there?"

"Of course, honey."

Mia hurried into the bathroom, brushed her teeth, splashed water on her face and ran a few runaway strands of hair behind her ears before heading to the kitchen. Will was waiting with a mug of steaming coffee while the contractors' tools buzzed behind him. His hair was slightly out of place, a golden glow of stubble on his jawline, his biceps peeking out from his T-shirt just before he slipped a sweater over his head.

"Thank you," she said, shrugging on her coat as she took the warm beverage into her hands. She held it close as she slipped on her boots.

"Good morning," he told her, grabbing his coat and following her outside. "I had everything that you wanted done noted except the stripes," he said as they walked through the snow, along the edge of the horse field, toward the lighthouse where the painters were waiting. The pounding of the waves as they crashed on the snowy shore was the only sound.

"I think either would be fine," she said, "but my personal choice would be horizontal."

"Stay right here and enjoy your coffee," he said. "I'll let them know."

Mia looked up at the shiny glass atop the lighthouse, and the crisp morning urged her to climb up there to take in the view. It had been years since she'd been to the top. Why she thought her flannel pajama bottoms and rubber boots were warm enough to make the hike, she had no idea, but she wanted to do it. Will walked back over to her.

"Shall we go up?" she asked, pointing to the catwalk that encircled the glass at the top.

He gazed upward, shielding his eyes from the sun. "You sure you want to drink your coffee while climbing hundreds of steps?"

"We'll go slowly," she said, the nostalgia of her childhood taking over. "My grandmother used to tell me that the stairs led to heaven, and every step we took sent up a little prayer for the boaters that passed."

"That's really nice," Will said, the freezing wind ruffling his hair as he took in the large structure. "Is it unlocked?"

"It should still be. She never locked it. Unless someone wants to steal a five-ton optic lens, there's no reason to."

Mia pulled on the handle and, sure enough, it opened. They stepped inside, the clap of the door shutting behind them echoing in the stairwell. A chill running through her, she took a sip of her coffee and peered up at the spiral staircase. The faint sound of laughter filtered in from her memory as she recalled playing tag on the stairs with Riley, Grandma Ruth calling down to them to be careful.

"Hey, I spoke to Kate this morning," he said. "She's on board to be the charity at your party."

"Oh, that's great," she said.

"Now we just need a buyer for the lighthouse."

"I wonder who will buy this place..." she questioned aloud. Would they know not to get their abrasive clothing near the lens of the light so they wouldn't scratch it? Would they know they needed to lift slightly to get the latch to move when they wanted to stop the rotation of the beam? Would they know how to position the filters to warn boaters at Lock's Bend? There were so many little things like that her grandmother had taught her... Familiar faces from last Christmas's party floated through her mind, none of them fitting the bill of lighthouse owner. "I can't imagine anyone but Grandma Ruth working in here," she said before Will had answered her question.

"You know how you go out and look for houses and none of them feels right until you get to the one you end up buying? The one that just seems to fit you."

"Mm-hm," she said, making each step carefully as she took another drink of her coffee, letting it warm her, the roasted, nutty flavor comforting her.

"The right person will come along," he said.

They continued walking quietly, his words settling between them, running over and over in her mind, the shuffling of their footsteps and the clank of the painters' scaffolding against the exterior as they set up in the background. She hoped she was doing the right thing and that Grandma Ruth would approve if she could see what was happening from heaven.

"I remember the last time my grandmother climbed these steps," she finally said, her memories getting the better of her. "It was right before she went into the hospital when her cancer was finally grabbing hold of her. We couldn't believe she could still walk these steps and we kept asking if she was okay." Mia laughed at the thought. "She said, 'I'd be much better if you stopped asking me. As far as I can tell, my legs still move and my feet still meet the stairs. Unless you're seeing something I'm not.'"

Will chuckled. "Sounds like she was a spunky woman."

"That she was."

They continued the climb until they'd reached the room just under the lamp. Mia set her empty coffee mug on the ledge and opened the door. Just like the main house, the interior still carried Grandma Ruth's scent, more memories of her tickling the edges of Mia's mind. If she closed her eyes, she could almost imagine Grandma Ruth walking in and plopping down in one of the chairs next to the tea table she'd set up for cold nights.

"Where are we?" Will asked, peering out through the windows

at the stormy gray sea. The winter waves pounded the shore around them, their whitecaps spraying up against the lighthouse.

"This is the watch room," Mia replied. "It's where Grandma Ruth stayed during storms. It's safer than being up with all the glass."

The room was minimally decorated, as it was quite difficult to get furniture up the massive circular staircase, but she had two chairs, a handful of small tables, and a padded bench.

"These views are incredible," Will said, leaning over to look out over the Atlantic.

"The blue sky is deceptive," she noted. It looked like it could almost be warm out there, were it not for the huge crests on the waves. The water rose and rushed toward the shore in angry peaks and summits. "Want some really great views? Let's go into the lantern room. The views up there are spectacular."

They ascended the rest of the way up to the very top of the lighthouse, opening the door and walking into the glass enclosure. With the electric-blue sky all around them and the occasional cloud slipping by, it gave Mia the illusion of swaying in the air. She walked over to the glass and, just like she'd done as a kid, she pressed her forehead to it, looking out at the immense expanse of sea surrounding her.

"I feel so small up here," she said. "It makes me forget about all my troubles for a second."

"Yes, it certainly does..."

When she turned toward Will, she caught the intensity in his gaze as he looked at her. It seemed to startle him as much as it did Mia, and he broke eye contact, turning his attention to a seagull that had perched on the gallery deck outside.

She looked back out at the sea. "I know that New York is where my life is, but moments like this one up here make me wonder..." Her ambiguous statement was deliberate. She was testing the waters, dusting off her emotional side she'd kept hidden away for so long. With just one look, Will could bring it out in her.

Will nodded. "I feel that way too sometimes."

She needed to look at him to see if his answer related to her, but she was afraid to let herself feel anything. She didn't need this —she knew that. But despite herself, she was starting to want it.

"Why don't you stay here with Kate?" she asked. "What's really taking you back to Seattle?" She finally gave in, and looked at him.

He clenched his jaw tightly, a look she'd never seen on his face before surfacing. He stood still for a few seconds, that contemplation she'd seen before coming back. Finally, he spoke. "My wife."

Mia lost her breath, her mouth falling slack before she realized it and snapped it closed. "Your *wife*?"

He swallowed. "My... late wife. Susannah." He shoved his hands in his pockets, suddenly looking lost. "Her family is in Seattle. I'm their connection to her. Her mother calls me at least once a day. She rang that first day I met you and I pulled over to the side of the road. She asks about my day, about how I am, and so I ask her the same. Her tears tug on my own grief, and it's difficult to know how I'm supposed to handle it..."

"I'd assumed that Kate was the reason you were late that day," she said, still trying to process all of this.

He smiled through his contemplation. "Sometimes Kate can make me late, but she usually understands that I have places to be. A lot of the time, it's Fran, Susannah's mom, calling me or asking me to hurry back."

"I had no idea. I'm so sorry." She put her fingers to her mouth, as if she could hold in her empathy for him. But it poured out from her anyway.

"How were you to know? And it was nice that you didn't. It let me catch my breath, pretend to be a whole person for a while."

"When did Susannah pass away?"

"A year ago. She had a brain aneurism. We had no idea it was coming. She was perfectly healthy one day and gone the next."

"Oh my God."

"It wasn't like she'd gotten sick and I had time to prepare and grieve and worry and freak out that one day soon I would be without her. I'd gone to work, spending the morning in the office to put a few new properties into the real estate listing system because our Wi-Fi was acting up at home. She called and told me she had a headache, and asked if I could pick up some milk on the way home so she didn't have to go out. She was going to take a nap..."

Mia held her breath, already aching for him before he'd finished the story.

"I remember seeing her on the sofa, and it was clear she wasn't sleeping. I knew because it looked as if her soul was gone. I dropped the carton of milk and it burst, spilling everywhere... I ran to her like I could help her, not understanding, utterly confused. And I remember the wave of fear and panic when she didn't respond, not wanting to admit that she was gone."

"That's so incredibly tragic," Mia said in a whisper, her own problems feeling completely inconsequential in comparison.

He cleared his throat, his chest filling with air as if to rid them of the sadness that had fallen upon them. Mia reached out and touched his arm, unsure of how to comfort him. There was no way to comfort that kind of loss.

"Sometimes, if I let myself, when I'm home, I notice the silence... I've noticed that I didn't want anyone around. Because that would mean that I had to move along with my life and I wasn't ready." He trailed off, looking into the distance before finding Mia again. "I've noticed that it's really easy to talk to you," he said.

She nodded, an unspoken solidarity in their gaze.

"I've not met anyone who could do that for me... But I'm not sure that I... that we..."

"Oh!" She waved her hands in the air dismissively. "I'm in no place in my life to meet anyone." Her face burned with the admission that she'd even put him in a category of someone she'd consider dating. "I just told my mom and my sister that I need to figure out who I am without my ex, Milo. I've been his wife for so long that I'm not sure what to do without him. You're perfectly safe with me." She gave him an understanding grin.

He gazed at her fondly.

"So, you don't stay on the sofa of all your clients?" she teased, trying to lighten the mood.

"Should I include that in the sales package?" he teased back.

"Maybe not..."

Something about sharing that moment with Will, at the highest point of the lighthouse, surrounded by the crashing waves, made Mia feel like she'd found someone she could trust. She knew it in her heart: they'd definitely be friends after this.

ELEVEN

When they got back to the main house, Will headed out to Kate's to take care of Felix, leaving Mia and her mother in the kitchen. The cabinet doors were all gone, the cubbies that remained covered in plastic, and the measurements were being taken for the tile backsplash.

"Wow, things are coming along already," Mia said, excited. She picked up one of the tiles and turned it over in her hand. "These are going to look amazing paired with the rustic hardwoods that run through the house."

"Mia, you've really chosen some gorgeous finishes. Makes me want to move in," her mother teased, rinsing her cup and setting it out of the way of the contractors.

"That ain't in my way if you wanna leave it out," one of the contractors said, eyeing the mug with his dark eyes. "But you run the risk of me fillin' it up during my break."

Mia's mother grinned at him. "I'm Alice," she said, holding out her hand.

The man checked his palm for paint, wiped his fingers on his shirt, and shook her hand. "Pete. And that fool over there is JP."

JP waved from his ladder as he touched up the wall over the fridge.

"If you want coffee, you don't have to nip my mug. I'll get you a cup," Alice told him. "The pot's still on if you want one."

"Thank you kindly," Pete said, his crop of dark hair falling across his forehead as he bent down to paint under the lower cabinet.

Alice reached under the plastic covering and pulled two more mugs down, filling them with coffee. "Cream and sugar?"

"We both take ours black," Pete replied, nodding thanks as he took one of the mugs.

"This place for sale?" JP asked from atop the ladder as Alice held his mug up to him.

"Yes, it is," she replied.

Pete whistled. "It's quite a piece of property. It'd be fun to live here..."

"It *would* be fun to live here, wouldn't it?" Mia said, her heart breaking all over again at the fact that was an impossibility for them. She wiped the counter down with a towel to help her mother clean up. "What's Riley doing?" she asked.

"She's finishing getting ready for work, and then I'm going to see if I can get her car out of the snow. It looks like it's low enough now, and I want to go to bingo tonight," her mother said.

Mia's phone beeped on the table.

"I missed a call from Mildred," she said, putting the phone to her ear to listen to the message.

"She wants to come Saturday around noon and stay the weekend."

Her mother's eyebrows bounced with anticipation. "Maybe she'll share some good gossip about Mom's early years. Think Saturday will work?"

"That sounds fine to me." Mia turned to one of the contractors. "You all should be finished by Friday, right?"

"Will said there was a rush, so we'll be out of your hair by tomorrow," Pete said.

"Everything is coming together," she said.

Alice gave her a squeeze. "It's because *you're* taking care of it. We can always count on you."

"Thank you," Mia replied, wrapping her arms around her mother.

"So should we go out and take a look at what needs to be done in the barn?" Alice asked.

"Definitely."

"All right," her mother said with a clap of her hands. "Let's start Riley's car and see if we can get it to move."

After Mia zipped up her coat, the two of them headed outside with Riley's keys. Alice unlocked the car door and slipped inside, starting the engine.

"We should be good to go now," Mia told her, assessing the snow. It had already started melting with the sunshine outside, and the tires were almost completely visible.

"I think so too," her mother said. "Thank goodness."

Mia had to admit that she hadn't minded catching a ride with Will over the last few days. He'd been such a gentleman in all this.

All of a sudden, Mia's phone went off in her back pocket. She pulled it out to view the caller and sighed. Milo.

"Hello?" Mia answered, putting the phone to her ear as her mother shut the car door, revved the engine, and put it in reverse.

"What's the status of the Christmas party?" he asked without a hello. "It's Monday—brief day."

Mia shook her head. "We're going to be ready. And I already have a charity lined up. The digital invites are coming in and we have one hundred thirty confirmed as of last night."

"Good," he said.

Riley's tires spun wildly as Alice twisted them back and forth on the snow, accelerating and tugging on the steering wheel until the car came loose and lurched backward.

"I'll see you at the party," she said.

"All right. See you then."

The line went dead, and she blew air through her cold lips and slipped the phone back into her pocket.

Alice pulled off to the side and the two got out, leaving the car running. "It was a little tricky getting the tires unstuck from the ice, but we should be just fine driving now." She took a few strides, nearing Mia. "Your face looks like a storm cloud. What's wrong?"

"I wish things could've ended differently for Milo and me," Mia replied. "We're completely over."

"How do you feel about that?" Alice asked.

"It's so weird. I just wish we could be more civil, you know?" She moved a loose piece of snow with her foot.

"You remember the old saying Grandma Ruth used to tell us about things ending badly? They have to. Otherwise, they wouldn't end at all... You are an amazing woman," her mother told her. "Don't put too much pressure on yourself too soon. Just feel your way through it."

Mia nodded, unconvinced. She didn't feel very amazing at the moment.

"Let's take a look at the barn before we freeze to death."

When they got to the immense brick-red structure with white trim, Alice slid the large door open. The barn was noticeably empty. It had been for some time—ever since Grandma Ruth had sold off all the horses when she couldn't take care of them anymore. She'd sold all but Delilah early on, and she hadn't needed a whole barn just for her when she had the smaller stalls on the other side of the field. Then Riley had found Delilah a home and she must've cleaned out the few bags of feed.

Rays of sunlight filtered through the slats of the building, lining the dusty, old wood floor in gold beams. The thick oak rafters stretched across the ceiling as if holding the entire structure in place, and the old general store feed bags hung on the walls, giving the whole place a down-home feel.

If Mia closed her eyes, she could still see Grandma Ruth in her Levi's and rubber boots, shoveling hay from one side of the barn to the other after deliveries. She liked to keep it on the shady side of the barn, which was under one of the two-hundred-year-old oak trees on the property, so the horses could keep cool while they ate. Delilah would follow her around like a puppy whenever Grandma Ruth was in the barn, and eventually Grandma Ruth would relent, and give the horse her full attention. "Here you go, darlin'," she'd whisper, "you just can't get enough love, can you?"

"I miss Delilah," Mia said, so she wouldn't have to consider how much she missed Grandma Ruth.

"She's in a good home," Alice replied. "It's just down the road. You could go see her."

"I think I will," Mia replied with a sentimental smile. She sucked in a breath of cold air. "So," she said, clapping her hands and changing the subject before she got misty-eyed. "Lots to do."

"Tell me what you're thinking for in here." Alice tipped her head back to view the A-frame ceiling.

"I want to clean up these floors." Mia waved her arms out at the large expanse of wood flooring. "The old knots and divots give it an incredible amount of character. I also want an enormous glass chandelier hanging down from the center peak, above the floor. I'm hoping I can somehow get one on loan. And Christmas trees in every corner—Leah can do that in her sleep. It's drafty, so we'll need to line the space with heaters so people don't freeze to death." She walked over to the west-facing wall. "And along here, I'd love to set up a bar service and a DJ playing Christmas music. We'll rent tables and chairs to place around the room. And fill it with flowers, candles, and string lights."

"And you have the budget for all the things you have planned?"

"Broadhurst Creative does. They spare no expense on their parties."

"It all sounds incredible. I'd love to see it with everyone enjoying it."

"You will. You and Riley are coming to the party, right?"

"Oh my! Whatever would we wear?" her mother worried aloud.

"We've got time to order you a few dresses online," she said with an excited smile. She'd love nothing more than to have her family around her to help her face Milo all night. Mia took her mother's hands and gave her a spin. "Wouldn't you love to dance under the Christmas lights?" She twirled her again, making Alice laugh.

"I'd love to," she said. "I can't remember the last time I danced." She pulled her daughter into an embrace and waltzed around the floor with her.

At that moment, Mia knew there was no other place she needed to have this party than right here with the ones she loved.

TWELVE

Farmer Owens stood in his denim bibbed overalls on the front porch of his farmhouse, both chimneys puffing smoke into the cloud-covered sky. He put his hands on his hips as Mia got out of the car and smiled through his wiry beard.

"How ya doin'?" he called out to her.

"I'm fine, thanks," Mia replied, pulling her coat tighter to keep the cold from slithering inside her collar as she made her way to him.

"Careful on the ice," he warned. "It's slippery."

Mia paced across the drive carefully, a layer of snow between her boots and the gravel.

"I hear you wanna see your horse."

She climbed the steps to meet him on the porch. "I'd love to."

"Well, come on in. We'll walk through the house to give you a little warm-up before I throw you back into the cold again."

He opened the door and she walked into the dimly lit entryway, stepping onto a thin tapestry rug that looked as though it was original to the home. A lamp glowed on the rustic entryway table.

"How did you find out Delilah was for sale?" she asked, as they made their way down the hardwood hallway toward the black-and-white checkered tile of the kitchen. "Did Riley call you?"

"I've been pestering your grandmother for ages to let me take care of Delilah for her," Mr. Owens said with a jovial smile. He stopped and kissed his wife on the cheek while she washed dishes, her hands sunk into a pile of suds. "You remember my wife Beverly?"

"Hey there," Beverly said, addressing Mia with a bubbly wave of her fingers. "Glad you could come by. I'm so terribly sorry about the loss of your grandmother. I adored her. The funeral was such a lovely tribute..." Her shoulder-length hair that had been curled under at the funeral was tucked into a bun at the back of her head.

"Thank you," Mia said, trying not to recall that day. Coupled with seeing Delilah, it might be more than she could bear emotionally. "It's nice to see you."

"How's the lighthouse coming along?" Beverly asked, dipping a mug under the water and scrubbing it with a sponge. "I'll bet you have a lot to go through."

"It's getting there," Mia replied. "Speaking of the lighthouse, we found some things from an old acquaintance of my Grandma Ruth. The woman's name is Mildred Beaumont. Have you ever heard of her?" Maybe she could get some scoop on Mildred before she came to visit.

Beverly consulted her husband and both of them shook their heads.

"I haven't," the woman replied. "What did you find?'

"Oh, just a few Christmas cards and some odds and ends. I was just curious." Mia wondered why, if Grandma Ruth was close with this woman, no one seemed to have heard of her.

"Sorry I couldn't be of more help." Beverly set a dish on the drying rack and wiped her hands on her apron. "I'll be happy to make y'all some hot tea if you're goin' out into the barn," Ms. Owens offered.

"Please don't go to any trouble for me," Mia said. "I won't stay too long. I just wanted to say hello to Delilah while I was in town."

Mr. Owens opened the back door for her. "She's in the barn. Want me to walk you out there or would you like to take it from here?"

"I'll go alone, if that's okay," Mia said.

Mr. Owens waved his hand. "Be my guest. Just knock on this door when you want to come back in. Beverly and I will be at the kitchen table playing cards."

"Okay," Mia said, throwing them a smile. "Thank you."

She stepped out into the cold, walking through the wide frozen fields toward the horse fence, her feet crunching on the cold ground. She let herself in through the gate, then latched it behind her and trudged across the pasture, until she reached the barn door. She stood there for a moment, gathering herself before walking in. Squaring her shoulders, she opened the door and stepped inside.

"Delilah?" she called. "It's Mia."

Delilah snorted from the other side of the barn and then began to clip-clop toward her, away from the other horses, her ears perked up, her jaw slackening the way it did whenever she was happy. The dark chocolate horse's tail swished gently as she met Mia and her large, deep brown eyes found hers.

"Hey, girl," she said, tears filling her eyes. "I'll bet you wondered where I'd gone."

The horse snorted again, closing its eyes halfway and nuzzling her.

"It's been a long time, hasn't it?" Mia said, fighting back tears. It felt like yesterday that she and Grandma Ruth had the horse brushes, making her coat silky.

The horse eyed her once more.

"I know..." Mia cooed, putting her arms around the horse's neck. "I missed you." She just hadn't realized how much until now. "You have a good home here. Farmer Owens and his wife are great people."

Delilah shook and then swung her big head toward Mia, her hooves stepping closer.

"The other horses being nice to you?" she asked, stroking Delilah's long mane.

The horse's dark eyes bored into her as if they were telling Mia everything she'd been through.

"I know you must miss Grandma Ruth," she said, the horse's ears twitching at the sound of her voice. "I do too. I miss her every day. I wasn't there with her in her last moments, and that will always stay with me, but I promise to be there for the rest of your life. Farmer Owens will let me come to see you any time I want—all I have to do is ask. Sorry it took me so long to get here."

Delilah snorted, knocking one hoof against the barn floor.

"I know," Mia soothed. "You're allowed to be upset with me. But you know what?" Then she dropped her voice to a whisper. "You've done great. You're a warrior just like us." She stroked the horse's neck, fighting back the tears. "I promise that I'll come back this summer and we can take a ride together, okay? We'll take a nice walk through the buttercups. How does that sound?"

Delilah's hooves shifted the way they did whenever she was happy.

"I've missed you, ol' girl," she said. "And I'm sorry for staying away so long. I won't do that again."

She made herself a promise right there that she'd never let anything pull her away from her family again. Even if life took her elsewhere, she'd always come home.

THIRTEEN

It was late in the evening by the time Mia got to the bakery. The pale gray light had given way to the blackness that was settling in, making the cloud-covered sky look like a sheet of velvet.

"Good day?" Will asked from behind the counter after she'd come inside.

Mia took her coat off and draped it on the old soda fountain stool. "Yes, I saw my horse Delilah in her new home with Farmer Owens." She sat down next to Kate and Felix, who was coloring. "I never realized how much I missed her."

"That's fantastic." Will smiled, grabbing three croissants with parchment and mugs of hot cocoa. He slid them across to where she and Kate were sitting, and put an extra big marshmallow in Felix's mug.

"Will tells me you might be able to help with the bakery," Kate said, picking at her croissant. Felix's crayon stilled and he looked up with wide eyes. "I'm so grateful for your support."

"If that's what you want. I'd like to try to make it profitable again."

"That's a tough job. Nothing I've done has helped. I've run sales, sent out print ads... I even paid for a billboard."

"I think we need to dig below that level," Mia said. "We need to consider how to reach the people in town. Will, do you have a pad of paper and a pen back there?"

Will opened a drawer and retrieved the items, setting them in front of Kate and Mia while little Felix looked on. The boy turned his paper over to a clean side, his crayon poised for working like the adults.

Mia clicked the pen and began explaining while taking notes. "What I suggest is that we give the place a facelift, and then find people in the community who remember it in its heyday and get them in here, sharing stories. Those quotes and video footage will be your advertising."

"Oh, that would be amazing," Kate said. "You have such a talent for this—I can tell already."

Mia smiled, completely in her element. "It's what I do," she said. "Once we get all that done, *then* we'll work on the ads. Will, could we book your photographer once we get people in here?"

"Yep," he said.

Felix wrote a mass of letters on his paper in a line. "I can help Mom with what she should bake," he said, writing a B on his paper as he mouthed the word *bake*.

"Excellent. Felix, we never made my grandmother's snicker-doodles. Let's put that on the list, shall we?"

Felix wrote "sics" and pointed to his word. "Got it," he said. "Snickerdoodles."

"Awesome, thank you," she said. "I have someone in New York that we use at our company who can take the video footage and set original music to it as well as an overlay of typography. We should probably have enough in the budget after the charity event to run a few local television ads. But before we do all that, we'll need to close."

"Close?" Kate asked.

Felix looked up from his paper.

"We'll want a grand opening with a lot of press. I'll help you arrange it. We'll get the word out on all the major local networks and put up flyers with your number, and we'll go door-to-door if we have to so that we can get people from town back in. We'll have balloons, free cookies, giveaways, live music..."

Felix gasped, drawing the attention of the three of them. "It's just like Santa said: Sometimes you have a shake-up—when things seem to go wrong, but really, they're just moving out of the way for something even better!"

"That's right," Mia said, surprised at how well he was following the conversation.

Kate looked on, tears forming in her eyes.

"Is everything okay?" Mia asked.

"I had no idea how we'd get the money. I didn't think this was ever possible."

"I'm glad I could help," Mia replied.

"It's not every day that a person in Winsted Cape gets a big-city PR person for free, along with a bucket of money."

Happiness bubbled up, a feeling of real purpose for the first time in a very long while settling over Mia. "I will need one thing in return," she said.

"What's that?"

"I'm going to need bakery catering for about two hundred people."

Kate's eyes widened. "I've never baked for that many people at once."

"Think you can do it?"

"I can definitely do it," she said.

"Awesome!" said Felix, and Mia gave him a high-five.

"I've got goodies," Mia said, letting herself in through the kitchen door of the lighthouse. She set a box of cookies that Kate had packed for her on the table. "Mom? Riley?"

"In here," Riley called from the living room.

"I brought home a box from The Corner Bakery." She plopped down next to her sister, only then noticing that Riley and her mother had brought over the Christmas tree from her childhood home, and Mia's presents were under it. The tiny tree was a stark contrast to the large space of the lighthouse, and that single image was a reminder of how far she'd come since the days of her childhood. "It feels very festive in here," she said.

Alice, who'd piled up a few pillows by the fire and was sitting on the floor, leaning against the hearth, twisted around to view it. "We thought we'd enjoy every minute in the lighthouse. It's different when I know the days are numbered. I want to savor every single minute."

How quickly things could change, Mia thought wistfully. In a year, they'd lost Grandma Ruth, had to give up the lighthouse, and things were over with Milo. She could've never guessed how the last twelve months would've unfolded. Not in a million years.

FOURTEEN

"Oh, look at this," Alice said as she came into the kitchen the next morning, where Mia and the contractors were finishing up. Mia's mother ran her hand along the gorgeous new sparkling white countertops. Riley grabbed a cup of hot cocoa and rushed out the door for work.

"Bye, y'all!" she said, as she kept the door open with one foot while she grabbed her bag. "I'll see y'all this evening."

"Bye, Riley," Mia said, as Alice waved her daughter off.

"The cabinet doors are out in the truck. They're going on in just a minute," Mia said to her mother excitedly.

The contractor joined in the conversation, adding, "We've just got a little clean-up to do on the tile work, and you'll have your new kitchen."

"Leah's already on a plane with two other stagers, headed our way," Mia said.

The kitchen door flew open and Riley came rushing back in, red-cheeked. "Has anyone seen my car keys?" she asked, racing past them down the hallway. "I've set them somewhere..."

Alice and Mia hurried after her, finding her in Grandma Ruth's bedroom, fingering through her things on the dresser.

"You sure they aren't in your purse?" their mother asked.

"I dumped it out on the seat in the car," Riley said, moving to her suitcase and digging around in it.

"I'll take you to work," Mia offered.

"That's okay," Riley replied, pulling her phone from her coat pocket. "I'll text them that I'm going to be late. I need to figure out where I've put the darned things."

Mia dropped down to check under the bed. "Hey, what's this little box under here?" she asked, before dragging it out into the middle of the room.

Mia opened the flaps and the three of them peered inside. She pulled out a small photo album and opened it. Inside the cover, in Grandma Ruth's scratchy script, was the name Abigail Carter.

"Who's Abigail Carter?" Mia asked, as she took in the old photos of a toddler with wispy curls and round cheeks. "She's adorable."

"I have no idea," their mother said. "We don't have anyone in the family named that."

"Hey, wait a minute," Mia replied. "Abigail Carter. A. C. Isn't that what's on the pendant of the necklace we found the other day? A. H. C., right?"

The first four pages of the photo album were all of the little girl. Some were taken by the sea, others on Main Street in town. Mia recognized the storefronts behind her. "Someone local with our last name?" she asked.

"Like I said, *I've* never heard of her," Alice said. "What else is in the box?"

Mia took out a little yellow sweater with embroidered flowers at the shoulders, its pearl buttons now a creamy gold color from age.

"Oh, how sweet," Alice said, leaning closer. "Was this one of our sweaters?"

"I have no idea..." Riley said. "It looks like something Mom would put on you."

"How would you know?" Mia laughed, before noticing something written on the lid of the box and pulling it toward her, reading what it said. "For safekeeping."

"I don't think it was one of yours," Alice said. "Maybe she'd gotten it for me when one of you was little and never gave it to me. It would be just like her to keep it for her grandchildren." She folded the sweater and placed it back in the box.

"We'll be sure to keep it then," Mia said. "If she wanted her great-grandchild to wear it, we'll make sure it happens, won't we, Riley?"

Riley smiled fondly, her eyes on the sweater. "Definitely."

"Whatcha doing?" Mia asked as she came into the kitchen and sat down next to Alice, who had papers spread across the table.

"Nothing you need to concern yourself with," Alice said, gathering the papers and stacking them up.

"What is that?" Mia tried to see, but Alice held whatever it was away from her.

"Show me," she said, cornering Alice so she could see what her mother had in her hand. "Bills?"

"I'm just helping Riley with the rent for her house. They did some cuts at the hospital and she can't cover all her bills right now."

"You'll burn through your savings, with you and Riley living on them," Mia worried aloud.

"I know, but she's my daughter. And I can't find a job to save my life."

Before Mia could reply, her phone vibrated on the kitchen table with a call. "I'm going to help you look for jobs today," she said, picking it up. "Ugh, it's Milo. Let me just get this really quickly."

"Of course." Alice made herself a cup of tea and took it into the living room.

"Hello? I don't need checking up on, Milo. I've got the party under control."

"It's not about that. I need to talk to you about Elaine."

The last thing she wanted to do was talk about the employee he was dating. "Whatever it is, can't you handle it?"

"I have handled it, Mia. Just let me get this off my chest."

Mia closed her eyes, the phone against her ear, willing him to spit out whatever it was that he was trying to say.

"I was sitting across from Elaine while we were out to dinner the other night, and—I don't know—it was as if something clicked..."

The familiar feeling swept over her, as though her food had settled heavier than a cinder block in her stomach. She chewed on her lip, feeling the blood drain from her face. She didn't want to hear that he was proposing or that he'd found the love of his life. Why was he telling her all this?

"I'm wasting my time with her," he said.

Mia held her breath. *What?* "And you're telling me this, why?"

"It took me until now to realize what a complete jerk I've been to you. I know I've snapped at you when it wasn't justified and I've been distant. I just wanted to say... I'm sorry." His soft tone made the hair on her arms stand up. She hadn't heard it in so long, she'd almost forgotten that he could sound like that.

"Thank you," was all she could get out, her voice croaking with conflicted emotion. Part of her wanted to pull her hair out and scream at him for messing everything up, and the other half of her was relieved that she'd gotten out of this marriage when she had.

"Maybe I should come to Winsted Cape before the party so we can talk."

"About what?" she asked, her words breathy with fear—fear that she'd make the wrong decision if he were in front of her.

"What do you mean, 'about what?' About us."

"You can't just make one phone call and suddenly decide to change the tables, Milo. We're nearly divorced."

"I'm not trying to change anything," he said gently, and her heart hammered in her chest when she didn't even get a rise out of him. "I just want to talk."

"Okay," she said, but the word was detached from her as if it hadn't even been her who had uttered it.

Their good days ran through her mind like an old movie reel:

the crinkles at the edges of his eyes when he laughed beside her on the carnival ride on their second date; the way he'd looked over his shoulder at her, his attraction so clear, when they were riding beach cruisers in St. Thomas that one summer; how he'd taken her in his arms in the rain on a street corner one night after they'd had more champagne than they could remember. But, despite it all, she did remember.

"I can't wait to see you," he said, pulling her back into the present.

"See you soon." Mia hung up the phone, wondering if her well-laid plans for Christmas would be as smooth as she'd thought they'd be...

FIFTEEN

"We need taste testers," Kate said, when Mia arrived at The Corner Bakery after Will had asked her to come and to bring her grandmother's snickerdoodle recipe.

All the tables in the bakery had been pushed together, covered in parchment paper, dusted with flour, and covered in Christmas cookies and treats at one end. The other end had a massive array of cakes—at least seven of them—all decorated in white fondant and colored icing in reds, greens, and metallics.

"It looks like Christmas exploded in here," Mia said, greeting Felix and Will while shrugging off her coat and hanging it on a hook by the door.

"I'm preparing for your party," Kate said, wiping chocolate off her cheek with the back of her hand. Her hair was pulled up into a ponytail with a bandana tied around it, her apron covered in flour. "Felix and Will have narrowed it down to these options." She swept her hand across the tables.

"Please help her," Will teased, "we can't ingest any more treats. We're stuffed."

"I could do one more cookie but that's it," Felix chimed in.

With a grin, Mia picked up a shortbread cookie piled with coconut and drizzled with caramel and milk chocolate. She took a bite, the warm creaminess of the chocolate exploding in her mouth against the sweet crunch of the coconut. Her eyes round, she held it up, nodding as she chewed.

"I like that one too," Will told her, walking over to her side of the table, his spicy scent overtaking the smell of the treats in front of her.

"It was the first one he picked up," Kate said, wrinkling her nose in amusement. "I guess the coconut bundles are a winner."

"See what you think about this one," Will suggested, pointing to something that looked like a small chocolate bar.

Mia picked it up and took a bite, immediately surprised by the taste of graham cracker and marshmallow inside.

"Those are our inside-out s'mores," Kate said. "What do you think?"

"They're amazing," Mia replied, trying to pinpoint the extra flavor. "They're like s'mores but better."

Kate nodded. "That's our Grandfather Platt's secret ingredient: a layer of brown sugar between the marshmallow and the graham cracker. But don't tell anyone. It's *secret*."

Felix pretended to zip his lips.

"What's your favorite, Felix?" Mia asked, perusing the table of delicacies.

"That Christmas cake," he said, pointing to a double-decker cylinder of white fondant with icing-drawn holly leaves and red berries all over it. "Try a piece."

"Okay," she said, already unsure of how she'd ever narrow these down any further.

"I haven't tried that one yet," Will said.

Kate slid the large knife into the cake, cutting a slice and placing it on a plate.

On her way to the counter at the back, Mia eyed the enormous triangular piece of what looked to be some sort of spice cake with stripes of icing running through it. She took a seat on one of the stools. "This is huge. There's no way I'll be able to eat it all."

Kate waggled a finger toward the counter. "Will, grab a fork. You two can try it together."

Will picked up a utensil and walked over, sitting down next to her. Shoulder to shoulder, he stabbed the cake and dragged his fork across the plate to get his bite. With the forkful of cake poised just in front of his mouth, he said, "Get your bite. On the count of three, we'll try it."

Mia piled the cake onto her fork and held it up.

Felix said, "Okay, ready? One, two... three!"

They both ate at the same time. She immediately noted the sugary sweetness and vanilla of the icing against the rich moistness of the cake, the flavors melding together in an explosion of rich, creamy deliciousness.

"This might be the best cake I've ever eaten," she said.

Kate squealed in delight. "It's my brand-new recipe. I've been working on it for the last month."

"It's really great," Will agreed.

"I'd love it if you could make this cake for the party."

"Of course!" Kate nearly floated around the tables. "That's a very good sign."

"A good sign?" Mia asked.

"My mother once told me about a time when we catered a large event for the bakery—a massive wedding with five hundred guests; it was huge. She came up with a unique recipe, and decided to surprise the bride. This could go either way but, Mama said, 'If the host enjoys it, it'll bring good luck to the bakery.' She could feel it, she said. So, when you asked me to cater the party, I saw it as a sign and got to work. With everything going on, we need all the luck we can get."

"I love that."

"Which is why I asked you to bring your grandmother's snickerdoodle recipe. Will mentioned you all had one, and I thought that if you, Will, and I worked out a variation of it, a little extra luck may come our way. Want to see if we can build a recipe that will knock their socks off?"

The thought of all her guests enjoying Grandma Ruth's snickerdoodle cookies while celebrating Christmas at the lighthouse sent a wave of happiness through Mia. "I'd love to."

"Great!" Kate clapped her hands with excitement. "Do you have the recipe?"

Mia reached into her pocket and pulled out the old recipe card she'd taken from Grandma Ruth's box back at the lighthouse.

"Excellent! Let me make sure we have all the ingredients. Keep trying cookies!" Kate said over her shoulder, as she popped into the back room and returned with aprons for everyone. She slipped Felix's over his head, folding the fabric to make it shorter and tying it at the back.

Will put on his apron and led Mia behind the counter. They washed their hands in the sink and got started pulling out the ingredients as Kate read them aloud. Kate set a large container of butter in front of them, followed by the cream of tartar, eggs, vanilla, and other ingredients. "It calls for cinnamon as the main spice," Kate said. "What if we mixed it up a bit? We could add clove, cacao, cashew and nutmeg." She pursed her lips, thinking before adding, "We could dip half of it in a super creamy milk chocolate and sprinkle orange zest on it just before it cools."

"That sounds absolutely incredible," Mia said. "You're a natural. Grandma Ruth would approve."

Seeing Kate in her element, Mia wanted to make this work more than ever. Baking was clearly Kate's destiny, and without help from her charity efforts, her talent might be lost forever.

"All right," Kate said, getting to work. "Felix, I'm going to fill this bowl with dry ingredients. Will you mix them together for me with the wooden spoon?"

"Yes," Felix said, stepping onto a small wooden box that put him at just the right height to reach the counter.

"Mia, you and Will crack the eggs into a bowl and whisk them. I'll grab the other spices."

Will handed Mia a whisk and began cracking eggs into a ceramic bowl. She leaned in and stirred as he added each yolk. "I used to do this with my grandmother," she said, recalling the times she'd stood on a stool just like Felix was doing, in the kitchen at the lighthouse. Grandma Ruth would wrap her arms around little Mia and say, "This is our family's special snickerdoodle cookie recipe, passed down from my own grandmother." Something about doing it now felt very right.

"I did too," Kate said, with a thoughtful look to her son. "I'm glad that Felix is getting a chance to do it." She ruffled his hair. "Are you having fun?" she asked as she dumped in the spices that she'd been combining.

Felix stirred the bowl with his spoon. "Yes. I want to make cookies every day!"

"Oh, shoot," Kate said. "The one-cup measuring cup is dirty. I used the last clean one for the final batch of cookies."

Felix frowned, looking worried. Then he hopped off his stool. "It's okay, Mama," he said, opening a drawer behind them and pulling out a tablespoon. "We can use this."

Kate laughed fondly. "Oh, honey. That's too small. We need a big cup."

Felix eyed the spoon, his little face crumpling in confusion. Then, he picked up the dirty one-cup measuring cup and began dipping the spoon into the center of it, counting on his fingers. "Sixteen."

"Sixteen?" Kate asked, confused.

"I think there are about fifteen or sixteen tablespoons in a cup —that's what it looks like to me. I'd go with sixteen."

Kate eyed Will, who pulled out his phone and searched for how many tablespoons are in a cup. His eyes round, he looked up from his phone. "There are sixteen tablespoons in a cup."

Felix handed the tablespoon over to his mother, his chest puffing out in pride.

"Did you learn that in Kindergarten?" she asked him.

He shook his head and shrugged. "I just guessed."

"That's a great guess," Will said. "What was the last thing your teacher taught you in math before break?"

Felix huffed out a sigh of child-sized tension. "She was telling us what all the shapes are."

"Do you already know all the shape names?"

"Yes. Well, the ones she talks about, anyway. But I asked her about the things that aren't on her list. Like a donut. What shape is that? She said a circle but it isn't, because it has rounded edges and the center is missing."

"Did you tell her that?" Will asked, still holding empty eggshells in his hands. He dropped them into the trash and washed his hands.

"Yeah."

Will grabbed a towel, his eyes on his nephew. "What did she say?"

"She told me I could pass out the papers since I knew all the shapes, and she'd help me answer my question later. The other kids were getting loud."

"Well"—Will reached around Felix, scooping him up and making him squeal— "the only shapes we're talking about today are circles!" He held Felix like an airplane and zoomed him around the counter, over the table of cookies.

Felix burst into laughter, reaching out to try to grab a cookie, but Will lifted him higher just before he could get one.

Kate leaned over to Mia. "That's the kind of thing I wish I could do with Felix. I'm so glad Will's here. He's such a good influence on Felix." She scooped up some butter on her spoon, adding it to the other ingredients she'd been combining. "I want him to know how to be a good man, you know?"

Mia thought about Will. If anyone could provide Kate's son with a wonderfully loving environment, it would be Will. She looked back at Will and Felix, who were now nibbling cookies. She'd never seen anything more wonderful than the smiles on both of their faces.

"Moment of truth," Mia said, putting one of Grandma Ruth's snickerdoodle cookies to her lips. She took a soft, chewy bite. Rolled twice in the sugary spice mix, it melted in her mouth.

"Perfect," she said.

Kate grinned wide. "We need to clean up and get all this boxed and into the fridge," she said, after they'd sampled all of the desserts. She took a pile of flattened Corner Bakery boxes out of a drawer and began assembling one. "It's time to head home and get some shut-eye. Felix is up past his bedtime."

"I'm okay, Mama," Felix said, his eyelids dropping before he forced them back open. "I want to stay."

"Tell me what to do and I'll help," Mia offered.

"I've got an even better idea," Will said, turning to Mia, taking the box gently from her hands. "Think you could drop me by Kate's on your way home?"

"Of course," she replied.

"Kate, why don't you take Felix home, and Mia and I can pack everything up for you."

"Oh, I don't want to make you two do that," Kate said, fatigue showing in her eyes despite her kind expression.

"You've been baking all day. Let us help you," her brother said.

"All right," Kate relented. "You sure you two can do it all yourselves?"

"Absolutely," Mia replied for the both of them.

Kate handed Will the remaining boxes. "I'd pack by type with only two types per box, and if you can, the large batches should be labeled and numbered. Stack those together, and try not to leave the kitchen a mess. The chocolate pot can be tricky. You sure you don't want me to stay?"

"Kate, we've got it," Will said, with an affectionate pat on his sister's shoulder.

"May I stay with Uncle Will?" Felix asked.

"No, honey," Kate told him as she gathered her purse and their coats. "We need to get you home and into bed. Where's your hat?" She opened his coat and he slipped his arms inside.

After Felix ran into the back room to grab his hat, he slipped the little beanie with a fuzzy ball on his head.

"Thanks, y'all," Kate said.

When Kate and Felix had left, Will turned to Mia. "Any strategic suggestions for boxing all this up?" He handed her a pair of plastic gloves.

Mia surveyed the tables full of treats. "Maybe we should do all the chocolate-covered and fruit-filled ones first so we can get them into the fridge. Then we can pack up the chocolate chips and sugar cookies." She surveyed the open kitchen area behind the counter. "Let's see if there's anything back there that needs to be taken care of first."

"Sounds good," he said, gesturing for Mia to lead the way.

She washed up at the sink and slipped on her plastic gloves before grabbing a container of cream and putting it in the fridge. "See if you can grab the butter over there too," she said as Will washed his hands.

He handed her the butter, also finding a jug of milk and a half-empty container of eggs.

While Mia secured them all in the industrial fridge, Will grabbed a couple of chocolate molds from under the cabinet and then fumbled with the chocolate pot, a massive, free-standing double boiler. She came over to see if she could help in some way.

He clicked off the machine that had been keeping the chocolate at melting temperature. "It unclips down here," he said, turning his head to see the bottom of the pot. "We'll pour the chocolate into these molds to save it... You just have to be careful because—"

He unclipped it and suddenly the whole thing tipped, swinging wildly on its hinges. The tipping motion hit an open jar of preserves, sending it slamming onto its side. Chocolate and strawberry preserves poured over a pan of croissants, soaking them in a sea of liquid, and spread along the counters, oozing down onto the floor. Will quickly righted the thing, rushing to catch the dripping chocolate and strawberries with the molds.

Realizing that any attempt to stop the roaming chocolate was futile, Mia covered her mouth, stifling a laugh. "Kate did say it was tricky." She giggled again, turning Will's frown of concentration into a grin.

"What am I supposed to do with this?" he asked, covered in chocolate himself. Then, something occurring to him, he walked over to the pan of croissants and picked one up, chocolate and strawberry jam sliding down his glove and onto his wrist. "This looks delicious now," he said, taking a bite, unbothered.

With a mess everywhere, she stepped over and eyed the new creation. Will picked up another one and held it out to her. "Bite?"

Mia leaned in and before she knew it, to her complete shock, Will wriggled it, smearing chocolate and strawberries across her mouth and cheeks.

"You were too clean," he teased. "I just wanted to make sure you felt included."

She gasped, but was momentarily distracted by the fact that the strawberry and chocolate-covered croissants were cream-filled, the vanilla custard mixing with the sweet berries and milk chocolate...

"I can't believe you did that!" she said, licking her lips and grabbing another croissant, cocking it like a quarterback before a Hail Mary throw into the endzone, the confection aimed at Will's face.

"You wouldn't," he said with a laugh.

"Carters are warriors—ask my mom."

He eyed the pan of croissants, clearly debating a defensive tactic.

"But even a warrior wouldn't risk missing and hitting the historical photo of the Platt brothers behind us."

"You're right." She lowered it, reaching for help to step over the puddle of chocolate.

He took her hand, guiding her across the spilled chocolate. "But I will do this!" She smooshed it right in his face. Throwing his head back, he laughed, stretching out for another one, but Mia jumped in the way. "I'm not letting you get any more!"

Stopping still, Will's arms fell by his sides. "If I want one, I can get one."

"You sure about that?" She shot him a look of challenge.

He lunged forward to take her by the tops of the arms but she dodged out of the way, simultaneously grabbing the entire pan of croissants, chocolate and strawberry jam, splattering the inside of the clear display case. But just as she moved to give herself some room between them, her boot slipped in the sauce, causing her to lose her balance. The tray flew out of her hand and clattered on the floor as she squeezed her eyes shut, bracing for the hard smack on the ground. Instead, her body was cushioned by Will's strong arms, the two of them toppling over onto the floor.

Mia opened her eyes to see Will staring down at her, a smear of strawberries still on his cheek. "Sometimes even warriors need help," he said.

She needed to get out from under him before she lost all her resolve and let him kiss her. "I could've handled it," she said, her words so soft she knew that they weren't convincing.

He nodded, his gaze not leaving hers. "I'm sure you could've."

"Yes," she agreed, trying to convince herself that she hadn't needed him just then. "There was no point in even catching me."

"Well, there actually was a point."

"Which was?"

He leaned down toward her, his breath on her skin. Fear pricking her, the uncertainty of letting him in nearly overwhelming, she closed her eyes and held her breath, but when his kiss never came, she opened her eyes, confused. "What was the point?" she asked, focusing on his grinning face.

Will held up a croissant. "I told you if I wanted one, I could get one." He wiggled it in front of her.

Mia playfully pushed him off her. "Come on, we need to get this mess cleaned up." But as they stood and began to wipe the chocolate off the surfaces, all she could think about was that kiss that never materialized.

SIXTEEN

The next morning, the bag of snickerdoodle cookies that Mia had brought home after leaving the bakery last night was nearly empty. Grandma Ruth's recipe and the added ingredients they'd put in them were incredible.

"Morning," Mia said, greeting her mother and sister as she walked into the kitchen.

Mia had gotten up early so that she could be ready when Leah arrived this morning. Her decorator and friend had flown in late last night and stayed in a hotel in Richmond before making the drive down to Winsted Cape.

"You can*not* bring those things into the house anymore," her mother playfully scolded her as Mia reached into the bag, grabbing a cookie.

"No joke," Riley added from her chair at the table. She was wearing her glasses, having clearly not put in her contacts yet, and her robe was tied loosely at her waist, her hands wrapped around her cup of Joe.

Alice clinked a mug of coffee down in front of Mia. "I won't be able to fit the dress I'm thinking about wearing to the Christmas party if I keep eating those."

"What are you going to wear?" Mia asked, pouring cream into

her mug and stirring the dark liquid until it had floating swirls on the top.

"A dress I found in Grandma Ruth's guestroom closet. It was hanging in a plastic bag at the back."

"Oh, really?" Mia dipped the last bite of the cookie into her coffee and popped it into her mouth, savoring the sugary sweetness and the rich roast, so relieved at how her mother was taking all of this.

"Yes. It's beautiful. It's red, has an Italian tag inside, and looks like it's from around the 1950s, but it could be a current style if you accessorize just so. Very Audrey Hepburn."

"I wonder if it was from her European travels," Mia speculated out loud. "I always wanted her to tell me about them. I even asked her once in the hospital to tell me about when she was in Italy, thinking it would take her mind off the pain, but she said, 'Ah, that was another life...' and then she closed her eyes and fell asleep."

"That time of her life seemed so magical," Alice said. "Which was why I was so excited to find that dress. I'll feel like a princess in it. It's just gorgeous."

A knock halted their conversation. "That's probably Leah," Mia said, getting up and opening the kitchen door. "Oh," she said to the delivery man standing opposite her, holding an enormous bundle of red roses with Christmas holly and baby's breath. "What are these?"

"Delivery for Mia Broadhurst."

"*Mia Broadhurst?*" She reached out slowly and took the bouquet.

"That's what the paper says. Is there a problem?"

"That's me." She forced a smile.

"Have a nice day," he said, obviously not worried about her utter surprise.

"You too..." Mia shut the door and set the flowers on the table, plucking the card from the top and opening it. She read the message aloud:

Sorry for being such a jerk.
Milo

"Well, that's a surprise," Alice said. "I didn't know you two were on sending-flowers terms."

"We aren't," Mia said, tossing the card onto the table. "He wants to try again."

"What?" her mother asked, both her eyes and Riley's round with interest.

Mia told them about the call with Milo. "If he thinks he can treat me like he has for the last year and then make it all better with a bunch of roses, he's mistaken." She shoved the card back into its holder, leaving the envelope on the table.

"I think he's just saying sorry," Riley said. "Don't read into it too much."

"They're very pretty," Alice said, her gaze on the bright red blooms.

Mia's coffee settled like acid in her stomach. "Maybe I should call him later."

"It's probably the kind thing to do since he did apologize, and he got you something nice," her mother said, pushing the vase into the center of the table. "They look nice there. Very Christmassy."

Another knock turned Mia's attention away from the roses. "*This* is probably Leah." She opened the door.

"Oh my goodness!" Mia's friend Leah said, as she stretched out her fur-draped arms and wrapped her manicured fingers around Mia's shoulders, kissing her on both cheeks. "I feel like it's been ages!" She dropped her Louis Vuitton handbag at their feet. Her salon-gold hair was pulled tightly in her signature power-bun, which accentuated her high cheekbones and perfect eye makeup. It was as if the city of New York had just blown in through the door, knocking over the southern charm like a whirlwind. "This property is to die for! It's just stunning."

"If you like it, it's for sale," Alice said, standing and holding out her hand while Riley ran her fingers through her hair. "Alice Carter. Mia's mom."

"It's lovely to meet you." Leah shook her hand.

"And this is Riley, Mia's sister."

Riley waved from the table.

"I hope I'm not intruding on your breakfast," Leah said, with a smile showing off her perfectly white teeth. "I just got so excited to stage this place that I couldn't wait another minute. Oh! Those are stunning!" she said, distracted by the bouquet of roses.

"They're from Milo. And it's perfectly fine for you to come now," Mia assured her, getting her off the subject of the flowers as quickly as possible. "How about if I take your coat and then I'll show you around."

Leah slipped the long fur coat off her thin frame and handed it to Mia. "Things are a little different here," Mia said, as she deliberated over where to place the expensive fur. She draped it on one of the kitchen chairs. Leah didn't seem to mind; she'd already turned to grab a measuring tape from her handbag.

Mia flashed her mother and Riley an excited smile before turning back to Leah and heading into the living room. She'd been waiting for this moment. This was when everything would finally flip over to the hopeful side. The lighthouse would get the wonderful upgrade that it needed, and she wouldn't feel so worried about the budget, knowing she could dip into the corporate party fund for more decorations to fill the space.

"So, the party's going to be here, right?" Leah asked, eyeing the mantle.

"Yes." She offered a smile to cover the fact that Leah had to like the idea because if she hated it, there were literally no other options.

"We'll want the space to still be like a home, rather than a venue," Leah began, to Mia's relief, "so let's fill it with white furniture and coastal-colored accents. I'm thinking we want a backdrop of neutrals with sand dollars, starfish, candles galore..." She turned to the wall that held framed needlework of various flowers. "I brought Alex and Rob to help stage. We'll strip the walls of the current pictures and replace what's there with simple, modern art. I've pulled some samples." She opened her phone screen and turned it toward Mia to show her the bright turquoise and navy splashes of color on white canvas.

"That's beautiful," Mia said, delighted to hear that Alex Wendell and Rob Cruse were with Leah. They were her top stagers.

"Are these hardwoods throughout?" Leah asked, dropping her phone into the deep pocket of her long sweater.

"Yes, they are. Thank goodness."

"Agreed. They already have a beige tone to them. Let's just add some white rugs." She walked into the center of the living room. "I say we have two oversized white sofas facing each other, a circular table in the center with an explosion of coastal silk flowers in a bright turquoise vase, and then you can do up some tall Christmas trees in either corner with silver and navy."

"That sounds like a plan. I'd love to do all silver serving trays with white linen napkins and very basic, unfrilly glassware for the party."

"*Gaw*geous." Leah threw her hand to her heart. "Great minds think alike." She moved around the room. "I think we need lots of lamplight." She stretched out the measuring tape, holding one end to the floor, measuring upward. Then she keyed in the numbers on her phone. As the tape snapped back into its holder, she paced over to Mia, sweeping her into a friendly hug. "I've missed you!"

"I know," Mia said. "Things have been so crazy."

Leah waved her arms around. "I can tell! You're living in a lighthouse!" Then her bright red lips dropped into a pout. "How's Milo handling you being all the way down here?"

"He's managing," Mia replied. She didn't want to hide the truth from her good friend, but Leah wasn't known for being discreet, and Mia didn't need any more trouble by having word get out. "What were you thinking for the dining room?" she asked, changing the subject as quickly as she could.

"I found a furniture company in North Carolina that has some really great pieces they can give me on loan." She swished into the dining area and rested her hands on one of Grandma Ruth's old cherrywood chairs. "I'd like to go light in here as well. It's popular these days to go more casual for dining. I'm thinking a rustic farm table with wildflowers and woven turquoise chargers under simple white plates."

"Love it." Mia leaned against the large window, her fingers resting on the sill. Feeling something under her touch, she leaned down to take a look. There seemed to be a child's writing scratched into the wood, very faint, spelling out *hope*.

Hope is where you find it.

"What are you doing?" Leah laughed as Mia bent down to see if there was anything under the window molding.

"I just thought I felt something," she said, running her fingers along the bottom of the sill, but there was nothing there. She pressed on the wall around the window.

"What did you feel?" Leah asked, coming closer.

Mia scrambled for an answer for her friend. "It felt unlevel," she lied, not wanting to get into the whole mystery right at that moment.

"It looks perfectly fine," Leah said. "We'll get this house whipped into shape in no time."

Mia smiled at her friend, ignoring the pinch that took over her chest at the thought of losing this house—and all their memories—for good. It hadn't truly seemed real until now.

Mia had spent the rest of the day securing the final details for the party's catering and rental equipment. With Leah going full steam in the interior, and the teams painting the outside, Mia called Will to see if he was still interested in helping to clear out the barn.

"Of course," he said when she asked him over the phone.

"When I rented the equipment for the party, they said they could drop the space heaters and extra propane by tomorrow morning. They're putting them inside the barn, so we can use them while we work."

"That's perfect," Will said.

"How's the baking going?" she asked, dropping onto the bed, the phone at her ear.

"I think Kate has finally narrowed it down to a nice even hundred options or so," he joked, making Mia laugh. The mental image of his face hovering above hers came to mind. "Good thing her semester's ended for the holiday. How about the rest of the catering? Everything okay with that?"

"I ended up using the Sea Shack. They can't offer a full menu on such late notice, but they can provide hors d'oeuvres with beer and wine. That'll work! So, all we have left now is the barn. Think we can get it into some kind of shape by Christmas?"

"We can definitely try. Should I come over first thing in the morning—say eight?"

"That would be perfect."

"All right, I'll see if I can get that power washer and be over at around eight."

"Sounds good. I'll see you then."

After they said their goodbyes, Mia lay on the bed, rapping her fingernails on the phone screen. She knew that the last thing she had to do today was call Milo, but everything in her body wanted to avoid it.

If she wanted to be truthful to herself, she was stuck—stuck between the old life that she had as the wife of a wealthy CEO in New York, and this other version of herself: the person who'd promised Delilah she'd take her for another ride; the person who was invested in the local bakery's success; the person, no matter how hard she tried, who couldn't imagine anyone but a Carter owning the lighthouse.

There was a knock at the door. Thankful for the diversion, Mia called out, "Come in."

Alice poked her head inside. She was holding a couple of old photos. "I found these in Mom's dresser drawer," she said, holding the photos out for Mia to see. "It must be that same little girl, just older." She sat next to Mia and looked over her shoulder at the images.

Mia looked down at a little girl with ringlets pulled into a giant bow, her cheeks still round like the baby she'd seen in the other pictures.

"Flip that one to read the back," Alice said, tapping the photo in Mia's right hand.

Mia turned it over. "Abigail—the same name as the girl in the other pictures."

"Yes." Alice gently took the photos from Mia and studied them. "This girl is everywhere here."

"Maybe we could try to find some information on Abigail Carter in town," Mia suggested. "Maybe on Riley's next day off, we should go out and ask around."

"Definitely!" her mother said.

Something in Mia's gut told her Grandma Ruth wanted her to find out.

SEVENTEEN

The next morning, Leah had brought Alex and Rob, and they were laying new rugs, rearranging furniture, and changing out lighting.

"Morning, sunshine!" Leah said as Mia entered the living room.

"Morning," she returned with a yawn. "Seen my mom or my sister?"

"They're in the kitchen," she said with bobbing, perfectly penciled eyebrows. "We're done in there, so you'll have to take a look!"

Mia padded into the kitchen and gasped. The white countertops were gleaming, there was a big bowl of red baubles and holly sitting at the end of the new bar, and a tiered plate of cookies was positioned in the corner. Linen towels with a simple pattern of Christmas trees embroidered in silver at the very bottom hung from the vintage oven, and a rustic farmhouse-style chandelier, draped in fresh greenery and red bows for the holiday, hovered above the farm table, sending a glorious glow over the chargers and plates Leah had set out. Mia reached over to touch the explosion of blooms in a glass vase in the center of the table.

"Beautiful, isn't it?" Alice asked.

"I'm speechless," Mia said. The lighthouse kitchen had never looked so incredible. "This party is going to be fantastic."

"Have you spoken to Milo any more about it?" Riley asked. She was wearing Christmas-themed scrubs for work, as if the holiday had just landed among them.

"I called him last night, but I didn't get an answer." She had finally worked up the courage to call him, and while she wasn't saying so, she was fine with him not picking up. "Has anyone heard from Will?" she asked, checking her phone screen. "It's after eight..." Knowing what she now knew, she couldn't help being worried about him.

"I haven't heard anything," Alice said, straightening the Christmas-patterned dish towel and admiring it.

"Me neither," Riley said, gathering her purse and car keys.

"Okay," Mia said. "Have the heaters been delivered?"

"Yes," Alice replied. "I saw them out there this morning."

"Great. I'll get them going and then start clearing the barn. When Will gets here, send him my way."

"Of course. Bundle up, it's cold," Alice said, handing Mia a travel mug of coffee and her coat before opening the door.

"Thank you," Mia said, slipping her arms into the sleeves of her coat.

The winter air blew off the Atlantic with what felt like gale force, blowing her hair back and causing her to lose all feeling in her face and neck, her skin numbing immediately to the icy temperature. She wedged the coffee cup between her arm and chest and fished her mittens out of her pockets, pulling them on as she trudged the winding gravel path to the barn. She stopped just outside to admire the new paint job. It looked amazing in dark red with bright white trim. She unlatched the large barn doors, swinging the right side open, and moved one of the heaters that had been dropped off and set inside this morning into the empty space in the center.

An electrician by trade, her grandfather had wired the barn so that he could have light out there to do his woodworking. She went over to the wall and pulled the old breaker lever he'd installed, a bulb in the A-line roof buzzing to life. The cans of white paint and supplies they'd gotten from the exterior painters lined one of the walls inside. The heaters were on rollers so she pushed one of the massive, six-foot metal contraptions to the center and followed the directions to turn on the propane.

She moved the old bridles and saddles that had been left after Delilah was sold, setting them off to the side. Then she began pushing the last few stacks of hay over to the door so she could dispose of them. With Grandma Ruth's old barn broom, a wide mass of bristles attached to a long handle that always leaned against the western wall of the barn, Mia began to sweep the huge wood floor to prepare it for power washing.

When she'd finished clearing the main floor, dust swirled around her as she leaned on the broom, taking in the space. A small crack between the boards on the back end of the barn let in a faint white light, in the same spot that allowed through a golden beam in the summertime. What struck her most was the silence. So many times she'd been in this barn, sweeping out the hay to the tapping of Delilah's hooves. The horse's snorts and whinnies were like music she'd taken for granted until now.

Grandma Ruth would come in, carrying a basket of fresh carrots she'd picked up at the farmer's market. The horses knew, clopping over to her excitedly, hovering around her while she handed them out.

"Sorry I'm late," Will's voice echoed through the space.

Mia turned around.

"It's becoming a habit, I'm afraid." He stood next to a power washing machine, holding a cardboard cup holder with two to-go cups from The Drip, the local coffee shop. He stepped forward, walking toward her with the cups outstretched in offering. "And I also seem to bring you treats to apologize," he said with a smirk.

She smiled, setting down the broom and taking the coffee. She dropped down onto the floor and held the cup with both hands, relishing the warmth of it through her mittens. "Everything okay?"

Will sat down next to her, contemplation etching his handsome face. "As okay as it's ever been." He frowned, looking down at his cup before fixing his gaze back on her. "Susannah's mother Fran must be struggling at the holidays. She really wants me to come back. It's hard to justify getting off the phone when nothing I have to do compares to the grief of a mother who's lost her child."

"That's tough, I'm sure," she said. "I can handle all this alone if you need to go home—I know you were planning to go back soon anyway. You can maintain the listing from there and I'll be here to show the house—if anyone even comes looking."

"That's very generous of you, but me going home isn't going to alleviate Fran's sadness. And while I'm usually there to help console her, Susannah's dad is there to help her. I don't want to leave Kate either."

Mia sipped her warm coffee, a nutty, caramel flavor washing away the taste of barn dust.

"I'll start at the back so the water can push the dirt out the barn doors," he said, standing up and getting to work. He grabbed the power washing machine and walked to the other end of the barn.

Mia wanted nothing more than to help Will, but without a solution to offer him, perhaps it was better to focus on the moment. After all, she was struggling to solve her own issues as it was.

"It looks amazing," Mia said, staring at the wet boards of the floor. They'd moved the heater around as they went, tossed the hay outside, stored away all the horse paraphernalia, and sprayed the floors until they looked new. "Better than I thought! I didn't even know the wood was ever this light."

"Imagine it full of tables," he said, admiring the space. He took out his phone and did a search before turning on "I'm Dreaming of a White Christmas," setting it in the middle of the floor. "And the chandelier you'd mentioned up there." He pointed to the bulb that illuminated the space. "This floor will be filled with people dancing in fine dresses." He took her hand and gave her a spin, making her laugh. Then he pulled her in and held one hand, his other around her waist as they danced in the middle of the barn, just the two of them.

Mia looked up at him and he beamed down at her. If only she were in a place where she could make this happen; the last thing she wanted was to break his fragile heart. With an apologetic smile, she twirled out of his grasp.

"And I was thinking that it would be gorgeous if we covered the whole back wall in white lights. We could staple right over the wires with a staple gun."

"We should definitely measure to see how many strands to get," Will suggested with a slight frown, allowing her to let go. "I've got a tape measure in the truck."

"You're pretty handy," she said. "How do you know how to do all this stuff?"

"Starting out in real estate, I needed to know how to save money when I put properties on the market. Then, once I was practiced, I flipped a couple of houses."

"You're a regular one-man band," she told him with a smile.

Will huffed out a modest laugh. "I'll get that tape measure." He glanced at her over his shoulder, and the tenderness in his eyes gave her a rush of butterflies she tried her hardest to ignore.

Mia poured the paint into trays while Will set up more heaters around the barn and brought the ladder over.

"It's positively toasty in here with all of the heaters running," she said, shrugging off her coat and mittens, the excitement that she might actually have created an actual venue bubbling up. She dipped her brush into the paint.

"It's perfect," Will said. He picked up a brush and immersed it in the paint, pulling it out and wiping the excess off on the edge of the can. "I'll go up the ladder and paint the top boards of the wall if you'll stand underneath and do the bottom," he said. "We can meet in the middle."

"Sounds like a plan." Moving to the left of the ladder, Mia began painting the interior walls in long, white strokes. "When I was a girl, I wanted to be a painter," she said, as she pulled the brush upward, arcing the bristles.

"Really?" Will replied. "So did I."

"You did?" she asked with a laugh.

He dipped his brush into the bucket that hung from the ladder. "Yep. I drew a squirl in art class and won a contest. It went all the way to the state finals. I knew, at the young age of seven, that I was destined to be an artist," he said with a chuckle.

"What happened then?" she asked, playing along. "How come you aren't on a street corner in Paris selling your wares, or opening your own gallery in New York?"

"Because I met a girl."

She stopped painting and looked up at him. "At seven?"

"Mm-hm. She had blonde pigtails and bright blue eyes."

"So, you settled down with her instead of following your dreams? What was married life like as a seven-year-old?"

He laughed. "Ah, I definitely didn't marry her. But she introduced me to baseball and taught me how to pitch. Her left-handed pitch was meaner than Whitey Ford's."

"Who's Whitey Ford?"

Will leaned down into her view, his eyes wide. "Only one of the best Yankees pitchers of the 1950s." He went back to painting. "I ended up playing baseball all through school and finally earning a scholarship to UNC Greensboro, where I played for four years."

"That's amazing," she said, seeing him through a slightly more casual lens. "So, the girl was good?"

"Yes," he said, setting his paintbrush on the paint tray of the ladder and climbing down. "Her name was Gabby Benson." He looked around for a moment before picking up his tape measure. "She taught me that if I pitch two and then, for the third, put my fingers like so..." he said, wrapping them around the tape measure. He reared back and lifted his knee in a pitcher's stance, his imaginary glove in the other hand. "...I could release it here." He stretched his arm out. "No one could hit it. That's how I got my scholarship."

She set her brush down, interested in his story.

"But what they didn't know was that all they had to do to hit it was choke up on the bat and swing."

"Like this?" she teased, raising her hands as if she were holding a bat.

He laughed fondly at her.

"Not quite." He stepped behind her, taking her arms and moving them into position. His face was next to hers, that spicy scent of his overwhelming her. He moved her arms as if she were swinging at the ball. "Like that."

Mia struggled to get her breath, her heart pattering.

"Hello," a deep and very familiar voice came from the large barn doors, breaking the magic.

Suddenly, Will let her go.

Milo walked in, assessing the half-painted wall. "Busy?" The word was laden with questions, his gaze sliding over to Will.

Mia's mouth hung open and she had to snap it shut.

"Will Thacker," Will told him, reaching out a hand.

Milo walked forward, his Maison Margiela loafers tapping on the boards with every step, and shook it. He took in a breath, running his fingers through his jet-black hair. "Milo Broadhurst."

"What are you doing here?" Mia asked.

"I thought I'd come see the venue," he said, sliding his hands into the pockets of his coat and pacing around the barn. "Not sure our city folks are going to be up for a hoedown."

He was jealous—she could tell—but she wouldn't allow him to affect her. "I'm not so sure they will either, so it's a good thing that Will and I are going to make it a classier holiday event."

"And have we hired Will?" he asked, giving Will a once-over before offering a cordial nod.

"He's the real estate agent who's selling the lighthouse," she explained. "But he's been more than gracious in helping out."

"That's very kind of you," Milo said, clearly on his best behavior now. He slipped off his coat, hanging it on the latch to the door and closing it behind them. "I don't mind rolling up my sleeves. What needs to be done?"

An uncomfortable air permeated the space all the way to the corners of the barn. The last thing she wanted was to work with Will and Milo under the same roof. "We've got it sorted out," she said. "Why don't you check in with Leah inside and take a look at what she's done?"

"I already have," he said, unbuttoning his sleeves and folding them up.

"May I speak to you outside?" she asked him, trying to keep her tone from giving away her frustration.

Will awkwardly turned toward the back wall. "I'll get back to painting," he said.

"Okay, Will. I'll be right back in. I just need to talk to Milo for a quick sec." Mia pushed open the door and waved her hand for Milo to join her.

The two of them stepped into the icy cold of winter, the warmth of the heaters shut inside behind them. "What do you think you're doing, showing up unannounced like this?" she asked.

"You're the one who asked, 'Can we talk when I get home?'" he said. "'Just strip away all the baggage and talk,' you told me. Remember? Well, I'm here now."

He opened his arms as if she'd run into them, but things weren't the same as they'd been that first night when she'd gotten there. So much had happened... "I know I said that..." She chewed on the inside of her lip while trying to keep from shivering to death. "Look, thank you for the flowers, Milo, but it's... too little, too late."

"It's never too late," he said. "You used to say that, remember? 'Nothing is ever too hard, ever too late.'"

"It's different now."

"You've always been a fighter, fighting for us every minute through our rough patch."

"I'd hardly call this a rough patch. We're getting a *divorce*."

His gaze fell down to the sloppy snow sludge at their feet. "What's changed?" Then he eyed the barn door. "Is it the real estate agent in there?"

"He has a name. It's Will."

He drew back, taking her in. "It is, isn't it?"

"It's not him."

"Then what is it?"

She exhaled, not really able to pinpoint it herself. "I just don't feel the same way anymore."

The hurt on his face sent a fire through her. How dare he look wounded when he'd been an absolute bear to her time and time again, never giving her a moment of sympathy.

"I've messed up," he said, shaking his head. "I'm not great at this..."

"Look. It's freezing out here, and I have a lot to do if we want to be ready for the Christmas party."

He nodded. "Sure you don't want my help?"

"I'll be fine. I'll let you know if I need you. Do you have a place to stay?"

"Yes. I've got a room at the inn in town."

"Okay." She bounced up and down for warmth.

"Let me at least take you to dinner later. No pressure or anything—just the two of us with time to talk."

She opened her mouth to object, but she didn't know how to say it.

"Please," he urged. "We owe ourselves that much, don't we?"

"All right," she finally relented. "I have to get back to work if you want to have a party."

He turned and headed toward his Porsche. "I'll call you later," he said over his shoulder. She watched the back of him as he walked away, realizing right then that much of her need to make their marriage work in the last year had really been her need not to fail at the marriage. When it came down to it, she didn't love Milo anymore.

"Everything okay?" Will asked once she'd come back into the barn, the warmth enveloping her.

"Yeah," she replied, holding her frozen hands up to one of the heaters to regain feeling in them.

"You sure?" He dropped his paintbrush into the bucket. She eyed the back wall, which was completely finished.

"I'm sure," she replied. "You started painting the wall while I was gone?"

Will smiled proudly. "Yes," he said, brightening. "That way we can finish early and, after we buy lights, I can offer to take you to dinner tonight."

"It must be my night for a good meal," she said.

The skin between his brows wrinkled adorably.

"Milo asked if he could take me to dinner."

"Oh?"

She blew air through her lips, a pinch forming in her shoulder. If she were being honest with herself, she'd much rather spend the evening with Will. Will was easy—he was kind and generous. He made her laugh. No strings attached. Milo, on the other hand...

"Yeah. We have some things to talk about."

She wasn't lying. She wanted to figure out what had caused this change of heart. It wasn't like Milo to flip-flop with his decisions, and she had to know if there was something more behind this return.

She could visibly see the withdrawal in Will's eyes, and she wanted to reach out and grasp him, tell him not to pull away. But then she told herself it was probably better this way. They both had too much going on. With his late wife's family pulling on him, and that huge amount of pressure, she knew it would only be a matter of time before he'd go back to Seattle. And with her own divorce and now Milo's renewed interest in their relationship... All of it sat like a brick in her stomach.

"Well," he said in the silence, pushing a smile across his face. "All done in here. It's time for lights and Christmas trees. Shall we go find some?"

"Absolutely." She couldn't wait to start bringing some Christmas cheer to the lighthouse. She, for one, was in desperate need of it.

EIGHTEEN

The ceilings of the light shop dripped with shimmering glass. There were small, teardrop-shaped chandeliers along one side of the store, the styles gradually getting larger until Mia and Will got to the back where the biggest ones were displayed. Mia looked up at an enormous round one—three-tiered, with rows and rows of beaded glass cascading down it like a display of royal diamond necklaces. She could just imagine it in the barn with the white wall as a backdrop and the exposed beams all around.

"That one is stunning," she said, pointing to it. "Think we could get it on loan?"

"Probably," he said. "I'll call the owner and ask. He's not in today." Will pulled out his phone and snapped a picture. "The Christmas tree lot is just across the street. Should we take a look?"

"Yes," Mia replied, getting excited.

Mia zipped up her coat, slipped on her mittens, and they headed out the door, crossing the road and reaching Donny's Tree Lot. She remembered running through the aisles of trees and hiding behind them in a Christmassy game of hide-and-seek when she was here choosing a tree with Grandma Ruth once when she was little.

Strings of festive lights arced over the aisles full of evergreens while Christmas music played on the loudspeaker. A line of people snaked around the trees, queueing up for hot cocoa. Mia took in a long breath of wintery air, blocking out the fact that Milo was in town and letting the holiday finally settle upon her.

"It's nice to have a little Christmas around," Will said, as they perused the first row of trees. "I didn't decorate last year." He gave Mia a meaningful look and she knew that he hadn't decorated since he'd lost Susannah.

"Are you okay looking with me?" she asked.

He smiled, raising his eyebrows in thought. "Yes. I'm very much okay. Although I can't guarantee I'm the best to help you choose."

"Why not?"

"I don't know your tastes," he said carefully.

Not wanting to stare into those honest blue eyes of his, she inspected a nearby tree. "Oh, look. Each tree has a number," she said, thinking. "Let's walk around and take mental notes of the numbers we think the other might choose. When we get to the last tree, we'll tell each other. There's a lot you can learn about a person by the Christmas tree they choose."

"Is that so?" he asked.

"Definitely. For example, are you a more modest guy, choosing a tall, thin tree like this one?" She pointed to number twenty-three. "Or would you rather be over the top and ridiculously festive with that one?" She nodded toward an enormous tree that towered over the others.

"I suppose you won't get an answer until the end," he said, the corners of his mouth turning upward sweetly. He gestured for her to walk with him, waving his hand across the aisle. "You first."

"All right," she replied, allowing herself to enjoy their easy banter. "I wonder if you'll be able to guess my choices," she said, as she toyed with the bristles on tree number twenty-seven.

He pursed his lips, thinking. "I definitely don't think you'd pick that one."

"How do you know?"

"Its branches are too far apart, and it wouldn't fill the room with joy..." He looked into her eyes just a tick longer than she wanted him to, so with a grin, she turned away and walked to the next tree.

"What about this one?" she said, gesturing to the one to her right, a Douglas fir, full with dark green branches.

"I thought we weren't telling each other," he answered with a laugh.

"You're right," she agreed. "That one is number twenty-nine in case you need to know."

He squinted at her. "You could be bluffing to throw me off the scent."

"I guess you'll have to rely on how well you know me to decide if I am or not."

He stared at her, a mixture of amusement and challenge in his eyes.

They walked along each of the aisles, stopping occasionally to look at trees, all the while chatting.

"What do you do on a random Tuesday night after work?" she asked, making conversation.

"Hm." He paced along beside her, his gaze on the trees. "I turn on some music, make myself dinner, and then read while I eat."

"What do you like to read?"

"Mostly non-fiction but sometimes I'll read a good crime novel. How about you? What do you do on a random Tuesday night after work?"

"Tuesday is my tennis day with friends, so I usually meet them for a game and then we have cocktails at the club bar after. Then I go home, shower, and work on my laptop until it's time to go to bed."

"So, you enjoy tennis?"

"I'm not sure," she answered honestly.

"You play every Tuesday, but you aren't sure if you like it?"

"I've never really thought about it. It was good exercise and it was something to do to get out of the house, so I went. I haven't missed it since I've been here, though, so maybe it isn't my favorite thing to do."

"What *is* your favorite thing to do?"

Mia tried to pinpoint the things in her life that actually gave her joy, and to her dismay realized she couldn't pinpoint anything. Seeing Will was the only thing that she could say made her happy, and she certainly wasn't going to say *that*.

"Okay," he said, bringing her out of her thoughts. "Your lack of answer speaks volumes. We need to figure out your favorite things."

She continued to rack her brain for ideas.

"What are you doing tomorrow?" he asked.

"Probably working on the lighthouse."

"We're ahead of schedule. I have an idea but I'm going to need you for a few hours. Think you can spare some time?"

Affection for him bubbled up. "What are you planning?" she asked, as she caught sight of a beautiful balsam fir.

"I'm not sure," he replied. "I need to make a few calls."

"Okay," she said, very curious as they got to the end of the tree lot.

"Know what trees you like?"

"There's one that stands out above the rest," she replied.

"Only one? In all these possibilities? I hope I can guess it."

"How many did you have?"

"Well, three, but come to think of it, one of those was better than the others, so I'll give you the same difficult task of figuring out my one." He grinned at her.

Mia caught the attention of the owner Donny, who had just returned from helping someone load a tree onto the top their car. She remembered him from when she was a girl. But back then, he'd been a lanky teenager, working with his dad and climbing into his truck at the end of the night to head to the beach, where he and his friends gathered around a bonfire on Friday nights. Now, he was a bibbed overall-clad lumberjack of a man with a red beard covering that youthful smile. "Excuse me," she said.

"Oh, hey," Donny said, coming over and clearly placing her. "How are ya?"

"I'm doing well! How about you?"

"Can't complain. Took over my dad's business. It ain't the most glamorous job in the world," he said as his gaze slid up and down her designer outfit, "but the hours are good. When I ain't sellin' Christmas trees, I bring our produce to the family market. In summertime, we've got peaches that'll knock your socks off."

Mia smiled, genuinely glad to have run into him.

"I heard about your Grandma Ruth," he said.

She nodded.

"Everyone has. She was one of our town legends. We swore she was a superhero when none of us was lookin'."

Mia laughed. "A superhero?"

"Yes ma'am. Can't you see it? She'd do a twirl and come out in a leotard with Lighthouse Lady on the front." He chuckled at his own joke. "Her superpower was makin' people feel good. I swear, I don't think that woman had any flaws at all."

"She was great, wasn't she?"

"Damn straight, she was. You takin' over as the new Lighthouse Lady?"

Mia pressed her cheeks outward to maintain her smile, her heart falling into her chest. "I'm not, actually. We're selling the lighthouse."

"Dang. That's a shame. It's been in your family for years, ain't it?"

"Mm-hm."

"Shame," he said again, as if to drive it into her heart further. "What can I help ya with?"

She sucked in an icy cold breath of salty air to refocus and introduced Will. "My friend Will and I are going to buy a Christmas tree, but we're playing a little game. May I tell you a tree number so he can guess it?"

He arched an eyebrow but played along. "Sure."

Mia whispered in Donny's ear, "Forty-one."

"I'm going to go out on a limb," Will said, playing the game. "I'm willing to guess that my number is your number."

"What makes you think that they'd be the same?" she asked, a little thrill zinging around inside her. Milo had never cared one bit about what kind of Christmas tree she'd had. In fact, he thought they were a waste of time, money, and energy—he'd used those three exact words once when she'd had one delivered to their Manhattan apartment.

"We've agreed on everything else so far," Will said. "Let's see if we agree on this. Twenty-seven is very nice."

Mia gritted her teeth playfully, shaking her head.

Will laughed. "You didn't let me finish. Thirteen is also really great."

A fizzle of happiness slithered through her when she saw his gaze land on the aisle with her tree.

"But forty-one is my favorite. Is that your number?"

Donny's eyes grew round. "You some kind of magician?" he asked Will.

Will threw his head back and laughed. "Was that really your number?"

Donnie clapped him on the back. "Yes, sir, it was. I reckon you should go buy a lottery ticket tonight with the luck you're havin'!"

"How about that?" Will said. "I guessed it."

She gazed up at him. "How about that?" she echoed.

Mia turned to Donny. "We'll take twenty-seven, thirteen, and forty-one. You can put them in the back of Will's truck for us."

Just then, Will's phone rang. He peered down at the number and turned the ringer off, contemplation sliding down his face. "It's Fran, Susannah's mom."

"Do you need to get it?" Mia asked, as she grabbed three tree stands and handed them to Donny.

"I'll call her back tonight."

"Okay." She thought about the bonds that held him and Susannah's family together. That was the thing with family. They'd always be a part of his life...

"I'll be happy to set the trees up for you, when we get back to the lighthouse," Will offered.

"Thank you," Mia replied, wondering what she would've done without him this Christmas.

NINETEEN

Milo's Porsche was purring like a kitten in the drive outside the lighthouse. He got out, walking up in his jeans and a casual coat, looking like he'd stepped right out of Mia's memory. It had been a long time since she'd seen him dressed down, and the sight through the kitchen window pulled at her heartstrings.

"My back is killing me," Riley said, rubbing her lower back through her scrubs as she sat down to a bowl of Alice's homemade stew, which she'd been brewing in the crockpot all day. "The right side keeps pinching. I've been on my feet way too long today."

"Your nerves go crazy when you're on your feet," Alice said, as she looked over Mia's shoulder at Milo as he neared the door. "And you're wearing those slip-on shoes. I wonder if you need some with more support..."

Mia straightened her shirt and made sure it was tucked into her jeans, then fiddled with her dangly earrings. She opened the door to let him in.

"Hey," he said, with that sparkle in his green eyes that she hadn't seen for years.

"Hi," she replied, avoiding his gaze. He didn't get to turn on his charm whenever he felt like it. There were levels to their relationship now, and they certainly weren't at the flirty stage. They were nowhere near it.

"The roses look nice on the table," he said before waving to Riley.

Mia's sister waved back.

"It's been a long time since the two of you looked like that going out," Alice said, coming over and giving him a hug in greeting, but her embrace was visibly more reserved than it used to be. "Where are y'all eating tonight?"

"I got us reservations at Alistair's," he said.

Mia's mother drew back, a glint in her eyes. "Wow."

Alistair's was a local steakhouse and seafood restaurant, boasting an organic menu and farm-to-table options as well as freshly caught fish and homemade bread. It was about forty minutes' drive through a few villages, in the larger area of Mott's Pointe.

"What's the occasion?" Mia asked.

"Just celebrating us," Milo said.

His over-the-top response used to be flattering, but now it made her feel uneasy. There was no "us." And the fact that he didn't seem to understand that made her question his sincerity.

"Well, have a wonderful time," Mia's mother said.

"Shall we?" Milo ushered Mia out the door.

Mia reluctantly waved to Riley and her mother and headed out behind Milo, who paced further ahead of her to open her car door as if it were their first date. In a way, it sort of was. She'd hadn't seen him like this in forever. She slid into the warm leather interior of the Porsche, snowflakes fluttering down again. As he pulled around, she caught sight of the barn, her mind going to the Christmas trees that Will had put up for her.

"How have you been?" he asked, causing her to swim out of her thoughts. Milo looked over at her with his big green eyes.

She held her breath so as not to lay into him. How had she *been*? "What kind of question is that?" she asked, her frustration getting the better of her.

Something flashed in his usually confident eyes that she'd never seen before, and he seemed unsure of himself. "I'm just trying to break the ice," he said before the two of them fell into silence.

The seaside dunes sparkling with the moonlight glistening on the snow slipped by her window, before the clouds covered it and they all turned gray again.

"I'm not sure how to do this," Milo spoke into the quiet between them. He kept his eyes on the road, snow coming down in front of his headlights. "I want to tell you I'm sorry for being so terrible. I want to show you that I'm not a creep. I'm definitely not the guy you were married to—I've changed. But for the better."

She couldn't help but be skeptical. Was this because things hadn't worked out with Elaine and he found himself alone? But she didn't want to fight tonight. She just didn't have it in her.

"I was awful to you so that I could push you away without feeling the guilt that swarmed me every time I thought about Elaine," he continued. "If I'm being truthful here, Elaine wasn't really the issue. You and I had stopped communicating long before she came into the picture. And when she took an interest in the things I said, it was... nice."

Mia considered this. Was that why she liked being with Will? Was it really the attention she craved? But then she thought about how much she enjoyed seeing him with Felix, how his eyes crinkled at the corners when he smiled at her... The way her heartbeat rose whenever he came around.

"When it came down to it," Milo said, "I realized that what drew me to Elaine was what I missed about *you*." He glanced over at her and then back to the road. "I missed *us*."

"You have a funny way of showing it," she said, looking back out the window, the black of night behind the seagrass slipping past. "If you missed *us*, you could've started again with me instead of Elaine."

"I didn't understand it at first. I just missed the good times and I know that now. I missed the way you always read me lines in your book, expecting me to laugh when I hadn't read the story. The way you told a joke but then forgot the punchline so you got frustrated, when really it was the most adorable thing. I missed the way you used to find me in the dark and kiss me just before you went to sleep..."

She didn't respond, at a loss for what to say, none of those things feeling natural now. Their happy ending was so far gone at this point that she didn't know if she could ever get it back.

They finished the rest of the drive, both of them sitting quietly. It was as comfortable a silence as they could have. The two of them had spent many mornings just like that, neither of them saying a word; Mia with her coffee, her eyes on her laptop while Milo had his morning smoothie, his nose in his phone.

They pulled up at Alistair's. Despite their conversation and then the lack thereof, Milo still got out and trotted around her side, opening the car door for her.

"Hello, Mr. Broadhurst," the hostess said when they entered and Milo had given his name. She nodded in greeting at Mia. "Mrs. Broadhurst."

It occurred to Mia that Mrs. Broadhurst didn't seem to fit her anymore. But for all intents and purposes, they might as well be married tonight. No one but her family knew they weren't. The only difference was that this time, she felt like she was an imposter walking in someone else's life.

Once they'd headed through the moody dining area, past white tablecloth-clad tables full of laughter and quiet chatter, they were seated at a lovebird-sized table with a flickering candle between them. The waitress came over, already holding two drinks: club soda with vodka and a splash of pineapple for her—her favorite go-to drink whenever they were out—and bourbon and Coke for Milo. Just like old times.

"You've thought of everything," she said from behind her menu as the waitress set them down.

"I'll give you two a minute," the woman said, before walking away and leaving them alone once more.

"Just wanted to show you that I'm willing to try." His finger hooked the top of her menu, pulling it down so that she had to make eye contact with him. "I *am* trying, Mia."

She set the menu on the table. "What exactly are you trying? What do you want from this? You want us to go back to New York together? Spend our days working and barely seeing each other so we can fall into bed on opposite sides, both of us asleep before our heads hit the pillow? That's who we've become." She picked her menu back up, hiding behind it to keep the tears from coming. "Today, I was asked what I liked to do and I didn't have an answer." She blinked and cleared her throat, not wanting to make a scene.

"What do you mean?" Milo asked.

"I don't have a clue what I like to do because all I do is work."

"What about when you go to the club to work out or play tennis? Or when you're working on the charities?"

"Those are things that are expected of me, but they aren't ideas that I initiated, that I'm passionate about."

"Okay, then what *do* you want to do?"

"I don't know," she snapped, her voice rising. She quickly dipped her head and focused on her menu, the words a blur in front of her.

"There's no rush to figure it out," he said quietly. "Do you want me to find someone else to take over PR at work so you can pursue something else?"

"I don't know," she said again, confusion swimming around in her mind, stealing her ability to form an answer. She gripped the menu, trying to find a way to explain. "If I close my eyes, I can remember riding my horse Delilah on the beach. I'd give her the command to run, just so I could feel the wind against my skin and the Atlantic would blur in my peripheral vision."

"You want to ride horses?"

"No," she said. "I want to feel that freedom again. Somewhere along the line, I lost it, and became what everyone expected of me."

"You're an absolute success, Mia. Is that so bad?" he challenged.

She nodded, frowning. "It is when I have no idea what I want or who I am."

"Is there anything I can do to help?"

"I don't think so." Not knowing was terrifying. She'd never dealt with this before, and she wasn't sure how to handle it. It would be so easy to slip right back into being Milo's wife, throw herself into her PR job at Broadhurst Creative, and her life would go back to normal. There was a certain calm that came from knowing what was ahead... Maybe she was going through some sort of breakdown after Grandma Ruth had passed. Maybe she missed her grandmother more than she needed the change, and the emotion of it was just coming out in a strange way. Was she being too dramatic? Should she and Milo simply move to the next phase of their life and should she simply get over these feelings?

The waitress returned to take their orders. Still lost in her own contemplations, Mia ordered pan-seared scallops, the first thing her eyes saw on the menu that sounded delicious. Milo ordered a filet. He always got the filet. He tipped his glass back and took a sip.

"Milo, have you ever thought about having kids?" she asked.

He sucked in a breath with his bourbon and swallowed wrong, coughing quietly into his napkin while his chest heaved. When he'd recovered, he asked, "You haven't even given us a chance tonight—I'm literally dying here, trying to show you how I feel about you, and you've been like a brick wall. And then you ask if I want kids?" He laughed. "Shouldn't we figure out the two of us first?"

"That's what I'm trying to do."

He sobered. "You're saying that you see a future with children?"

She shrugged, but her mind went to Felix and his little laugh that was like bubbles in the air. "Maybe."

"I'd think you'd want to be sure first."

"I'm just asking. Are you open to possibly having kids one day, or is it completely off the table?"

He huffed out an indignant chuckle. "This is a ridiculous conversation. If I say no—I know you: that will be it. But you're putting me in a tough spot because you can't even say you want kids. So should I lie and say yes?"

"Do you want kids?" she asked again, outright, already knowing the answer.

He shrugged, imitating her earlier answer. "Sure." But she knew it wasn't true.

Frustrated, she asked, "You just want to go on living every day the same way you already have been?"

He leaned forward, his forearms on the table, the flames dancing in his eyes. "Sometimes the grass isn't always greener on the other side. Sometimes, your life is pretty damn good."

"That's an interesting perspective, given your decision to see if it was greener with Elaine. Is it *pretty damn good* to have a husband I never see and a job that takes up every waking minute of my day, except for the few things I schedule in to give me"—she made air quotes—"down time?"

"Those are things we can change. We have a house in the islands. I flew here in an hour on a private rented jet. You lunch at the best spots in the city and get your hair and nails done whenever you call, even though the salon has a waiting list months long. Our lives are pretty amazing, if you ask me. And we've worked hard for what we have."

She considered Riley and how hard she worked for pennies on the dollar, how she had to work like crazy to be the best at what she did to keep her hours at the hospital. She thought of her mother, who barely had enough to make ends meet, both of them desperate to sell the lighthouse that meant so much to them just so they could live comfortably. And then she contemplated her life with Milo. Together, they didn't have half of the trouble her family did. Could Milo be right?

TWENTY

Riley bounced at the end of Mia's bed the next morning. "Get uuuup," she whined. "I want to leave and I know you're gonna at least want a cup of coffee before we go."

Mia's eyes burned as she tried to open them. She'd tossed and turned all night, trying to figure out what was wrong with her and if she was going through some kind of early mid-life crisis. With a groan, she pulled the pillow over her head.

"You can do it," Riley said, bouncing again and making Mia's head throb. "Get up." She yanked the pillow off of Mia's face and tossed it to the end of the bed. "We're going into town together."

That got Mia's attention. With a yawn, she sat up and blinked to sharpen her sister's blurry face.

"There she is!" Riley sang. "Little Miss Sunshine!" She took Mia's hands and pulled her out of bed. "Mom made breakfast casserole!"

"What are we doing in town?" Mia croaked, running her hands over her face, still attempting to focus.

"Trying to figure out who Abigail Carter is," Riley said, linking arms with her sister as they entered the kitchen. She relayed today's plan to their mother, who was wearing two large oven mitts and holding the steaming, bubbling casserole in her hands, the spicy scent of sausage mixed with onions and salted butter floating into the air.

"Oh, I want to go." Alice set the casserole onto the counter along with the mitts, and sunk a large serving knife into the dish, plating three generous portions. She carried them over to the table.

"Should we check the records office?" Riley asked.

Mia scraped up a bite of the sausage, egg, and cheese casserole. "If you want to. That's a great idea. We could also take a look at historical newspaper articles at the library."

"I'll get ready right after breakfast," Alice said.

Mia got up and poured herself a glass of orange juice, returning to the table. "It'll work perfectly if we're out of the house this morning, too. Leah said she's finishing up today and bringing in all the Christmas decorations."

Alice put a hand on her heart. "Oh, what a present this will be!"

A heavy-set brunette woman peered past the pair of readers perched on her nose and over her desk at Mia, Riley, and Alice. She hadn't introduced herself, only calling out the words "Next, please," as the line snaked down the hallway behind them, but the nameplate on her desk said Trisha Jones.

"I don't see anything in our records for an Abigail Carter," she said after a few lackadaisical keystrokes on her computer. "You could try a private online genealogy service," she suggested.

"You sure?" Mia asked, leaning over the desk. "This is really important. Can you check one more time?"

The woman relented, her shoulders dropping just slightly in a meager attempt at empathy. With a pout, she tapped her keyboard again, scrolling down and squinting at the screen. Another few taps. Scrolling...

"I have an Andrew Carter..."

Disappointed, Mia eyed her mother and sister.

"That's our grandfather," Riley said.

The woman's hands stilled on her keyboard. "I'm sorry. Like I said, there isn't anyone fitting that description in our county record. Next, please," she called over their shoulders.

"It makes sense that the child might not have been born here in Winsted Cape if she's some long-lost family member. But I'm not sure where to look," Mia said as they left the building. "It's like finding a needle in a haystack."

"We're going to have to have faith that Mildred Beaumont has some answers for us," Alice said, holding the door open as they stepped into the icy cold air.

Mia opened her rental car door and they all climbed inside. "I wonder, is she out there somewhere—this Carter woman that none of us know? Is she like us? Does she know we exist?"

"Think it's worth looking at the library?" Riley asked.

Mia adjusted her rearview mirror and put the car in reverse. "Definitely. I don't want to leave a single stone unturned."

The library yielded no new leads, so to console themselves, Mia, Alice, and Riley went to The Drip for a coffee. But when they arrived back at the lighthouse, their spirits were lifted.

Mia gasped when she pulled up outside. The lighthouse looked as though it were on the cover of a Christmas card. The porch railings were draped in enormous swags of fresh greenery with long, swooping bows pulling it up at every post. The doors were adorned in festive wreaths of spruce and berries. Lights lined every edge and doorway, and small glistening Christmas trees flanked the front door.

Mia parked the car and they hurried up to the kitchen door, rushing in like children on Christmas morning, past the table that looked like it was set for Christmas dinner and into the living room, where their mother's little holiday tree had been replaced with one that towered over them, its tip crowned with an angel with feathered wings that reached all the way up to the vaulted ceiling. Mia's presents for her mother and sister sat on a velvet tree skirt underneath. The mantle was draped in more greenery and cream and red candles, with four stockings in beige stuffed with candy canes.

Festive music played throughout the house, and it smelled like cinnamon and cloves. A fire burned in the fireplace and candles were lit around the room.

"Leah, this is stunning," Mia said to her friend as she came in from another room.

"Glad you like it!" Leah said with a grin that split her beautiful face. "I just finished."

Mia ran her hand along one of the silver-stemmed lamps. "The light fixtures are amazing. It all just blows me away."

"It looks like something out of a magazine," Riley said, spinning around. "I can't believe it! I feel like we've won some sort of Christmas vacation! It's so pretty!" Her lip wobbled and she wiped a tear from her eye.

Alice rushed over to her daughter. "Oh, don't cry," she said with a laugh.

"Grandma Ruth would've loved this." She reached for Mia and her mother, embracing them.

Leah put her manicured hand to her face. "Oh my goodness. I've never had a response like this." She swished over to them. "You've made my day."

"You've made my year!" Riley said.

"And mine." Mia gave her friend a hug. "Thank you for dropping everything to do this for me."

"I'd do it any time for you."

"Want to stay for the Broadhurst Christmas party? You're more than welcome to."

"I wish I could, but I've got to bolt. I'm decorating someone's holiday home in Colorado in two days."

Mia smiled. "Busy lady." She knew all about that kind of pace. She'd kept it for years. And she had to admit that she'd felt calmer since she'd gotten to Winsted Cape. If only she could bottle it and take it home with her to New York.

. . .

"Wow, the lighthouse looks wonderful," Will said as he opened the door to his truck for Mia.

The afternoon light filtered through the snow clouds, casting a white shine on everything. The painters had just finished. With all the decorations, and the falling snow, it looked like a postcard.

"Where are we going today?" she asked, climbing in.

"Well, it actually isn't just one place. We're on a hunt."

"A hunt?"

He looked over at her, those blue eyes sparkling in the winter light. "A hunt for things you like to do. Open the glove box. I've got a score card in there for you."

Curious, she unlatched the glove box and peered inside. Sitting on top of the automotive documents was a piece of paper on a small clipboard. Written across the top was a score chart from one to five, with one the worst and five the best. Below, the page had rows numbered one to three. A pen was clipped at the top. She put it in her lap and closed the glove box, a fizz of excitement snaking through her as she wondered where they were off to.

Just out of town, Will pulled into the parking lot at another small coffee shop called The Local Bean. It was quaint, with a large pair of oak doors and picture windows on either side showing off the dark-wood tables with candles flickering in the centers. They got out and walked inside.

"You're getting me coffee as the first item on our hunt?" she asked.

"Nope," he said with a grin, throwing a hand up to the barista. "This is Jacob," he said. "He's going to teach us how to make a latte of your choice."

"Nice to meet you," Jacob said from behind the counter. "Come around and wash up!"

"Oh," Mia said with a laugh. "Lattes are my favorite!"

Will chuckled. "I *knew* they were."

She grinned over at him before turning to Jacob. "We're actually going to make one?"

"Yes, ma'am," Jacob said.

After Mia and Will took off their coats, they went over to the sink. As Mia washed her hands, Will dipped his fingers in on top of hers and flicked water at her. She jumped back, giggling.

"Stop playing, you two!" Jacob said, beckoning them over. "This is the espresso machine," he told them. "It's what we use to get espresso shots for your latte. Have you ever used one before?"

Mia shook her head, offering Will her paper towel.

When he took it from her, his hand grazed hers, both of them locking eyes before Mia forced herself to glance away.

"Cool. You'll learn something today then," Jacob continued. "Here you go."

He picked up a large sack of coffee beans and lumped them into Mia's arms, causing her to wobble. Will jumped in and put his hands under hers, bracing the bag.

"Pour some of those into the espresso grinder," Jacob directed.

With Will's help, Mia stood on her tiptoes and dumped them in, returning the lid to the grinder. Will's breath at her neck, she had to work to keep her focus. The next thing she knew, she had a handled object in her palm.

"That's a portafilter. We're going to fill that with the grounds and lock it into the espresso machine." Mia did as she was told, filling it, applying pressure to pack it down, and snapping it into place.

"Will, you're not getting off easy. Grab one of those silver steaming pitchers and fill it with milk for me." After Will did as he was told, Jacob dropped a thermometer into it and pulled out the steaming wand. "Put the milk under there and froth it until I say stop."

Will stepped up next to Mia, their sides touching, a smile surfacing on her lips. He noticed, his eyebrows rising in amusement. The wand hissed in the milk as Will gave it a whirl.

"Take a look at the flavors and let me know which one you'd like. They're all house-made," Jacob told them. "Will, you're good to stop frothing."

Mia picked up two brown apothecary-style pump bottles—one

labeled with lavender and the other with vanilla—and set them beside the two to-go cups that Jacob had placed next to Will. He mixed the lattes and handed a cup to Mia and the other to Will. "Here you go!" he said.

"Thank you for letting me do this," Mia said.

"Will tells me you're in PR. Any chance you'd want to change careers? We could use another barista."

She laughed. "I can't say I'd be terribly efficient at it, but it was definitely fun to try." She glanced up happily at Will.

"Darn. Because I could use you today," he teased.

"Sorry, man." Will held up his cup in thanks. "I'm stealing her. We have more to do!" He turned to Mia. "Ready for the next stop?"

As they grabbed their coats and took their lattes to the truck, Mia couldn't help thinking that Milo would never have done this for her. Grandma Ruth's words circled around: *Hope is where you find it.* She wondered if this was what she'd meant: finding hope in the little things. For the first time in a long time, Mia couldn't wait to see what the rest of the day held.

TWENTY-ONE

Will pulled to a stop at a small beach bungalow on the edge of town, nestled along a shady, icy street far enough away from the sea that the breeze was only a faint reminder that the ocean was near. The faded sign out front said, "Palm Readings and Spirit Discovery."

Mia chuckled. "What is this?"

He cut the engine and turned toward her. "We need to see if you might have a hidden gift as a mind reader," he said with a teasing smile as he opened his door.

"Wait," she said, stopping him. "Wouldn't I know if I were a mind reader?" She put her fingers to her temples and pretended to channel her thoughts. "I'd have known we were coming."

He laughed, taking her coffee from the cup holder and handing it to her.

"Maybe you've never tapped into it."

"You can't be serious," she said. "We're not going in there..." She eyed the peeling paint on the door.

"Are you afraid of what she might say?" he kidded.

"Absolutely not." She opened her door and hopped out of the truck, trying to be a good sport, but if she allowed herself to admit it, she worried that the psychic would see through the walls she'd built up and try to tear them down. She wasn't sure she could deal with that.

Will opened the door, the hinges creaking, and they walked inside. The place was musty and dark, a tattered tapestry rug lining the entryway. A table sat opposite them, covered in purple velvet and cluttered with glass trinkets.

"Hello!" an old woman said as she shuffled in from a back room. She had on a kimono-style robe that accentuated her large hips, her wiry hair pulled upward tightly, making her cheekbones stick out despite the extra weight on her face. "I'm Madame Simone," she said with an odd wave of her hand in little circles. "And what brings you by today?"

"My friend here—Mia—is wondering if she's a mind reader."

Mia sucked in a breath, and she could feel the humor radiating from Will despite his stoic exterior. She shot him a playful look.

"Ah, come in," Madame Simone said, waving them into the sitting room where she sat behind a low, round table supporting a massive crystal ball. She gestured to a tasseled pillow that would double as Mia's seat.

Mia grabbed Will's elbow and yanked him down with her as she lowered herself onto the pillow.

The woman studied her with a curious eye. "Put your hands on the glass ball, dear," she said. "I need to get your aura."

Reluctantly, Mia did as she was told.

Madame Simone squinted at it as if she were reading small text. Then she sat back, satisfied. "Ah, you are in search of your happy ending."

"Aren't we all?" Mia countered.

The woman frowned, her red lips pulling on the age lines that surrounded them. "The thing that everyone gets wrong in this life is that they confuse their physical being with their soul."

"What do you mean?"

"We believe in happy endings—it's in our nature to think that things should end happily. But that's our soul speaking to us."

"Isn't that a good thing?" Mia asked. "Shouldn't we listen to our soul?"

"Of course. It's our essence. But we misunderstand it." She traced an imaginary line on the crystal ball. "I do think we'll get our happy ending in what comes after this life. But in *this* life, we're not always meant to have a happy ending because this life isn't all we're given. Our lives don't end here with our physical bodies."

"Then what's the purpose of this physical life, as you call it?" Mia asked.

"We're meant to learn about who we really are and who we want around us. That's what we take into the next phase." She took Mia's hand from across the table. "You are looking for who you are right now, aren't you?"

Mia pulled her hand back, surprised by the woman's observation. She nodded subtly, unsure of whether to admit it or not.

Will watched her with a curious expression.

"When you find who you are, dear, *that* is your happy ending in this life. And reading crystal balls isn't your destination. Look within you and discover that thing that makes you feel whole. It'll find you. I can hear a wise woman's voice..."

Mia perked up. Could she have heard Grandma Ruth? *It'll find you... Hope is where you find it.* Did her grandmother mean that she could find hope within herself?

"Thank you," Mia said, the woman seeming more knowledgeable than she'd originally given her credit for. "How much do we owe you?"

"I didn't tell you anything that your heart didn't already know," the woman said. "No charge at all."

"Thanks so much," Mia replied, standing up.

They walked outside into the falling snow, the flakes as big as the emotions she felt after hearing Simone's reading.

"Well, now that we're caffeinated and we know our future," Will said, opening the truck door, "I suppose we should go to the next location and see if your destiny finds you." He flashed a smile that made her wonder if she'd found it already.

"Why are you doing this for me?" she asked when he'd gotten in on his side.

"I'm not really sure," he answered honestly. "I just feel like I should."

"You've already got so much going on but it's very sweet, thank you."

He pulled back a bit at her compliment. "I want to do things for you but I also don't want to lead you on in any way. I'm not ready for anything..."

"I know," she said, tucking away the surprise disappointment she felt. "And I'm not trying to start anything either." She gave him a sad smile. "Remember what Madame Simone said: We aren't always meant to have happy endings, right?"

He nodded.

"Maybe I'm supposed to help you figure out who you are too."

"Hm," he said with a smile. "Maybe."

"We'll do it together."

"Coffee and a palm reader. What's next in my day of self-discovery?" Mia asked as they bumped along the main road, headed away from the last village. She'd rated her first two stops on her score sheet.

The pine trees bent over under the heavy snow, the truck's wipers keeping time while they cleared the flakes off of the windshield in two large arcs. The road led them even further away from the ocean, into the vast expanse of rural farmland, where the fields glistened white.

"You'll have to wait and see," he said, turning up the Christmas music on the radio. "Carol of the Bells" played, giving her a magical feeling, sitting beside Will. This man had been a complete stranger to her only a few days ago, yet now here they were, driving around like old friends. "What did you score the coffee and Madame Simone?" he asked, alternating between trying to see her score and paying attention to the road.

"They both got fours," she replied.

"Four. Hm. Wonder what has to happen to get a five."

She giggled. "I don't want to give a five right off the bat because I might do something that's even better than these."

"Fair enough," he said. "Well, I'm hoping this will be your five."

He turned down a narrow road dusted with snow. At the end of it was an old farmhouse, with windows that glowed the color of champagne and smoke puffing from its chimney. When Will pulled up in front of it, the door opened and an older woman appeared. She waved.

"This is Kitty," Will said after they'd gotten out of the truck. "Kitty, this is Mia."

"Well, hello, Mia," Kitty said. "I've heard a lot about you." Then she squeezed Will's arm. "And I haven't seen you since you were a little guy. How have you been?"

"Good," he said, offering a polite smile. There was an undercurrent of familiarity between them.

"Well!" Kitty clapped her hands together. "It's not our usual season for goat visits, but definitely fine with me!" She beckoned them inside.

They walked through the old house, the wood floors stunningly discolored from years of traffic, giving them a warm and friendly finish that no manufacturer could ever achieve. She walked them past the hardwood staircase with its curved railing and the living and dining areas. Then, they walked out the back door, headed for the small structure just outside.

"We have a special platform to keep them warmer out here," Kitty said over her shoulder. She tugged the door open and they were immediately greeted with the "maaaa" of the goats. "Will thought you'd be most interested in the babies."

"He did?" Mia looked over at him and he shrugged.

"I thought you looked more like a baby goat person."

Mia laughed. "What about me makes you think that?"

He peered into her eyes and, for a moment, it was as if he could see straight into her soul. "You just seem... nurturing."

"Like a great mom," Kitty said, lifting a thin baby goat with tan fur and a white chest from the pen. Gingerly, she handed it to Mia, who immediately cradled it in her arms, the feeling as natural as her own laughter. "And he was right," Kitty said. "Look at how it's taking to you, Mia. You must have kids of your own."

In that moment, the absence of children in her life hit her like a punch in the gut. She swallowed. "Uh, no. I don't, actually."

"Oh," Kitty said, clearly surprised. "You're a natural."

The goat looked as though it were smiling, its little limbs hanging from hers so easily, as if she'd raised it from the day it was born.

"You're holding Stella," Kitty told her. "One day, we hope she produces milk as well as her mother Bubbles. And on that note, let's go inside and wash up. I've got more for you."

Mia set the goat down and followed Kitty, Will stepping up next to her. "Having fun?" he asked quietly.

"Yes," Mia replied. If she were honest, she couldn't remember the last time she'd had as much fun as she'd had today so far.

"So, is this a five?"

She chewed on a grin. "I'll have to let you know."

Inside, Kitty pulled out a large platter full of cheeses, grapes, and crackers. "These cheeses are all made here on site," she said, pointing them toward the sink to wash up. "We have cranberry goat cheese—that's my favorite but I hardly eat it because it takes so long to make. And this one is my second favorite; our original, salted goat cheese." She dished up the cheeses and accompaniments. "Have a seat. I'll get out the wine." Kitty took a bottle of white wine out of the fridge and poured each of them a glass.

"Is this your first date?" she asked, handing Mia her Sauvignon Blanc.

"Oh, we aren't dating," Mia said.

Kitty shot a curious look to Will. "I just thought..."

He stared at her, clearly perplexed.

"Well, you said on the phone that you wanted to do something nice for a woman you'd been seeing."

"A woman I've been seeing over the last week or so," he corrected. "Seeing, as in literally seeing her, hanging out with her... What do we call it?" he asked Mia.

Kitty's grin widened in amusement. "Taking a woman on a day of mini excursions? I'd call that a date."

Seeing the discomfort in Will's face, Mia told Kitty, "I think he's being a great friend. That's what I'd call it." Even though *friend* didn't sound like the right word to describe what they were. What exactly would they label what they were?

TWENTY-TWO

"Leah called while you were gone," Alice said brightly when Mia came into the kitchen at the lighthouse, the space filled with the scent of oregano and cheese. "She's sending the photographer over to do the photo shoot tomorrow morning." She lit one of the Christmas Cookie Dough candles Leah had put out on the counter, sending a plume of deliciously sweet fragrance into the salty air. "How was your afternoon?"

Mia grinned despite herself.

Alice raised her eyebrows. "That good?"

"Will took me to three very unique places to see if he could figure out what it is I like to do." She told her mother about the coffee, the fortune teller, and the goats.

"And did you ever rate one of them a five?"

"I did," she replied, sitting down in the chair. "The goats were a five... Because they helped me realize the questions that I needed to ask myself."

Her mother pulled out a chair and took a seat, leaning on her forearm. "Which are?" Alice scooted over the napkins and silverware for four.

"Who makes me smile? And when do I feel the happiest?"

Alice looked lovingly at her daughter.

"Why are there four place settings?" Mia asked, suddenly noticing them.

"Milo's asked to come over. He stopped by today while you were gone."

Just the mention of Milo caused all the cheerful thoughts she'd had to spin like a funnel, disappearing into thin air.

"I see your face, and I already know, but I couldn't say no."

"He's the one who decided to come early. That's on him."

"Yes, but it's Christmas," Alice countered.

"Yes, it is!" Riley said, as she bounced into the kitchen and took a seat next to Mia. She put her elbows on the table and sunk her chin into her hand. "What are we talking about?"

"Milo," Mia said.

Alice pulled a large dish of lasagna out of the oven and set it on a trivet on the counter, just as a knock on the door sent their attention over to it. Getting up, Mia opened the door.

"Hey," Milo said, handing her a clear bag of Christmas chocolates wrapped in gold, red, and green foil. "I saw these and thought you'd like them. They're truffles."

"Thank you," she replied, taking the bag reluctantly and shutting the door behind him. She set them on the table.

He took off his coat and hung it on the back of one of the kitchen chairs. "It smells divine, Alice. Did you cook this?" He leaned over the lasagna.

"I sure did. Y'all wash up and dish yourselves a plate." Alice moved the roses from the center of the table and replaced them with the candle while everyone got up and headed over to the kitchen sink.

As they piled lasagna onto their plates, another knock at the door stopped them all in their tracks. Who could be coming by unannounced this late in the evening?

"You forgot this," Will said from the other side of the doorway once Mia had opened it. He held out the piece of paper with her ratings on it.

"You came all the way out here to give this to me?" she asked, trying to keep her smile at bay while taking it from his fingers.

"And to ask you if you want to grab a burger with us." He nodded toward the truck, where Kate and Felix waved from the front bench seat.

"I can't," she said, opening the door wider to reveal Milo and her sister sitting at the table.

Will clamped his eyes on Milo. "Oh, I'm sorry to intrude." He backed away awkwardly, raising his hand in goodbye. "Enjoy your dinner."

"There's plenty if they want to come inside," Alice suggested, loudly enough that her voice could reach Will.

When Mia looked inside, her gaze landed on Riley, who gave Mia an oh-my-gosh-she's-crazy look and cleared her throat. Mia couldn't agree more.

Alice walked over and poked her head out the door. "Y'all come in," she said, waving Kate and Felix inside.

Before Will could tell them otherwise, they opened the truck door, and Felix had run over and wrapped Mia's legs in an embrace. She gave him a squeeze and kneeled down. "How have you been?" she asked, wrinkling her nose at him.

"Great! There's no school and Mom's been busy baking—my favorite!"

"Well, hello, Felix," Alice said. "Are you hungry?"

"Yes!" the little boy said, unwrapping his scarf. "I'm starving." Felix bounced up and down while Kate introduced herself to Alice and Riley.

"I'm glad because we're going to need someone to help us eat all this lasagna."

Kate tipped her head up and surveyed the lighthouse kitchen as she entered. "It's gorgeous in here," she said. "It's like something out of a Christmas movie."

"I'm glad you like it," Mia said. "My designer could give us some ideas for the bakery if you'd like. She's a close friend." She turned toward the table. "Milo, this is Kate, who owns the bakery we're sponsoring for the charity event this year."

"It's nice to meet you," Milo said, standing up and offering a firm shake. His curious glances bounced between them all. Mia's heart pounded as she ushered Will to a seat next to hers at the table. He placed his coat on the back of the chair.

"All right," Alice said, clapping her hands together. "Felix, if you and Will want to wash up first, your mom can go after you all. Let's eat!"

Milo sat stiffly at the table, watching everyone while Will lifted Felix, turning on the water and putting the little boy's hands under the stream.

"Oh, what are those?" Felix asked, pointing a soapy, dripping finger at the chocolates in shiny paper. Will rinsed his hand and wrapped it in a paper towel to dry it off.

"Milo brought those for Mia," Alice explained, "but I'm nearly certain she'll share some with you after dinner."

Will stared at the chocolates with contemplation in his eyes. Even though they had decided neither of them was ready to pursue anything, Mia wanted to run over to him and tell him they didn't mean a thing. She could only imagine what it seemed like with her ex-husband at the table for dinner, roses over on the counter, and a brand-new bag of chocolates.

"What's left to do in the barn?" Alice asked, adding more place settings to the table.

Felix climbed into a chair beside Will.

"The chandelier can be delivered as early as tomorrow," Will said. "I can help you hang it."

"Thank you," Mia said, trying to ignore Milo's prying glare. "And we also have to string up the lights on the back wall, call the florist and put in our order, design the banner for the charity, and get the party rental company to set up the tables and chairs." Then it suddenly hit her, her pulse rising. "Oh my gosh, I haven't checked in with the DJs to confirm yet."

"Why not?" Milo asked.

"I've been a little busy," she replied quietly.

"Running around town on dates?" he mumbled.

She let it go. The last thing she wanted was to start anything now in front of everyone. When they'd been together, he wasn't even a jealous person—it was his desire to win that was fueling this.

"Sorry," he whispered.

"It sounds like you've gotten everything done for the most part," Alice said brightly.

"Do we have wait staff?" Milo asked.

Mia laughed. "In Winsted Cape? No. But that's the charm of it. It'll all be help yourself."

Milo scooped up a forkful of lasagna with a skeptical look. With the bite hovering over his plate, he asked, "Who's going to pass out the champagne?"

"It'll be in buckets of ice and our guests can pour it themselves. I think they know how to pour a glass."

Milo's eyes grew round, and she could tell that he wasn't at all thrilled with the idea.

"We'll talk about the specifics later," she suggested. "Felix, how's the lasagna?"

The little boy gave her a thumbs up with his cheeks full of food like a chipmunk, and the sight melted away her anxiety over Milo for the moment.

Mia was relieved that Milo didn't say anything more because she knew what he was probably thinking: they were supposed to be catering to their clients and they needed to pull out all the stops— but something told her that it would all be okay in the end.

Will's phone went off in his pocket and he silenced it.

Kate offered a sympathetic glance.

"I'm terribly sorry," Will said, setting his napkin by his plate. "Can I just get this very quickly?"

"Of course," Mia replied.

Will stood up and excused himself, walking into the living room with the phone at his ear. "Hi, Fran," she heard him say. "Yes, I'm doing well."

Susannah's mother.

A heaviness settled over Mia, and she suddenly wondered what things would be like once the holiday was over and Will returned to Seattle. As she looked over at Kate, it seemed that his sister might be wondering the same thing.

TWENTY-THREE

The next morning, Kate sat down across from Mia at The Drip, her hands wrapped around her latte. They were meeting to go over the specifics of the charity and finalize the dessert spread for the party. With the photo shoot in a few hours and Mildred Beaumont coming later today, Mia had a full day ahead of her.

"I'm planning to dress up and help behind the dessert table if you'd like," Kate suggested. "I know you don't have any staff. Felix was asking if he could help out as well. I could rent him a tuxedo."

"That would be amazing, thank you," Mia said.

"Felix will be so excited. You know, this project has really helped him. He's been baking with me like crazy and it's all he talks about. It's been so great that I find myself worrying more and more about how he'll be after the holiday when he has to go back to that school."

"I wish he wasn't dealing with all that at such a young age," Mia said.

"There's a private school that I want him to go to. They'd build a curriculum around his strengths. But there's no way I can afford it. Especially paying childcare once Will goes home, and I'm back in classes and working at the bakery full time."

"Well, until I get a handle on what I'm doing, I could probably help you out. I'm sure my mother would also step in. I'll ask her today."

"You're a life-saver. I'd take private childcare in a second."

Happiness bubbled up inside Mia as she realized that being a life-saver was one of the things that fulfilled her.

When Mia returned to the lighthouse, her mother's and sister's bags were packed and ready to be loaded into their cars.

"I'm just going to run home and get us more clothes so we can stay on through the holiday, and I'll be back for the party," Alice told her. "The photographers are already taking pictures and there's a drone flying through the house to do video."

"Excellent," Mia said. "Need any help getting these into the cars?"

"That would be amazing."

Alice lugged the suitcase over to her sedan and popped the trunk, hoisting the bag inside with a thud. Mia lumped in two smaller bags.

"Have you thought about what you want to do for work after the holiday?" Mia asked.

Alice turned around and pursed her lips in thought. "I have no idea, if I'm being honest."

"Have you ever thought about being a babysitter?"

"Why?"

Mia told her mother the idea that had been swirling around in her mind since she'd spoken to Kate. "You could watch Felix and Kate could pay you."

"It sounds fantastic, Mia, but I don't have anything at my house to entertain Felix. There's no way I could keep that bright little boy busy all day."

Mia remembered the long summer days at the lighthouse: swinging on the tree swing, riding horses, playing in the surf. Then she thought about the dingy little home she'd grown up in. The lighthouse had been her saving grace, the place she'd run to whenever she needed to feel the freedom of childhood. She couldn't believe it was actually going to be sold.

"You might have a point," Mia said, disappointed.

That evening, Alice fussed with a plate of cookies she'd made for Mildred Beaumont and her daughter, while Mia secured the DJ and designed the banner for the bakery, then sent it off to her guy who could print it for her and overnight it if needed. She shut her laptop.

Mildred and her daughter were coming in late, held up by traffic. Mia's mother took the old photos and Christmas cards, the baby sweater, and the necklace with the pendant they'd found and stacked them neatly next to the cookies, before heading into the living room.

"Oh my stars," Alice said, finally relaxing into a chair. "I'm so looking forward to meeting Mildred and her daughter. I'm literally giddy about it." She put her head back and rested.

The lighthouse looked like a Christmas wonderland. The fire was going strong in the old stone fireplace and all the Christmas trees and candles were lit, glistening against the inky night sky through the glass of the windows. The smell of chocolate chip cookies still filled the air, and Alice had holiday music playing low on the stereo.

"It looks gorgeous in here," Mia said, finally able to take it all in. Her fingers were still pink from the cold. She'd spent the last few hours directing the chandelier installation in the barn, setting up the tables and chairs, and hanging the lights. Will hadn't been able to help in the end, so he'd sent someone else from the lighting shop.

"Something tells me that we're going to hear some wonderful stories today."

"You think?" Mia asked, taking a cookie from the plate and rearranging them so that they were displayed well again. She took a bite, the warm, buttery dough mixing with the milky cream of the chocolate chips.

"Yes, I do. And I hope she has answers for us about these photos and the Christmas cards we found."

"And the pendant," Mia added.

Alice nodded. "I just know there must be a history behind them, or Grandma Ruth wouldn't have kept them."

Riley came into the room and plopped down beside her mother just as the front bell rang, which never happened: all three of them knew who it was. Alice jumped straight up and answered the door, Riley and Mia following behind her.

Instead of a bright smile like Grandma Ruth's, they encountered a withered old woman, hunched at the shoulders, whose shifty eyes darted between the three of them, and another woman roughly Alice's age.

"I'm Mildred Beaumont and this is my daughter," the woman said, her words broken with age.

"Please," Alice ushered them in, "come in and get warm."

Mildred's daughter clutched a shoulder bag tightly to her side and came in after her mother. They eyed the place and looked at each other flabbergasted, as though they'd never seen anything quite like it, before sitting down on the sofa opposite the three Carters. The meeting wasn't exactly as Mia had imagined.

"You're welcome to a cookie," Alice said, pushing the plate toward them, but they didn't take one.

"Do you all live here?" Mildred asked.

"Only through the holiday," Riley said. "We're getting it ready to sell."

The old woman's eyebrows flew up and she shot a look over to her daughter, who glanced around in shifty silence.

Alice stood up uncomfortably. "I've got some pictures and Christmas cards I'd love to share with you," she said, rushing off into the kitchen to get them. She returned quickly and handed them to the younger woman. "And I've got this necklace and a little baby sweater." Mildred looked over her daughter's shoulder at them.

"Ah yes. I remember those well," the old woman said, her expression wary.

"Could you tell us about them?" Alice asked.

"Well, that's why we're here," Mildred said. She turned one of the photos around and pointed to the baby. "This is my daughter Hope." Then she tapped the woman. "And this is me."

Mia's breath caught and her blood ran cold. *Hope.*

"You were such an adorable baby," Alice said. "I wondered why my mother had so many photos of you."

Mia's stomach turned with unease as she'd expected a smile from Hope. Instead, the woman stared at Mia's mother as if assessing her.

"My given name is Abigail Hope *Carter*," she said, the final word slow and enunciated. She ran her finger over the pendant in her palm.

Remembering the initials on the pendant, Mia was dying to know if she had a distant cousin or something. She took in Hope's slightly olive skin and her dark hair, but her coloring was nothing like the rest of the family. She considered Mildred, trying to see past the woman's old age to what she might have looked like when she was young, but her face and nose were such a different shape from any of the family, so it would be very surprising if she was some long-lost sister of Grandma Ruth's. She stopped contemplating scenarios only when Mildred spoke up.

"I adopted Hope when she was born," Mildred said to Alice. "Your mother had gotten pregnant by a man in Italy and she'd never seen him again, as far as I know."

The three Carter women stared in disbelief, none of them saying a thing through their shock.

"We kept in touch through the years, as she asked. She went on to marry and had you." Mildred nodded at Alice. "But we continued to check in every few years. She told us once that she regretted giving Hope up, but she'd been so young, I can't imagine how difficult it would have been if she'd have raised a baby alone. She was only eighteen."

"That's... incredible," Alice said as she locked eyes with Hope, the two of them both suddenly noticing their shared thin fingers and the way they were both sitting with their signature long legs crossed.

Mia took in every inch of her new aunt, her mother's sister, little bits of Grandma Ruth floating forward: the slope of Hope's shoulders, the point of her chin, her perfectly round hairline. Mia took in a jagged breath, emotion welling up. Grandma Ruth had carried this around with her every single day. Mia searched her recollections of her grandmother, trying to see this story lurking behind the smile in her memory.

Clearly noticing, Hope uncrossed her legs and cleared her throat.

"We're glad you told us of her passing. We didn't know..." Hope said. Then she took in a breath that stuck in her chest as if she were nervous about something.

"Are you okay?" Alice asked.

"I am, yes," Hope replied. "I'm worried about the three of you." She dug down into her shoulder bag and pulled out a stack of papers that were held together by a staple. "This is Ruth's will. The lighthouse was left to me."

"I'm sorry, what?" Alice said, her face crumpling in disbelief. She reached for the paperwork and scanned it, flipping pages. "This can't be." She ran her finger over Grandma Ruth's signature. "That doesn't make any sense. She willed it to us."

Alice turned to her daughters, the three of them wide-eyed as they took in this information, everything they knew about Grandma Ruth and her wishes now coming into question.

"There's no way..." Mia whispered in complete denial, feeling overwhelmed.

Alice shook her head, too stunned to reply, tears welling up in her eyes.

"This is ridiculous," Riley said, shaking her head and

addressing the whole group. "I was with my grandmother in her last days. I read over her will with her. She made it right there in the hospital. She okayed it all."

"I have a clear record here," Hope said. "When Ruth got sick, she started getting her affairs in order and made sure I had the will if the cancer took her. ...And I have this." She reached into her bag and pulled out a postcard. "Ruth gave it to my mother. It's from my father." She handed it to Alice, who held it out for her girls to read.

Mia cara Ruth,

Ti auguro tutta la felicità del mondo.

Tutto il mio amore,

Antonio

Below the message, in Grandma Ruth's scratchy handwriting, it said, *To Hope, from your father.*

"What does the message say?" Mia asked.

Riley translated. "It says, 'My dear Ruth, I wish you all the happiness in the world. All my love, Antonio.'"

Alice stared at the words in their curly Italian script, her eyes rounding. "May I speak to my girls for just a quick second in the kitchen?" she asked, handing the postcard back to Hope. Mia and Riley got up and followed her.

"I don't even know what to say," Riley said quietly once they were alone, her hand on her heart as if she were keeping it inside her chest.

"It's quite a shock, to find out I have a sister. And I can't believe what my mother went through..." Alice rubbed her eyes and then turned her attention to her girls, who both wrapped their arms around their mother.

"It's incredible, isn't it?" Mia asked.

"Yes... We have to talk quickly," she said, clearly trying to swim out of her emotion and switch gears. "It occurred to me that if we allow Hope to have the lighthouse, we don't have to sell it," she whispered. "And she will inherit the debt accrued. It'll kill me to let it go, but we'll walk away free."

"There has to be another way," Riley told her in a hushed voice. "I think I was always hoping that we could somehow save it, that no one would buy it and we'd never have to let it go."

Mia put her hands on her sister's shoulders. "None of us want to let it go but we have to. I hate to say it but there's no way to keep it. And at least we would still be able to leave the lighthouse with family that way."

"She's not our family," Riley said through gritted teeth.

"Let's just see what they say," Mia suggested.

They returned to the living room, taking their seats, Mia's heart racing.

"What did you all decide?" Hope asked, folding her hands in her lap as if this were the easiest thing in the world. Because she hadn't grown up here, she hadn't spent Christmases nestled in next to the warm fire while the sea raged outside; she hadn't sat at their family dinner table and passed dishes full of Grandma Ruth's homemade recipes at the holidays; she'd never danced through the house like all of them had, the music blaring so loudly it drowned out their laughter.

"After Christmas, we'll consider moving out and letting you take the house," Mia said, attempting to be the voice of reason here. It went against everything she felt was right, but there was no other way to do this.

"Well, technically, it belongs to us now."

"Technically," Mia said, "we don't know who it belongs to because we have two wills."

"Until we settle this legally," Hope said, "given the... changes you've already made to the house, we can't risk any further damage to the property."

"Damage? You call this damage?" Mia waved a hand in the air, the sparkling tree glistening alongside the fresh white interior.

"It's best that no one occupies the home to prevent any further change to the property. We got that advice from our lawyer. He advised that all parties should vacate the property, and he's willing to move quickly. We'll have an order within twenty-four hours."

Alice jumped up, her lips set in a straight line. "I'm going back to my house to get our copy of the will so that I can read it word by word. There's no way I'm leaving my mother's home—the one she adored—until I'm good and ready."

Hope bristled. "Because the lighthouse is not your primary residence, and there's doubt as to who inherits the property, both of us must vacate the premises until we can settle this in court," Hope said. "I'm sorry."

"Why do you care if we're here a few extra days?" Mia asked.

"Because we follow the rules to a T." She eyed Alice. What was behind that stare?

"This has to be a fake," Riley said, standing up, snatching the will from the table, looking down at it and tossing it next to the plate of cookies. "I was with Grandma Ruth when she wrote the will in the hospital! No one seems to hear that!"

Mia hopped up to settle her sister. "It's okay," she soothed. "I'm sure there's some rational explanation for all of this." She put her arm around Riley and lowered her down slowly, the Broadhurst Creative event now flooding her mind. If they had to leave, they couldn't have the Christmas party. The whole place was deco-rated, the furniture rented; the invitations had gone out; the charity had been set. People had booked plane tickets to the middle of nowhere.

"I was there," Riley repeated. "I helped Grandma Ruth with all her paperwork at the end." She gritted her teeth, shaking her head.

Suddenly, something clicked in Mia's memory. "Wait a minute," she said, standing back up and pacing around, getting her thoughts straight. She looked over at Riley. "'Tell your sister, hope is where you find it. If you'll look.'" She quietly uttered Grandma Ruth's words, her eyes on her sister.

"What?" Riley said, her eyebrows furrowed.

"You told me when you were going over the paperwork, Grandma Ruth said, 'Tell your sister, hope *is where* you find it...'" Then, realization dawned in full force. "Not, 'is where,'" she said aloud. "You misheard Grandma Ruth. I think she might have said, 'Tell your sister... Hope'"—she pointed to the woman—"'I swear you'll find it if you look.' She wanted us to find evidence of Hope."

Riley gasped, her gaze slowly rotating to Hope and Mildred before snapping back over to Mia. "But why?!" Riley said, clearly frustrated. "So she could rip the lighthouse out from under us?"

"Wait." Mia stopped them, holding her hands in the air. "Riley, did Grandma Ruth say anything else before that statement that you can remember? What were you two talking about?"

Riley shook her head. "Nothing, really. Just how much she loved us, and how..." She chewed on the inside of her cheek, thoughts clearly whirling in her mind.

"How, what?" Alice asked, leaning forward, her expression intense.

"How she wanted to make sure everyone in her family was taken care of. She said that she had faith in the three of us, and she knew Mia could keep everything running." She swallowed. "But I remember her saying over and over that everyone needed to be taken care of. Then she grabbed my arm and said that line about finding hope."

Mildred spoke up finally, nodding. "It would be just like Ruth to make sure Hope was included. That's all she wanted in life, and that's why I sent her cards and pictures regularly. I wanted to assure her that her daughter was cared for."

"Would Grandma Ruth have left the lighthouse to Hope, assuming that Mia would take care of us?" Riley asked, turning to her mother. "Was she setting everyone up financially?"

"But I'm in no position to take care of you all; that's the problem," Mia said gently, trying to hide her disappointment that she couldn't fulfill Grandma Ruth's wishes.

"Right, but Grandma Ruth didn't know that."

Hope stood. "You all have a lot to talk about. We'll leave you with my number." She jotted it down on a scrap of paper from her purse and then helped Mildred stand and gather her things. Taking the will off the table, she slipped it into her bag.

"We'll give you twenty-four hours to vacate, and then we'll need to discuss the next steps," Hope said as Alice helped them to the door. "Maybe we can grab a coffee," Hope suggested, her tone softening as she addressed her half-sister.

Alice nodded, obviously at a loss for words. She watched them go and then shut the door. When she turned around, her face was as white as a ghost. "I know what our will says. I just didn't want to tell them. It clearly says we are to receive all assets. It doesn't state the lighthouse explicitly. We need to get a lawyer."

"We'll think of something," Mia said, her stomach plummeting. "We have to."

TWENTY-FOUR

The sun hadn't even come up the next morning when Mia awoke, every muscle in her body feeling as though she'd just run a marathon. She hadn't slept, thinking about everything, her mind full to the brim. She'd used money she didn't really have to pay Leah to decorate the lighthouse; Will was staying on, expecting a sale—he'd put all that time into helping them get ready; the party was up in the air, and there would be absolutely no way she'd find another venue. Two hundred-plus of Broadhurst's top clients would be at the very least angry, but also probably wanting refunds for their flights. She'd have to face Milo and tell him she'd ruined the event, and probably the next few years while he built his reputation back up. The bakery wouldn't get the charity money she'd promised, and it would close. Felix would be devastated, and Kate would be out of work...

If that wasn't enough to deal with, thoughts of Grandma Ruth had zoomed through her mind all night as Mia contemplated the sacrifices her grandmother had had to make at such a young age, and how she'd gone through so much in her life that none of them had known anything about. Little things began to take shape in her mind, like why she cared so much about that cuckoo clock, the red dress with the Italian tag, the inscription in that book: *All my love...* It was all because of Antonio—and Hope.

Mia's head throbbed with it all as she slipped on her boots and coat, and quietly left through the kitchen door, headed for the barn. She needed to get out of the lighthouse and clear her head, suddenly feeling like she was being caged in.

The coastal air was freezing, whipping through her like knives as she trudged through the newly fallen snow, but she didn't mind because it took the focus off her aching temples. She threw open the barn door and walked into the magical space she'd created, then clicked on the lights, the place coming to life like some sort of magical festive dream. The tables were all set up, waiting for people; the trees glistened in the corners; the chandelier sent beads of champagne-colored sparkles across the empty space in the center of the room that she'd left for dancing. Dancing that would never happen.

She sunk down to the floor and started to cry. She'd never let herself cry before—not like this. Huge, deep sobs rose from within her as if a lifetime of sadness had been waiting to escape. It couldn't end like this. She'd come too far for everything to fall apart. But just like she was now, it had all begun to unravel.

Her life was literally unrecognizable from the one she'd led for so many years, and she didn't know what to do. She repeated it over and over in her head: she didn't know what to do. She always knew. Everyone trusted her to know everything. But at this moment, she didn't know anything. She put her face in her hands, more tears escaping her. How was she supposed to fix all of this? Were all the signs pointing to her getting back with Milo? It would solve all her financial issues, and she'd have her house and her life in New York again...

Then suddenly, a shuffle across the barn made her freeze, pulling her out of her moment of panic.

"Whatcha doing out here?" her mother asked, tugging her coat tighter to keep warm.

"I don't know how to fix this," Mia admitted, spreading her arms wide, tears brimming in her eyes. She cleared her throat, pushing them back down. "If I'm being honest, the thought of selling the lighthouse tears my heart out, but I don't see any other way. Maybe if Hope takes it from us, we can at least visit..." Her chest felt so tight it could explode. "We have to be out of the lighthouse *today*. I need to talk to Milo."

Alice's eyes grew round as she realized what being out of the house by the end of the day meant. "What are you going to say?"

"I haven't thought it through yet," she answered honestly.

"You two will figure it out," she said, coming over to her daughter and putting her arm around Mia's shoulders.

Mia put her head on her mother's shoulder like she had when she was a girl. "I hope so," she replied, her voice hoarse.

TWENTY-FIVE

Meeting Milo at The Drip was safe. He couldn't freak out or lose his mind in a public coffee shop, and she could hide behind her cup when she broke the news.

He rushed inside in a flash, giving her a very unexpected kiss on the cheek. "Hello, darling," he said. "What would you like?"

"What?" she asked, taken completely off guard.

"Coffee. What would you like?"

"Oh. Um." She draped her coat on the back of her chair.

"I'll get you something great."

Before she could respond, he was up at the counter, putting in the orders. He flew back over to the table. "I brought something for you," he said, rifling through the pockets of his trench coat. He pulled out her chair and gestured for her to sit, then set a small gift box in front of her.

She stared at it, trying to come up with reasons he'd bring her a gift. A few people shuffled in, excusing themselves as they squeezed past Mia to get to the ordering counter.

"What is this?" she asked.

"Open it."

There was a part of her that wanted to push the box right back toward him and blurt out all that was on her mind. If he stopped for a second and paid attention, he might notice the red rims of her eyes that she'd been unable to cover when she'd done her makeup this morning.

The barista called Milo's name and he disappeared again, jogging up to the counter to retrieve their coffees. All his restless moving around was making her edgier. Not to mention the jewelry box sitting in front of her. Milo returned and set her coffee in front of her. She took a bitter sip, choking it down. "What did you order me?" she asked.

"I got you a black coffee."

But she didn't drink black coffee. Her mind went straight to Will, and the day they'd made lattes together.

He shuffled himself into his seat and produced a smile as he focused on her for the first time.

She stared at him, not sure how to even begin the conversation. "What is in this box?" she asked again, nervously fingering the velvet.

"I knew you'd come back," he said. "I was so sure of it that I got you that." He nodded toward the box. "Open it."

Trying to hide her trembling fingers, she reached out for it quickly and lifted the lid, placing her hands into her lap. In front of her was an enormous diamond, bigger than any she'd ever worn. "I don't understand."

"I want us to forget about all this divorce stuff and renew our vows."

She counted to four in her head to measure her calming inhale and then let it out slowly. "That's not why I called you here today," she said as evenly as she could. "I *don't* want to get back together."

He laughed as if she'd misspoken and he was waiting for her to correct herself. But when she didn't, his smile fell, and he snapped the box shut. "Why did you call then?"

The words rushing out as if they were pushing against her lips in a stampede, she blurted, "I'm cancelling the Broadhurst Christmas party."

"What?" The question exploded from him a little too loudly

and he sank down in his seat, picking up his cup of coffee. "What in the hell are you talking about?" he asked more quietly.

"We don't have a venue anymore." She explained about Hope's will and how that had changed everything. "We have to pack up our things and leave the house by tonight until the matter is resolved."

"I've got a potential new client coming to this who has a quarter of a million to use on ad spend for his new minor league football franchise. This party *has* to happen."

"And if it doesn't?" she asked.

"There is no 'if.' It *will* happen, Mia. I'll sue that Hope woman for all she's worth."

"On what grounds?"

"Libel. Our legal team will eat her alive. I'll wrap her up so tight in a lawsuit that she'll be too busy to know if we're on the premises or not."

"It's probably not a good idea to get caught up in this kind of legal battle," Mia warned. "It's costly, and our will doesn't actually state that we have been given the lighthouse. You'd be spinning your wheels and wasting money trying to sue."

"I'd consider it an investment in my clients."

"But what if Broadhurst loses? What about the bad publicity? The company we've worked so hard to build could crumble under the weight of legal bills and this cancellation. It looks bad. No one wants a PR company that gets wrapped up in lawsuits for the sake of one party."

"We don't lose. That's the point. If she wants to take us on, then let's have a meeting with her right now and get it started."

"Let me see if I can talk to her," Mia suggested, Milo's ruthless side making her stomach churn with unease. "Let's at least give her a warning and a chance to run." But in the end, she knew that with the wording of the wills, Mia and Milo didn't have a leg to stand on.

"I'd call her right now, Mia," he said, standing up and slipping on his coat.

Mia pointed to the ring. "Don't forget this," she said.

"It's not mine anymore. It's yours." He took his coffee and headed out the door.

"What's this?" Alice said, picking the ring box up off the coffee table and opening it. "Oh my goodness!"

Mia walked over to her, trying not to notice the packed bags sitting in the middle of the room, next to the newly decorated coffee table. "It's Milo's consolation prize for everything he's done. He wants to get back together."

"And what are your thoughts?"

Being with Milo could solve some of her problems, but she pushed the thought away and shook her head. "He can't just buy his way back into a relationship with me. It takes time and effort, neither of which he's willing to put into it. He's trying to force his way back into my life, and while I don't know exactly what I want, I'm pretty sure it isn't my old life."

"It's definitely stunning."

"Yeah..." Mia set the ring back down on the table. "Do you have that paper Hope left with her number on it?"

"Yes, it's in the kitchen. Why?"

"I'm going to try to convince her to let us stay for the party."

"Have you spoken to Will about it yet?"

"No, I need to talk to him too. He's been awfully quiet. I'm going to call him right now."

"Sounds good, honey. Let me know if you need me."

Mia kissed her mother on the cheek and headed down the hallway, letting herself into her bedroom and closing the door. Flopping back onto the bed, she called Will and he answered on the first ring.

"Hey there," he said, his hello like a warm hug in all of this. She realized, after hearing it, that she missed him. "Everything okay?"

"Well…" She trailed off, unsure of how to begin. "Why don't we meet somewhere?"

"All right," he said. "I'll pick you up in about twenty minutes."

"Okay."

She ended the call and stared at the photo of her on Delilah. What would she say to that little girl with the braided hair and big smile if she could? Would she ask her to do anything differently so she could avoid what she was dealing with now?

With all the energy she could muster, she pulled herself out of bed, fluffed her hair, and went to wait for Will, bracing herself to give him the news that he probably wouldn't be selling the lighthouse and she wouldn't be saving the bakery either.

TWENTY-SIX

Mia peered up at the modern glass structure sitting in the sand with the Atlantic crashing on the other side of it. The building towered over the shoreline, the minimal lines of it blending well with the surroundings. "Where are we?" she asked.

"A house I'm selling." Will jumped out of the truck and went around to open her door. "I figured it's quiet so we can talk."

They walked up to the door and he typed in the code to enter. Once they were inside, he turned on a lamp and a soft glow bathed the interior. The lights were all modern, like the house: track lighting and sleek, simple designs.

"The architectural goal of this home was to remain neutral so that the ocean could provide all the texture and color." He slipped his coat off, hung it on a hook next to the door, and then took hers.

"It's incredible," she said, looking around. "Very different from the traditional style of the lighthouse. I didn't realize there was anything like this in Winsted Cape." She sat down at the marble bar.

"As far as I know, there isn't. Which makes it difficult to sell. People come to Winsted Cape for the rural lifestyle."

"I wonder what made the owner build it here." She walked over to the back wall of glass, noticing it could be opened, exposing the entire rear of the house to the sea.

"The owners wanted to build a family home near their loved ones. This was their second home, but now they don't have a need for it." He slid his hands into his pockets, joining her at the back window with the view of the restless Atlantic.

"And it's okay to be here?"

"Yes, it's empty." He walked over to the bar, pulled out two stools, and sat down in one. "What did you want to tell me?" The mixture of concern and interest in his eyes gave her a fizzle of affection for him. But the reality of what lingered on her lips to say instantly broke the spell.

"It seems that the lighthouse isn't actually ours to sell."

He frowned in confusion. "What are you talking about?"

"There's a second will," she explained, filling him in on everything. "I have to speak to Hope as soon as possible to see if I can change her mind. At least until after the party. But either way, I don't think we should list the property now."

Will nodded, contemplative. "I'm so sorry you and your family are being faced with this."

"It's unbelievable," Mia said, still struggling to come to terms with it.

"If we do end up listing it later, I think the party was a lost opportunity, given how wealthy the audience will be, but I can list it in a few high-end magazines and some historical ones. We'll get the word out."

"Okay." She looked up at him and forced a smile. "I feel so terrible that this isn't turning out the way we'd hoped."

"Nothing ever turns out the way we think it will," he said. "That's how life is. We're beings who thrive on consistency and routine but life is madness—random and sudden, like the sea. It hits us when we least expect it."

"Mm," she agreed. Suddenly, in Will's presence, knowing what he'd faced in his life, her problems paled in comparison to losing the person he'd vowed to spend the rest of his life with.

Will's phone rang and he silenced it.

"Did you need to get that?"

It was as if he suddenly realized what he'd done. "Uh, no," he said. "I can call the person back if they need me to."

"What if it's Fran?" she asked, suddenly worried.

She was surprised by his smile. "I've talked to Fran, and if she calls and I don't answer, she'll understand."

Without warning, as she tried to focus on his smile, she was overcome, tears filling her eyes against her will. She jumped off the chair and coughed to cover it. She couldn't help thinking about how Will was dealing with the loss of his wife, yet he could smile despite all this and here she was falling apart. She'd always been the strong one. If she couldn't be strong through this, who was she at all?

Will jumped up and patted her back. "Are you okay? What happened?"

"I just swallowed wrong," she said, righting herself and wiping her eyes.

But just like the day they'd met, he seemed to read her. She knew that he could see through it.

Mia hung her head. "I always thought I had it all together. Everyone counted on me to take care of it all, and I was good at it. But now... I can't fix anything. And the worst part is that I can't stop crying over it."

"It's okay," he said, putting an arm around her and pulling her in. Even though she didn't want to, Mia jerked away for fear that his soft embrace would cause her to completely fall apart.

"You've lost your wife, yet you can still smile. How do you do it? How are you not in pieces right now?"

"I was in pieces. And part of me still is, but I have to tap into the part of me that is still here in the present rather than the one in the past with Susannah. Where is this coming from?" He tried to reach out for her arm but she wouldn't let him.

"I should be able to handle this and I can't."

"Handle what—the lighthouse? We'll meet with a lawyer and figure it out. I'll stay through to the end. Kate won't mind having me."

She offered a weak smile. "Not just the lighthouse. My whole life!" She threw her hands up in the air in surrender. "My job, or lack thereof, my mother, my sister, Milo—I don't love him," she said, pacing across the room. "I don't miss him when he's gone..." The words were right there in her mouth and she wanted to say it: she missed Will when he wasn't there. She'd felt his absence, which didn't make any sense because they'd only just met. But something about him made her feel like she'd known him forever.

"I feel like I'm spiraling," she said. "I have no idea what the purpose of all this is or what I'm supposed to do about it." She'd veered so far from the warrior woman she once was that she didn't recognize herself anymore.

He took a step toward her. "Maybe the purpose is to show you what I saw the day I met you."

She looked up at him when he stepped closer to her, her breathing growing calmer. "What did you see?"

"The vulnerability in your eyes."

She lifted her chin, quietly defiant.

"Vulnerability isn't a bad thing. Does it help if I tell you I couldn't get out of bed for months after Susannah died? That I thought my purpose was gone? We're all vulnerable, and let me save you the suspense: even though your problems aren't life-threatening, they're still real, they're still stressful. And it isn't your job to make it look easy. Fall apart if you want to—I don't mind. I've seen worse in my own mirror, I can promise you."

"How did you finally manage?" she asked, taking in even breaths to get herself together, dying to hear the magic bullet that made him better.

"I decided that, like it or not, God left me here, so there must be more that I need to do. And right when I decided that, Kate called and told me Felix said he missed me." He smiled gently. "So, that day I got up, cleaned the house, showered and shaved, and then packed my bags for Winsted Cape. I went to see Kate and Felix. And at night, after Felix was asleep, I cried on her shoulder, but during the day, I played with that kid like I never had and I soaked in all that joy until it was enough to sustain me."

She stared at him. "You are the strongest person I know... I feel like I've been doing it all wrong my whole life."

"What do you mean?"

"I've been thinking I was strong when really I wasn't at all. I just pushed everything down and hid it. But you—you moved through it, let the pain consume you, and then came out on the other side. That's real strength." Then she dipped her head, her gaze falling to the shiny hardwood floor. "I'm so confused about who I am," she admitted to him. "I don't know anymore."

"I do," he said. "You're the girl who wants to be heard. And what she doesn't know is that while she thinks no one is listening, we all hear her. You're the girl who loves people by taking care of them, and that's why you're having such a hard time right now. You feel that being able to support your family is how you show your love for them. But they all see it anyway. Your strength is in the glow that radiates from you when you walk into a room. It's magical because we all see it—it blinds us—even if *you* don't see it." He wiped a tear from her cheek, his words hitting her hard. "Your presence is strong enough that you took a man who didn't think he could ever feel again and made him so excited to face the day that he couldn't sleep at night. *That's* who you are."

She locked eyes with him, searching for evidence that he was only saying the right words to make her feel better, but all she found was truth. He leaned down, his lips brushing hers, his breath at her skin, but she pulled away.

"Where were you over the last few days?" she asked, focusing on her breathing to slow her racing heart.

"I was at Kate's, terrified."

"Of what?"

"Of how you make me feel." The openness on his face made her want to draw him in right there and then, and kiss him. "There. I said it out loud."

Mia hesitated, struggling to find the right thing to say.

"It's all a bit difficult, isn't it? I know you and Milo are still dealing with things, and I have Susannah's family... That's a tough call to make, and I'm not sure if I want to face that yet."

Mia knew there probably wasn't enough in Winsted Cape to enable Will to stay past the holiday. There wasn't enough real estate to keep him afloat. And she was the same. The prospects for high-end PR work were near zero in the small village, even if the thought of leaving her sister and mother was getting harder by the day.

"We don't need to face any of it yet," she said aloud. "Let's take it one thing at a time and focus on work first—it'll give us both time to think. Then we can figure *this* out." She waggled a finger between them.

"Yes, that would be good," he agreed.

"I'll talk to Hope and if I can't get her to change her mind, we can figure out our next plan together."

He smiled, looking down into her eyes. "Together. I like that."

The evening atmosphere at The Drip was cozy. A fire was crackling in the fireplace at one end of the dining area and only a few tables were occupied, most of them by singles with their laptops and earbuds. A lone woman read a book in one of the oversized chairs at the back.

When Mia arrived, Hope was already there, sitting at the table next to the coffee bar, the will stacked up in front of her as she sipped a bottle of water.

Mia waved to let her know she'd seen her and then walked up to the counter and ordered a decaf latte.

"Thank you for meeting me tonight," Mia told her, as she reached the table and sat down after ordering.

Hope looked at her sideways, both hands gripping her water bottle, her nervousness clear.

"How amazing that I have an aunt I never knew about," Mia

said with a smile, hoping to appeal to her softer side, but Hope's face remained neutral as she nodded.

The barista called Mia's name, so she popped over to the bar to grab her coffee and then headed back to their table, taking off her coat and getting comfortable.

"Were you all able to clear the property in time?" Hope asked.

"That's why I wanted to speak to you," Mia replied. "I need your help with something."

A guarded interest flickered in Hope's eyes as she sat with her back straight, her hands moving protectively to either side of the will.

"We'd originally remodeled a bit to put the house on the market, and we don't have to do that now, but there is one event that I'd like to follow through with." She explained the Broadhurst Christmas party and how important it was to Milo and his clients. "We have over two hundred people coming into town from all over the country, tomorrow. We can't reschedule this and we have no other options."

Hope took in a quiet breath and let it out. "I called my lawyer and he said that due to the fact that you all have been renovating the property, there will be a rush to resolve this."

"Meaning, you want us out no matter what?"

"Yes." Her stare was unwavering.

"Does family mean anything at all to you?"

A prick of something hit her when Mia asked that, but she clearly worked to hide it. "I'm terribly sorry for your circumstances, but the lighthouse wasn't yours to begin with. We'll have it signed, sealed, and delivered in a matter of days."

Mia swallowed the lump in her throat that was forming. "What are you going to do with the lighthouse?" she asked.

"I'm going to live there."

"You're going to move from South Carolina to Virginia? Do you know how to work the light? Do you have any clue how much work it takes to maintain the grounds?" She could've asked a hundred more questions, but she stopped herself there.

"All of that is my concern, not yours."

Mia stared at the brown ring forming around the inside of her mug as the foam dissipated, feeling hopeless. "I have a photo of my Grandma Ruth holding you when you were a baby," she said. "She had your little yellow sweater—still. She kept it all these years. She loved you so much that she gave you a better life than she could provide for you at such a young age. And she loved us too. This isn't what she would've wanted for either of us. She'd be torn apart to know that we'd do anything to hurt one another." She stared at the table, the words coming out faster than she could think them through. It didn't matter; they were from the heart. "So, tell me, what's going on to make you want to take this house so quickly? I just can't imagine you're a horrible person—you're a Carter!"

"I don't know you," Hope said. "And my motivation is personal."

Mia had hit her breaking point. "Listen," she said, leaning across the table. "I'm having that party tomorrow, even if you have to have them carry me off the premises. I grew up there, I helped my grandmother there—my grandmother who lived there right up until her death, and if she were still here, would have loved for this party to happen—and now, I'm asking for one final day." She stood up. "You're going to have to shut it down yourself if you want it to stop. Have a good night," she spat. Leaving her coffee on the table, she grabbed her coat and left.

When she got back to the lighthouse, she burst through the door. "Unpack your things," she said to her mother and Riley as they were preparing to leave. "We're staying."

Riley brightened. "Hope's will really is a fake?"

"Nope," Mia said, handing her mother a suitcase. "The will is probably real. But I told Hope she'll have to come over here and kick us out. We're having the party. Tomorrow morning, we'll need to be ready. We've got the event company setting up with table-cloths and decorations, the florist putting out arrangements at noon, and catering's coming in at two. I texted Kate and told her two as well so she can collaborate with the caterer."

"What happens if Hope shuts us down?" Riley asked, clearly worried.

"I don't know." Mia picked up another bag.

Alice walked over and put her hand on Mia's, gently putting down the suitcase. "Invite her."

"What?" Mia asked, aghast. "I met with her and she's not a nice person. We don't want her at the party."

"Something in my gut is telling me to invite her. Please, Mia. Remember what you said about Grandma Ruth—she wanted you to find her. She would want her to be included."

One thing Mia knew about Alice was that she could trust her mother's gut reactions. But this time, given how Hope had acted, she couldn't imagine her mom was right.

"If you don't, I will," Alice said.

"Then maybe you should do it," Mia said. "I don't want to speak to her again."

TWENTY-SEVEN

When Mia came into the kitchen the next morning, she found her mother and Riley buzzing around. Alice was wiping down the windowsills while Riley straightened the decorations that Leah had staged.

Her mind going a hundred miles an hour with everything she had to do today to finalize the party, Mia took two pieces of bread and popped them into the toaster without saying a word. Alice wiped the crumbs before she'd even gotten the twist tie back on the bread bag.

"We've been up for an hour already," her mother said, tidying the place for the party.

"What time is it?" Mia asked with a yawn as she took a plate from the cabinet.

"It's six thirty," Riley said, putting the plate back for Mia and offering her a paper plate. "To cut down on using dishes before the party," she explained, handing her plastic utensils. "We don't want the dishwasher running when everyone's here. It's like a freight train."

Mia took the utensils and buttered her toast, going over the mental list: *Finalize the song list with the DJ, check in on the florist and the caterer, check that all deliveries have been made...*

Riley stacked up the last few plates and put them in the cupboard. The toaster had already disappeared under the cabinet.

"I texted Hope and invited her tonight," said Alice. "I haven't heard back."

Mia shook her head as she grabbed her cell phone, which she'd left charging overnight. "Oh," she said, scrolling through the notifications. "People are arriving. I have notifications from the app that tell me when they've checked into the hotel." A shot of panic zinged through her. She *had* to pull this off.

"Milo's on his way over too. He said he tried to text you but didn't get you."

Mia's shoulders slumped. "For what?" she asked, scratching some more butter onto the slices of toast and coming over to sit with her mother and sister.

Alice moved the flower arrangement over to give them a clear path for discussion. "He didn't say."

Mia took a bite of her toast and swallowed. "I need to talk to Will. It hit me when I got up that we need to find a lawyer sooner rather than later. I wonder if he can work on finding us one. It'll be tough right at the holiday, but I'd like to have someone I can call if Hope shows up, deciding to shut us down." She didn't even want to think about lawyers' bills on top of everything else. She'd figure it out later.

"It's all so awful," Riley added. She wasn't in her scrubs today, her Christmas break having started. "Here we were, trying to do a good thing by contacting them…"

"We would've faced this eventually, I'm sure," Mia said, holding her toast between her fingers. "And who knows—legally, we should probably be out of the house, but I can't believe that she wouldn't do this for us. It's heartless."

There was a knock at the door.

"I'll get it," Mia said, standing up. She answered it, letting Milo in.

"Good morning," he said warily, offering a tray of to-go coffees while he sent a steely glance at Mia. "I thought I'd come by and see what's going on with the party. With no news, I assume it's a go."

"Sorry," Mia said. "I've been so busy that I haven't gotten you up to speed. Yes, everything's fine." She eyed her sister and mother, telling them with her stare that it would be better not to mention the fact that the authorities could show up and shut it all down. "Thank you for the coffees."

"You're welcome," he said. He gestured toward the living room. "Can we talk?"

Mia didn't want to talk. She wanted to call Will and get ready to assist the staff with preparing for the party. But after five years of being with Milo, she owed it to him to listen, so she left the remainder of her toast and followed him out of the kitchen.

"I'm coming on too strong," he said the minute they were alone. "I'm sorry. I've hurt you and I understand why you're not jumping at the chance to take me back."

"Milo, it's more than that," she said. "I'm not the same person who boarded that plane a couple of weeks ago, nor am I even the same person who filed for a divorce. And I think that if we tried to have another go at this, we'd both find that we didn't... fit anymore."

"You've outgrown me?" he said.

"I guess so."

"Isn't it worth it to make sure?" he asked.

"I've never been surer of anything in my life." Without Milo's money and without a job, she had no idea how she'd make ends meet, but what she did know was that she'd rather have to figure that out than be with the wrong person.

"I'll go," he said, defeated.

Despite everything, there was a small part of her that wanted to console him.

"I'll see you at the party."

As he walked away, the reality set in that it could be the last time she saw Milo Broadhurst, and the very last moment of the life she'd led for so many years. And the thought of that was surprisingly exhilarating.

.   .   .

By midday, the barn looked like a fairy tale. The tables were covered in white tablecloths, enormous bunches of red roses in the centers of them, with candles flickering everywhere. The chandelier was lit, along with the lights on the back wall and nestled in the Christmas trees. The DJ had set up against the wall and beside that were all the tables filled with serving trays and stands, ready for the dishes that were going to be set in them. Kate had stopped by quickly to set up cake stands, cookie trays, and all sorts of stunning vintage plates. And Mia had picked up the charity banner from the post office and had it all set up next to the donation register.

Mia walked around wide-eyed, taking it all in.

"What do you think?" the party planner asked, coming up from the back.

"It's more than I'd imagined."

"Wonderful. Later today, we'll begin setting up the main house and assist the caterer with getting the food prepped and on the warmers at two o'clock."

"Hey," Will said, coming up behind her. "Wow, this looks amazing."

Mia broke out into a smile, but it was more at the sight of him than his compliment.

"Do you want us to blow out the candles before we go and relight them before the guests arrive tonight?" the party planner asked as he packed up his things.

"I'll get them," Mia said, briefly turning her attention to the planner. "Thank you! See you tonight."

"See you tonight."

Mia did a little spin of happiness at the sight of the barn. Will grinned, his eyes on her. "It's gorgeous, isn't it?" she asked.

"It's going to be a great party, I can feel it."

"I hope you're right," she said.

"Speaking of the party, Felix is dying for me to come. Does the invitation still stand?"

While she worried about Milo's reaction to Will being there, the need for him to be by her side if Hope came knocking in the middle of the party outweighed her anxiety. "Of course," she said. "I'd love to have you there." She meant that.

"Excellent." Will looked around the barn. "Are we standing on a dance floor right now?"

"We are," she said, trying not to imagine the two of them in their party clothes, him pulling her in and twirling her around. But by the way he was looking at her, he seemed to be thinking the same thing. He reached over and took her hands, bringing her near him. He took a step toward her and started to sway. Then, before she could process it, he dipped her right there.

Mia let out a squeal of laughter, lifting all the stress right off her. She hadn't found anyone else who could do that.

"I feel like a rebel," Riley said, as she curled up on the sofa in the living room of the lighthouse. "We aren't supposed to be here, you know? It feels weird."

"Has anyone heard from Hope?" Alice asked.

"I haven't," Mia said. "Her silence makes me worry that she's building her legal forces. I just hope she waits until after the party. I really don't need that kind of drama just before announcing Milo's and my divorce in the coming weeks."

"If she shows up, we'll try to keep it quiet until the end of the event for you," Alice said.

"Thanks." Mia hoped everything would go off without a hitch, but she wouldn't let her guard down until the last guest had left the lighthouse tonight.

TWENTY-EIGHT

Alice had made them all lunch on paper plates in the living room with sandwiches and fresh fruit. Grandma Ruth's dress that she'd planned to wear was hanging on the door. Mia finished her final bite, taking in the moment. This was probably the last time all three of them would have a meal at the lighthouse. For so many years, she'd taken moments like these for granted, like all the days she'd nearly run straight through the kitchen on her way out to ride Delilah. She never realized that one day, they'd come to an abrupt end.

When they got to the kitchen, Alice, who'd had her phone to her ear, turned to them. "I got us hair appointments and they can fit us in right away. We need to get out of the way of the caterers anyway." She bustled around the kitchen, straightening up while the caterers walked around them, setting little bowls of mints and sampler trays with other nibbles throughout the lighthouse before they moved on to the barn later.

"Hair appointments?" Mia asked, tossing her plate in the trash.

"I got us all appointments at the salon downtown. I went ahead and scheduled three just in case you wanted to go too, but you can cancel any time. You're with a woman named Sheila. Riley and I have Marlene."

Mia had been into the salon once. She'd gone with Grandma

Ruth, who went in regularly for her weekly wash, blowout and style. The salon was an old, 1940s one-room shop on Main Street, with a picture window that allowed a view of every salon hairdryer bowl and the woman sitting under it. The quaint village salon was a far cry from Mia's New York hairdressers, but relaxing in a chair with her family for a few hours sounded great.

Riley fluffed up her hair. "I hope Marlene makes my hair big enough that people don't notice the size of my lower half. I tried on the dress I wanted to wear and I can't get it zipped all the way. Darned holiday food."

Mia reached into her handbag sitting in the corner of the kitchen, pulled out her wallet, and handed Riley her credit card.

"What's this for?" Riley asked.

"So you can get yourself a dress that you love for the party today," Mia told her with a smile. "I dragged you into this. The least I can do is make you feel fabulous while you're there. We can look at the boutiques while we're in town."

"You don't have to do that," Riley said.

"I know I don't, but I want to make my little sister feel like a princess."

Mia knew by the smile that broke out on Riley's face that she remembered all the times Mia had told her that while they'd gotten ready for school in the mornings. If Mia was super busy during the mornings, packing their lunches or finishing up her homework, Riley would say, "I don't need you to braid my hair today," but Mia always told her, "It's fine. School's better when you feel like a princess."

She tried to block out of her mind the fact that the whole party could be shut down by Hope and Mildred before it had even gotten started.

"Look at you!" Mia said, as she met the miniature tuxedo-clad Felix in the barn. The DJ's Christmas music had already started, the lights twinkling everywhere as people began to filter in.

Felix did a little dip and then giggled. "I'm in my fancy-man clothes," he said.

"Yes, you are." She took his hand and gave him a twirl, her own midnight-blue gown fanning out along the dance floor. She'd had Sheila give her a sweeping updo with tendrils that fell around her face, showing off her single-stone teardrop diamond necklace and matching earrings.

"Did you help to organize all those Christmas cookies over there?" Mia asked, pointing at the array of baked goods fanned out in front of Kate.

"Yes! Can we eat them yet?" he asked, already running over to the table.

Mia headed over to his mother, who was standing behind the confections. But as she neared her, Mia stopped in her tracks at the sight of Will in his tuxedo, his blue eyes sparkling as he laughed at something Kate had said. His expression was so relaxed, a Christmas cocktail in his hand, and she had to work to keep their little dance from earlier out of her mind.

But then, like a needle slide across a forty-five, Milo brought her view to a screeching halt.

"You look fabulous," he said, smiling at her with a reserved fondness in his eyes that she hadn't seen in years. He took her hands and held them out, turning her around before kissing the back of one of them, his gaze lingering on her empty ring finger. Clearly regrouping from the memory, his eyes met hers again. "Thank you for such a fantastic job. This party might be one of the best locations we've had so far. People seem to really love it." He waved an arm at the crowd.

Mia nodded hello to Eloise Faulkner, heiress to a billion-dollar diamond importer. Eloise held up her glass of champagne from under her fur shawl as she sampled a lobster fritter. Sam Edison, the up-and-coming actor, and his wife posed for a photo in front of the Christmas tree at the back. R. T. Ingram, the owner of a boutique hotel chain that was rapidly expanding across the country, came up to them, clapping Milo on the back and congratulating him on a wonderful holiday party. That was when Mia remembered no one knew yet that she and Milo weren't an item. She looked back over at the spot where Will had been standing but he wasn't there anymore, and the crowd was growing by the minute.

To keep everyone's attire holiday-ready, the party planner had set up cones in a semicircle outside the barn doors so that the hired cars could drop their passengers off, the guests stepping onto a red carpet-covered piece of plywood leading to the door. The view outside was an endless string of shiny luxury cars, guests still arriving.

Eloise made her way over to Mia and Milo. "Gorgeous party, darling," she said with an air kiss on Mia's cheek.

Milo excused himself, leaving Mia and Eloise together.

"It's so... rustic," Eloise continued. "Have you tapped into a new trend—rural living for the rich and famous?" She laughed in a circular pattern, her humor wrapping around Mia and making her feel festive.

"I hope so," Mia said, taking a flute of champagne from Riley, who joined them. Mia introduced her sister to Eloise.

"I heard this magnificent place was for sale," the woman said, her penciled eyebrows bouncing up and down. "What's the asking price?"

"I'm not entirely sure that's true anymore," Mia said. "It seems it was left to someone when the owner passed away."

"With the right offer, dear, anything is for sale," Eloise said. "Who owns it?"

"She might be here tonight," Riley said with a forced smile. "We invited her."

Just the idea made Mia's skin crawl.

Harriet Newhouse, designer for the stars, caught Eloise's attention and she swished off to say hello.

"Do you think she'll show up?" Riley asked, clearly worried.

"Let's not worry about it," Mia said. "Have you seen Will?" She tipped her head to see above the crowd but couldn't find him.

"He was over with Kate," Riley replied. "But I don't see him now."

Suddenly Milo was back, slightly out of breath. He thrust the ring box into Mia's hand. "Put this on," he said. "Quickly."

"Why?" she asked.

"Preston Schwartzman and his wife are here. Remember him?"

Mia tried to connect the name to the life that now seemed like a blurry, faraway memory after the few weeks she'd just had.

"He's the one who we're waiting on. If he signs with us, it's a huge deal—millions. But remember his wife, Sophie?" He leaned in closer to her. "The blonde who's half his age—the dancer?"

"Oh yes," she said, slowly sliding back into the Mia Broadhurst she'd been in New York. "She wanted me to handle their launch party, right?"

"Yes. What Sophie wants, Preston gives her. And she wants you specifically for that party. If we don't look married, he might not sign. I'd rather get his signature and then break the news that you may or may not be with us."

Mia knew how big this account was to Broadhurst, and it was for customers like these that they even had the party. With a sigh, she opened the box and slipped the ring onto her finger. Milo's shoulders relaxing, he slipped the empty box into his coat pocket.

"If anyone asks, your band is being set with more diamonds and you only have your engagement ring at the moment."

"No one will ask," she assured him.

He nodded, drawing her fingers to his lips and kissing them. "Thank you," he said. As he pulled away, she realized that she didn't feel a spark at all.

"Aren't you two the power couple," their former client Anita Rodriguez said as she passed them, rushing off to say hello to another guest.

"Oh, look." Milo pointed to the door. "Nicholas and Madeleine are here. That's a good sign."

Nicholas Whitman owned a music production company in

Nashville, and they were considering Broadhurst Creative for their PR next year when they unveiled a top-secret star they'd signed.

"Let's go say hello," Milo suggested, taking her hand.

Unable to get away, Mia had spent the last hour mingling with guests. With the party now in full swing, she finally had a moment to breathe. She still hadn't had a chance to speak to Will, so she decided to head into the lighthouse to find him before Milo could corner her again. She darted out of the barn and followed the newly lit path to the lighthouse. But as she made her way in through the kitchen door, instead of finding Will, she found someone else, her heart plummeting into her stomach.

Mia zeroed in on her estranged aunt, who was standing with Alice. The sounds of the crowd faded away below the buzz in her ears as she stared at Hope, praying no one had caught wind of the fact that she was there. She peeked out the window for any sign of the authorities, but all she found were the twinkling lights in the trees outside.

Someone took her arm and then she was being pulled into the sitting room at the front of the house. She looked up at Will, simultaneously panicked and relieved to see him. His gaze flickered to the rock of a diamond she was wearing, a flash of hurt shooting across his face, but before she could say anything, he whispered to her, "I wasn't going to mention it unless she showed up, but I've got some information on your new family member, Hope Beaumont."

"Oh?" she asked, her pulse racing, her heart pounding.

"I searched her address and looked her up in our real estate management system."

She stared at him, her mind abuzz with so much that she didn't know where to start. She hadn't even announced the charity yet, and she really didn't need anything to go wrong.

"It seems that her house in South Carolina is on the market. As a *foreclosure*. There are no other known addresses for Hope or her adoptive mother."

Mia digested this bit of information. "Where are they living then?"

"I'm not sure," Will answered.

"That could be why they want us out of the lighthouse so quickly," she breathed. "They don't have anywhere to live. Why didn't she just tell us that?"

"Your guess is as good as mine."

Suddenly, she felt awful about her little rant in the coffee shop over throwing the party. "I need to talk to her before she does anything," she said.

"What are you going to say?" Will asked.

"I haven't a clue," Mia answered honestly. "But maybe if I let her know that we're here for her, and that we're willing to help her and Mildred in any way we can, she'll ease up." She looked him in the eye. "Thank you for telling me."

"If we're telling each other things," he said, eyeing her ring, "I have to admit that I was disappointed to see that ring on your finger."

"Oh," she replied, looking down at the rock on her hand. She opened her mouth to explain, but his phone went off in his pocket and she noticed *Fran* on the screen. He held his phone up helplessly.

"It's okay," she urged him. It was so close to Christmas that Susannah's mother would probably need a shoulder.

With surrender in his eyes, Will put the phone to his ear, answering.

Mia darted out of the room to find Hope. When she reached her in the living room, that same closed-off look lingered in her eyes. "May I speak to you privately?" Mia asked, telling her mother with a nod that she was okay.

Hope followed Mia past the sparkling Christmas trees to her bedroom, and Mia closed the door.

"I'm sorry for how I treated you at the coffee shop," Mia said when they were alone.

Hope stood quietly without a reaction.

"I'm not a callous person," Mia went on. "And I can imagine that you aren't either..." She paused, trying to find the right words. "Where's Mildred tonight?"

"At the hotel," Hope replied softly.

"And how many nights have you all been in hotels?" Mia ventured. By the flicker of fear in Hope's face at the question, Mia knew that her assumption was right on the money. "What happened to your home?" she asked gently, while the distant noise of chatter and music from the barn filled the space between them.

Hope didn't speak, but her eyes glistened with emotion. She pursed her lips and went over to the window, turning away from Mia.

"There's something you may not know about who you are," Mia said to her back. "By blood, you're a Carter, and even though you were raised by someone else, you're bound by your family." She walked over to her and stood beside her, gazing out at the glimmering lights of the party. "We're warriors," she said. "Carter women are the strongest people on the planet. We don't always have it easy, but no matter what, we make it through by sheer grit and determination. We don't wait for someone to save us. We save ourselves. I see that trait in you."

Hope turned toward Mia, a tear escaping down her cheek.

"You know what else?"

Hope waited, hanging on Mia's every word.

"We are strong, but we're even stronger in numbers. If you need somewhere to live, all you have to do is tell us. The lighthouse may be yours, but so are we. You have two nieces now, and a sister who cares what happens to you and Mildred. We won't let you fall."

In that moment, Hope broke down, and just as Mia had fallen to her knees in the barn that day, Hope too was letting that wall she'd built fall down around her. "I lost my job," she said with a jagged breath. "Mom needed surgery on her heart and the bills were so high. They took the house." She sobbed as the words escaped her.

Mia knelt down next to her and put an arm around her. "What do you do for a living?" she asked.

"I'm a bookkeeper." She sniffled. "I prayed so hard for relief when I lost my job, and then Mia called with the news that my birth mother had passed. I got out my will and began researching the lighthouse. I read that sometimes nonprofit groups fund it and I could get a salary as a lighthouse keeper if I kept it running. My prayers were answered."

Mia smiled sadly. "It's mostly automated, but I can show you how to run it. Although, it's privately run and there's quite a bit of debt wrapped up in the house. You'd be taking over some pretty hefty mortgage payments. The debts have to be paid before the home can be officially signed over to you."

Hope's jaw slackened with the news and more tears rose in her eyes, her lip wobbling.

"That's why we made all the changes to the interior. We were going to sell it, pay off the debts, and distribute the remaining profit. Look, the lighthouse is yours, but we can still sell it if you want us to. One of the party guests—her name is Eloise Faulkner—asked about it tonight." She tried not to think about the beautiful memories she had here or the fact that someone like Eloise would replace all Grandma Ruth's things with her own...

A knock on the doorframe interrupted their conversation.

Kate peeked in. "Mia, I came looking for you because a group of guests were talking to your sister about the lighthouse, and she told them how bittersweet it was to get rid of it. She told them about the burden of the mortgage. A couple of investors were wondering why the bakery was the only business included in the charity this year."

Mia looked at Hope. "Before I had a venue, I stalled and said the venue and charity were a surprise this year." Her PR wheels were turning. "We could unveil the theme, 'A Christmas surprise,' and have a new charity reveal."

"Does anything need to be set up to add the lighthouse to the charity?" Kate asked.

"Nope. It's a simple form that I fill out for Broadhurst. The money is funneled through the business account." She got up and grabbed her laptop from her bag, opening the screen. "All I have to do is add the lighthouse to the form. See?" She typed in "Winsted Cape Historical Lighthouse." She consulted Hope. "This is your lighthouse," she said. "What do you want to do?"

She gave Mia a meaningful look. "I want to keep it in the *family*," she said.

Mia gave her an encouraging smile. "Let's do it."

Mia, Hope, and Kate entered the barn. When they stepped onto the open floor, heading toward the DJ so Mia could use the microphone, Will grazed Mia's wrist, stopping her.

"Everything okay?" he asked.

"Very much so," Mia replied.

He took in a breath as if he were battling a thought. "After things die down, I have something I'd like to tell you." The uncertainty in his delivery gave her pause. "Later," he said, smiling, but something else lurked behind it.

She nodded, her mind full of questions. But, refocusing, she headed over to the microphone. "Ladies and gentlemen," she said, tapping it, "I have a fantastic charity surprise for you!"

The crowd quieted down and began to gather in front of her, all the diamonds, sequins, and glasses of champagne as festive as the Christmas lights on the trees.

"Tonight is about holiday surprises and the wonderful blessings we can bring. If you all will look to your left, you'll see a banner for The Corner Bakery. Be sure to take a card with the facts about the history of the establishment, and feel free to sample their confections here." She waved a hand toward Kate's table full of treats. "They ship domestically and internationally, and can cater everything from birthday parties to weddings."

Kate eyed her, her gaze asking, "We do?"

Mia gave her an encouraging nod.

"But, as I said, tonight is a night of surprises," Mia said. "We don't have just one charity. We have two!" She unclipped the microphone and stepped out from behind the DJ's table. "The lighthouse on the very grounds on which you are standing has been here since 1870. In order to keep it running and within the same family that has run it for decades, we'll need your help..." Mia went on with her speech, noticing Milo had moved to the front of the crowd.

When she'd finished, he raised his glass. "To the amazing Mia Broadhurst, party planner extraordinaire," he called out. How his tune had changed...

The guests all cheered and toasted her.

"Thank you very much," she said graciously. "There are iPads set up on the table there for donations. Let's make this the biggest charity event of the season!" The crowd popped holiday confetti poppers and cheered again.

Mia handed the microphone back to the DJ, who started a jazzy version of "Have Yourself A Merry Little Christmas" as she made her way over to the iPad station to answer any questions the generous donors might have. The crowd gathered around excitedly, the whole place buzzing. Mia looked over at Hope, and for the first time since she'd met her, Hope broke out into an enormous grin.

Chairs sat askew in the middle of the confetti-covered barn floor, the tables littered with plates and half-empty glasses of champagne. The guests had mostly gone, with only a few lingering as they awaited their rides to their hotel. The DJ had packed up, and most of the food had been boxed.

Mia took one of the iPads over to Kate and Hope as they stood next to a plate of Corner Bakery cookies, nibbling the leftovers.

Felix ran up to Will, who gave him a fist bump as they joined Mia. Will gave her a meaningful look and she remembered that he'd wanted to speak to her. His jacket was long gone and his shirt-sleeves were rolled up, and he looked incredible just like that, but his serious look was making her heart squeeze. She wanted to talk to him right now to hear whatever it was he needed to get off his chest, but it wasn't quite time.

"I have good news," Mia said. "We've made enough money to cover the outstanding lighthouse debt *and* the renovations to the bakery," she said, quietly excited.

Hope clapped a hand over her mouth, tears filling her eyes.

"Really?" Kate asked. She threw her arms around Mia. "I cannot thank you enough for this. You know, people come into our lives right when we need them sometimes." She gave Mia another squeeze.

"Definitely," Hope said. "I can't wait to go back to the hotel to tell Mom about tonight."

"No more hotels," Mia said, giving her new aunt a big hug. And Hope hugged her back. It was the best feeling Mia had felt in a while.

Milo got her attention, beckoning her over to the barn doors. "I'm headed back to the hotel," he said. "Thank you for making this an incredible night. I didn't put enough faith in you, and I'm sorry."

"Thanks for the apology," she said. Looking at Milo in that moment, she realized how far she'd come this holiday. And she knew she had to do one last thing. Mia wriggled the ring off her finger and handed it to him. "We'll make the official announcement at the end of January," she said. "That should give you enough time to find a great PR replacement."

"What are *you* going to do?" he asked.

"I'm not sure quite yet for long-term, but I'm starting with a bakery relaunch."

"Given what you've done here, it should be amazing," he told her. Then he gave her a final kiss on the cheek. "I'll see ya."

"See ya," she said.

As he walked away for good this time, she felt a sense of relief. When the last person had left and her family gathered in the main house, Mia stood in the warmth of the barn, all the lights twinkling, feeling so blessed. The party had gone off without a hitch, the lighthouse was saved, and she'd been able to get what she needed to help Kate overhaul the bakery. This Christmas certainly had turned out to be magical. She looked up at the chandelier, wondering what Grandma Ruth would've thought of all this.

Then suddenly, the sound of footsteps on the wood floor brought her out of her contemplations. Will walked toward her. The top button of his crisp white tuxedo shirt was undone, his bowtie loose, the tails of it hanging around his neck. He stopped when he reached Mia and took her hands, surprising her.

His thumb grazed her empty ring finger and he gazed down at her curiously. "No ring?"

She shook her head, moving her fingers to intertwine them with his. "Wrong guy," she said.

He pursed his lips thoughtfully and nodded. "Too bad. For him." He allowed fondness to swim across his eyes. "I spoke to Fran tonight," he said.

"Yeah?" She nodded, remembering the call back in the sitting room.

"I asked her what she wanted for me. She told me that all she wanted in life was for me to be happy—that's what we're all trying to be, right?"

She nodded, looking up into his gorgeous eyes.

"I told her how wonderful her daughter was, how she stopped me in my tracks and made it hard to think about anything else when she was around. I also reminded her how low I got after she died, because meeting someone who can have that kind of effect on you isn't easy—the opportunity doesn't come around often—and after Susannah, I didn't think there was anything left. She agreed, telling me that lightning doesn't always strike twice." His thumb found her empty ring finger again. "I told Fran that for me, lightning *had* struck twice. I explained to her that I'd met someone who gets me up in the mornings, someone who makes me smile just thinking about her. And she gave me her blessing." He took a step toward her, closing the gap between them. "But this someone I found—I don't know if she feels the same way."

"Is that so? What if she did something like this," she said, putting her arms around his neck. "Would that help?"

He grinned down at her and then pursed his lips in that adorable way of his. "I'm not sure... She's a pretty strong-willed woman, so it's hard to say."

"She's definitely a strong-willed woman," Mia agreed, playing along. "What about this?" She reached up to his neck and pulled him toward her, but just before their lips met, she lightly kissed his cheek. "Better?"

He shook his head. "I'm just thinking I'll have to go for it and test her reaction."

"Fair assumption," she said with a laugh.

And there on the confetti-covered floor, under the sparkling light of the chandelier, the Christmas trees shining all around them, Will put his hands on Mia's face and drew her in, pressing his lips to hers. For the first time in her life, she felt true fireworks, that lightning feeling that Will had explained. As their breath mixed, the warmth of his soft lips on hers and his strong hands holding her, it was as if she'd been waiting for this moment her whole life. And she knew without a doubt that being with the ones she loved gave her more strength than anything else she'd ever tried.

When they slowed, she pulled back and looked up at him. "Seattle's a long way from here," she said.

"Yes."

"And it's a long way from New York."

"Is that where you're planning to live?"

"I'm not sure anymore. I think I might stick around Winsted Cape to be close to my mother and my sister." She grinned but it faded at the thought of Will going back to Washington.

"Seattle is definitely a very long way from Winsted Cape," he said, leaning down toward her. Then, into her ear, he whispered, "So it's a good thing I'm not going to live there."

"What?"

"You know the house I showed you down the road—the one I'm selling? It's mine from before I was married. When Susannah and I married, we moved into her house in Seattle. Susannah had convinced me to sell mine and I'd just never gotten organized to do it. Finally, just before you contacted me, I put it on the market. But I've since taken it off the system. Just like you, I realized how important it is to be with family."

"So, we're both staying in Winsted Cape, are we?" she asked, a fizzle of happiness zinging through her.

"Looks like it." He leaned in for another kiss before spinning her around the floor of the old barn. And she knew that this night was only the first of many they'd spend together.

EPILOGUE

A YEAR AND A HALF LATER

The old barn doors at the lighthouse were open wide in the heat of late May, the entry draped in gardenias and white roses that cascaded down each side. Inside, rows of white chairs held guests who fanned their faces with their monogrammed programs while they sipped on mason jars of lemonade, tied with white bows and sunk in buckets of ice at the end of each row.

In her satin heels, Mia stepped onto the pathway of rose petals leading into the barn, a bouquet of white wildflowers in her hand, her satin and lace dress fanned out behind her. Inside, she could see Felix in his tuxedo and shiny shoes, grinning from ear to ear. Her heart nearly burst at seeing the happiness bloom in that little boy over the last year.

The Corner Bakery relaunch had been so successful that it had become a hotspot for vacationers. It had also landed on the pages of *Travel History Magazine* since it was on the national historic register, and it stayed busy year-round. The bakery was doing so well that Kate had been able to renovate an apartment above it, hire a babysitter for Felix while she worked, and send Felix to the private school last year; he was excelling in every subject. Both Kate and Will now worked there, and they'd brought Mia onboard for full-time PR, which Mia balanced with her new online PR company, specializing in publicity strategy for small businesses.

"Did you really think that fortune telling and latte making were viable options for my skillset?" she'd asked Will one night with a laugh, as they reminisced about that day he'd taken her around town to figure out who she was.

"Absolutely not," he told her, those blue eyes light and excited. "But by showing you what you're not, sometimes it helps you to see what you are. I could see it all along."

"So by not being a barista, I'd learn I was best at PR?"

He shook his head. "No. That day had nothing to do with palm reading, coffee, or goats. You had *fun*. I was showing you that you weren't that woman from New York. You were still the girl from the little house in Winsted Cape. You just needed New York for a while to shape you into the person you're really meant to be."

Will could always see her.

As Mia entered the barn, she was met with the sound of the violinists and the beaming faces of her friends and family. Leah was wearing an incredible hat, and Hope and Mildred were in the front row by Riley and her mother, all grinning at her from their seats. And the last chair in the front row was empty, but hanging on the back of it was Grandma Ruth's yellow sweater with the pearl buttons. Mia choked back tears.

"I want Grandma Ruth to see the wedding," Mia had told her mother when they were planning earlier that year. "I want her there with us all—her whole family."

Alice had her hand on her heart while dabbing her eyes with a tissue. But it was the breathless surprise and undeniable love on Will's face at the end of the barn as he stood in his tuxedo, his face clean-shaven, his hair perfectly combed, watching his bride enter, that would make everything else fall away for her.

She barely heard the rest of the service, her entire focus on her future husband. And as she looked back through her life until this point, it all seemed to have been leading her here, to this moment, with this man.

"William Mason Thacker, do you take this woman to be your

lawfully wedded wife, to have and to hold from this day forward, for better or worse..."

The words wrapped around her, like her happiness, and she knew that Grandma Ruth could see it all. She could feel it. Before she'd gotten ready for the wedding today, the lighthouse buzzing with activity as everyone prepared for her big day, Mia had stopped for a second and run her finger along the phrase that was framed on the mantle. She'd had it made for Hope as a house-warming gift. It read, "Hope. I swear you'll find it." They'd all found hope that year, in different ways.

The next thing she knew, it was her turn, and she looked deep into Will's eyes. "I do." Will slipped the diamond and platinum band that matched her engagement ring onto her finger.

In an instant, his hands were on her face, his lips meeting hers, cheers lifting into the air like champagne bubbles. And while she knew she had a day ahead of her full of laughter and excitement, she couldn't wait until it was all over so she could walk into the home on the beach that Will had built for a family and begin the life they planned to build together. They hadn't decided how many kids they wanted to have, but one thing was for sure: if she had a girl, she'd teach her the Carter strength, but she'd let her know that she could be just as strong with someone wonderful by her side.

A LETTER FROM JENNY

Hi there!

Thank you so much for reading *A Lighthouse Christmas*. I really hope it had you snuggling up with your favorite mug of something warm and got you wanting to make memories with your own family and friends.

If you'd like me to drop you an email when my next Bookouture book is out, you can sign up here:

www.bookouture.com/jenny-hale

I won't share your information with anyone else, and I'll only email you a quick message once a month with my newsletter and then whenever new books come out.

If you did enjoy *A Lighthouse Christmas*, I'd be very grateful if you'd write a review online. Getting feedback from readers is so exciting, and it also helps to persuade others to pick up one of my books for the first time. It's one of the biggest gifts you could give me. If you enjoyed this story, and would like a few more happy endings, check out my other novels at:

www.itsjennyhale.com

Until next time,
Jenny xo

KEEP IN TOUCH WITH JENNY

www.itsjennyhale.com

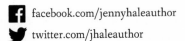

facebook.com/jennyhaleauthor

twitter.com/jhaleauthor

instagram.com/jhaleauthor

ACKNOWLEDGMENTS

I am forever grateful to the people and teams that I've worked with over the years, for shaping me into the person I am today and inspiring me.

To my amazing editor Christina Demosthenous, I couldn't have had a better person to help me get this story into its best version.

To Gil, who helped me through the legalities of two wills, I thank you!

And to my husband Justin, I am blessed to have his support. He always handles my level of crazy like a champ and is always in my corner, cheering me on to follow my dreams as far as they'll take me.

Made in the USA
Middletown, DE
29 November 2021

53750304R00154